An Ode for Orchids

James Fant

An Ode for Orchids
A Novel
Copyright © 2012 by James Fant

Published by James Fant Books, LLC
Summerville, SC

About the Author

James Fant loves telling good stories. He lives in South Carolina, where the mountains and the beaches have befriended him. His books include:

Simon's Splinter

Fourteen Pages

An Ode for Orchids

Close the Door

The Secret Branch

The Mended Fence

If you want to get an automatic email when James' next book is released, sign up here. Your email address will never be shared, and you can unsubscribe at any time.

Word-of-mouth is vital for a writer's success. If you enjoyed the book, please consider leaving a review at Amazon, even if it's just a line or two; it would be very much appreciated.

You can also visit his website, follow him on Twitter, connect on Facebook, or send him an email: james@jamesfantbooks.com

To the Wives that Love Us
To the Mothers that Nurture Us
To the Sisters that Have our Backs
To the Grandmothers that Teach Us the Way
To the Aunts that Invest in Us and Pour in to Our Lives
You Are and Will Always Be...
...Our Orchid

Prologue

It was still dark when Geneva Cole awoke from a measly three hours of sleep. But she was not weary at all. She was too excited to be tired because three of her granddaughters, Cicely, Brook, and Dawn, would arrive in the afternoon.

After getting out of her bed, she took light steps across the hallway to check on her youngest granddaughter, Karen. In the morning, Geneva would ask her how she slept. Karen would reply that she had sweet dreams. However, the dishevelment of her bed sheets and the glossiness of her skin betrayed her reply. Karen was not sleeping well at all.

After leaving Karen's bedroom, Geneva made her way downstairs to tend to her orchids. Her Paphiopedilum was quite beautiful. It filled the air with a light rose-like scent. Her Cymbidium was robust and very pleasing to the eye. Her Dendrobium was also extremely attractive and floriferous. Her Cattleya was queenly, enjoying even temperatures and appreciating the coolness of evening air. Each species of Geneva's orchids was uniquely beautiful. Yet she loved them all the same.

As she entered her living room, her orchids seemed to beam with life, welcoming her, wanting her love and attention. And so, she watered each one. She massaged their soil and gently caressed their leaves. She gave them a gentle spritz with a mister to keep them moist. And then, just because she really felt like they enjoyed it, she sang to them a little song.

Chapter 1

"What does every girl have that every guy wants?" Cicely asked her three cousins. When Karen, Brook and Dawn replied with playful shrugs, she turned around and wagged her backside to reveal the answer.

Karen said, "You are *so* nasty."

"But it is *so* true. It's like my momma always said, 'You have to use what you've got to get what you want from a man.'"

Of course Cicely's mother never said those words directly to her. Surely that is not something a mother would tell her 12-year-old daughter. Besides, how many 12-year-old girls would know the meaning of that phrase if they happened to hear it?

Cicely's statement hung in the humid June air as the girls walked up Big Cagle Street toward the basketball courts. The sun, sitting colonially in the center of a cloudless sky, pitilessly showered them with piercing rays of radiation. Heat enveloped them. Perspiration pooled on Cicely's top lip. She quickly wiped it away because she also remembered overhearing her mother say, "Never let them see you sweat."

"My feet hurt!" Dawn said. She was not a big fan of walking. Every now and again, she would stop and rub her arches, which throbbed and itched.

"You shouldn't have worn those jelly shoes," Cicely replied with disapproval. "Jelly shoes are so middle school."

"I *am* in middle school. And why are we out here in this heat anyway?"

"It's not that hot to me," Karen said, skipping up the sidewalk ahead of them. "I love being out in the sun."

Cicely replied, "You *should* love being out in the sun, as pale as you are. And why are you skipping. Stop skipping! You're 12 years old!"

"Why are you so snappy all of a sudden?" Brook asked. "First it was Dawn's jellies and now it's Karen's skipping."

But Cicely kept walking, her focus shifted. Her chest lifted and lowered as she labored to breathe. Her long lashes fluttered as if sending Morse code. Perhaps she was sending a distress signal to those boys on the basketball court. Those tall boys. Those high school aged boys. Those experienced boys.

Cicely Shaw was hot and bothered. And that pitiless summer sun had nothing to do with it.

***

Cicely, Brook, and Dawn were spending the summer with their grandmother; they called her Ma Geneva. The petite and lively old lady lived in a little neighborhood called New Town in a gray and black house that sat at the bottom of a street named Big Cagle. Looking east from the front porch, the girls could see the 25-story Daniel Building. To the north, they could see Paris Mountain. The surroundings were modest, yet enchanting and the scent of honeysuckle and freshly hung linen always softened the air.

The corner of Big Cagle and Willard Street never made a ruckus; some would call it boring. But the girls had been looking forward to their stay for quite a while and hoped that it might become a ritual. Karen, however, didn't have to look forward to the summer at all. That modest yet enchanting house with its scents of honeysuckle and linen was now her home.

While the girls made their way to the basketball courts, Cicely's mother, Susan, stood on the front porch. A lit cigarette at her fingertips. Smoke flowing through her pursed lips. She could not smoke in the house. Smoke would destroy the delicate air mixture and could, quite possibly, decrease the air's humidity. Besides, cigarette smoke left a stench in the air not easily removed. Most importantly, Ma Geneva's orchids would not like the smell.

Susan was ready to leave before she got there. Her plan was to drive up from Atlanta to Fountain Inn; pick up her twin nieces and their mother, Diane, who didn't drive by the way; drop off the girls at Ma Geneva's, staying just long enough to kiss the old lady on the cheek; leave the house with tires screeching; drop her free-loading sister back off in Fountain Inn; and then hightail it back to Atlanta before dark. However, Diane had other plans. She liked to linger, wear out her welcome so to speak.

"Momma, I'm taking some of your orchids home with me," she said as she lounged on the couch in full linger mode.

Ma Geneva just ignored her, continuing to roll the dough for her famous biscuits.

Susan entered the door smelling of freshly sprayed Chanel. She said, "Um, Diane—why did you take off your shoes? Are we not leaving soon?"

"Hush. Can't you see grown folks are talking?" Diane turned back to Ma Geneva. "You are giving me this Cattleya, aren't you, Momma?"

Ma Geneva sucked her teeth. "Those flowers would stand a better chance if I planted them somewhere out in the woods."

"Will you at least let me borrow the Paph?"

The old woman furrowed her brow. She thought to herself, how does one borrow a flower?

"No I will not," she replied. "You aren't taking my flowers all the way back down the road so you can kill them. You're barely taking care of those girls!"

Susan laughed. But Ma Geneva didn't miss a beat when she said to her, "Sue, you don't have to be afraid

4

to come in the house. We all know you're still smoking. And Diane, get your feet off of my couch!"

Diane rolled her eyes, making sure her mother did not see it.

"She would have a given the plants to Adele though," she jokingly said to her sister. "You know Adele was always the favorite."

"What did you say?" Ma Geneva came into the living room wielding a skillet. "What—Did—You—Say?"

"I was just playing, Momma."

Diane stiffened. Her eyes shifted from her mother to the skillet. Silence settled as if sound tiptoed out the room for its own safety. Seconds mimicked hours. The room darkened as Ma Geneva held that skillet up to Diane's head.

"Don't play like that!" Then she and the skillet walked into the kitchen.

Diane took a few shallow breaths before she said, "I think I just peed on myself."

"She is *definitely* not giving you one of those orchids now."

"You think?"

The grandfather clock resumed its ticking. The ceiling fan, its whipping: *whip, whip, whip.* Sound had snuck back into the room. The coast was clear.

"She hasn't gotten over it yet."

"No," Susan replied, "it is still as fresh as yesterday."

The two sisters spoke quietly in the living room, conversing mainly about Karen's mother, Adele, and how she spiraled into drug use and promiscuity. How no one knew the identity of Karen's father, the sadness of the situation. They spoke softly about the little girl who would have to grow up without her mother. Finally Diane asked, "Are we going to confront Momma or what?"

"You sure you want to do that? She came close to decapitating you."

5

"That was all part of the plan to soften her up. We have to deal with this. We have to deal with this once and for all!"

Susan took a deep breath. Now she really wanted to leave. She wanted to run back to her Mercedes and chain smoke all the way back down Interstate-85.

"Okay. Lead the way," she said with extreme reluctance. And with that, the two sisters entered the kitchen, unsure of what would happen next.

"Um, Momma. How's Karen holding up?" Diane asked.

The answer to that question was simple. Karen was not holding up at all. At times she was eerily silent and extremely distant. At other times her timbre was quite terrifying, especially at night. The screams would wake Ma Geneva, who would instantly begin to plead the blood of Jesus. But Karen's panic attacks scared her far more than the fluctuations of her mood.

Ma Geneva remembered the first one very well. As they headed out of the door to go to church, Karen started to tremble as if she were freezing. Her eyes widened. She retreated until her back touched the vinyl siding of the house. And even though she could go back no further, she continued to take steps. She wheezed and pounded on her chest. And then, as Ma Geneva looked on in disbelief, Karen collapsed and stopped breathing.

"How's Karen holding up, Momma?" Diane repeated when Ma Geneva did not answer.

"Best she can, I guess," Ma Geneva replied as she continued with the biscuit dough. "It's been hard for her. She has a ways to go."

"You see, that's what Sue and I want to talk to you about."

Ma Geneva slowly glanced up. She closely inspected her daughters, their wariness betraying them with every passing second.

6

"Like I said; she has a ways to go. That's part of the reason why I wanted the girls to stay here with us this summer."

Susan found the courage to interject. "You are not young anymore, Mom. And it is just you in the house now since Daddy is gone. Diane and I were thinking that maybe Karen should live with one of us. Look at me and Cicely: we have plenty of room. Karen will want for nothing."

That was a lie.

Diane chimed in. "Or she could come to Fountain Inn and stay with me and the twins. I mean—don't you think she would do better around younger folks like me or Sue?"

Ma Geneva would hear nothing of it. She felt that Cicely's mother paid too much attention to her career and not enough to her home. She hated the fact that Diane constantly subjected the twins to loud parties that occurred on school nights. And she especially hated the fact that Diane had a new boyfriend every other month. She wished that she could adopt her other granddaughters and raise them as well as Karen. But the summer visits would have to do.

***

"But have you ever French kissed before?" the tall boy with the faint mustache asked Cicely as she played with her Shirley Temple curls.

"Jail bait!" yelled another boy from across the basketball court.

"What's a French kiss?"

"You know, when you kiss and your mouth is open, and your tongue is dancing around."

"Oh you mean tongue kissing?" She smiled. "Oh I've done that."

"Stop lying!" The boy stepped into Cicely's space. His sweaty tank top inches from her Izod shirt.

7

"I think we better get going," Karen said, pulling at Cicely's arm. "The street lights are on."

Cicely snatched her arm away and shot Karen a glare.

"Maybe she's right," Brook said nervously.

"Screw Karen!" Cicely shouted. "The sun is still up. We have time."

Cicely was the oldest by several months. She was also the biggest of the four cousins. So her word was rarely challenged. Karen shrugged it off and returned to watching the game with the twins as Cicely and the tall boy made their way under the bleachers.

Karen and Brook watched the lay ups and slam-dunks while Dawn snuck a peak at what was going on below them. The tall boy leaned down to Cicely as she tilted her head back. Their mouths came together and the two youths began French kissing.

"Ugh!" Dawn said with disgust.

Karen looked beneath the bleachers and saw her cousin's face meshed with a boy that had to be at least three years her senior. With that, she grabbed Brook and Dawn and made her way down the bleachers.

"It's time to go, Cicely!" she shouted.

Cicely made no fuss, breaking the vacuum between her and the lanky boy. She smiled and then began walking toward her cousins.

They all walked down the street in silence. As they approached the house, Cicely stopped. "Y'all better not say anything either!" she ordered.

"If you want to catch the cooties from a boy you don't even know, that's on you," Karen said.

"Did he really have his tongue in your mouth?" Dawn asked.

Cicely said nothing, but smiled and played girlishly with the curls of her hair.

"Ugh," Dawn said again. And though she would never admit it, she was a little curious of how it felt.

***

The evening wore on, Diane and Susan were long gone, and the girls were content to crowd around Ma Geneva on the couch. They listened as their grandmother wove interesting tales about the good-ole days: mostly about the courtship between her and Papa Norris.

"Yes, we first started talking to one another seriously when I was thirteen years old," Ma Geneva recalled.

"Thirteen?" Cicely said. "You weren't too young to be interested in boys at thirteen?"

The question was full of sarcasm and Ma Geneva instantly knew that it wasn't really directed at her.

"No. As a matter of fact, you should be interested in boys at that age. But I must say that these little knuckle-head boys now-a-days are too mannish for their own good. That wasn't the case back in the day. Boys were respectful for the most part and young ladies were much more selective than they are now. We didn't just let some knuckle-head boy from off the street put his hands on us, much less his crusty lips."

Cicely coughed.

"No, things were much slower back then. We had respect for proper courtship."

Brook chimed in. "I bet Papa Norris used to come by and visit you every day, huh?"

"Every day without fail. We'd sit out on the porch and talk for hours about everything."

Dawn began deducing. "Courting, visiting. So I guess Mr. Henry is courting my Momma."

Brook snuck a glare at her twin, hoping she'd be quiet.

Mr. Henry's name never came up when Ma Geneva spoke to Diane. Deciding that it would be better to leave well enough alone, she pressed on.

9

"Anyway, we'd sit on the porch and drink fresh lemonade. Or we'd sit and talk in my parent's parlor if it was too cold outside. But we preferred the porch, with my brothers always in the parlor and such."

"Why didn't you just take him to your bedroom if you wanted privacy?"

Brook shoved Dawn in her side for that question, which without Dawn's knowledge, revealed so much about their mother's personal life. Finally, she picked up on her twin's messages and shut her mouth.

"My bedroom?" Ma Geneva asked. "Heavens no! Back in the day, young men weren't even allowed to see their girlfriend's bedroom."

The girls absorbed it all: hanging onto their grandmother's every word. Karen would laugh and interject all throughout the conversation, showing that she was slowly coming out of her shell. Ma Geneva's plan was working and she could already see that a strong and loving bond was forming between the girls.

But the summer eventually ended and it was time for the girls to return to their homes. And after the car was loaded with cousins and suitcases and Susan had pulled out of the driveway, Cicely sat in the passenger seat, looking in the side view mirror as Ma Geneva and Karen became smaller and smaller. All at once, with a left turn onto Willard Street, they disappeared from her view.

This would be the ebb and flow of the next four summers. The girls would come to Greenville, to the quiet house and the loving grandmother. And at the end of each summer, they would go back home...and Cicely would hate Karen even more.

Chapter 2

Susan zoomed up Interstate-85 driving ninety miles per hour as she talked on her car phone.

"You know, Karen is getting on my last nerve with those quote unquote panic attacks," she said to Diane. "She worries our mother unnecessarily."

There was a space where Diane undoubtedly gave her own opinion and then Susan continued.

"She just wants attention. Mom should let her live with me so I can straighten her out. She is spoiled just like Adele was."

Even though she spoke quietly and even though the music of Luther Vandross played loudly through the car speakers, Cicely heard every word. And a few times throughout the conversation between her mother and her aunt, Cicely rolled her eyes, as if she agreed with every spiteful word she heard.

***

Four summers had passed. As was their custom, Cicely, Brook and Dawn were in Greenville for the summer. They had been back for a month and everyone was in good spirits, especially Karen. Her glow screamed euphoria. Her aura emitted a pleasant vibe that anyone near her had to acknowledge. A song filled every nook and cranny of her heart; she could not ignore its harmony. Aaron, her boyfriend, gave her a happiness she once thought impossible.

They met in Atlanta during the previous Thanksgiving holiday. Ma Geneva and Karen were there visiting Susan and Cicely when in church she met Aaron. He approached her, they exchanged numbers, and started going steady that same day.

They were determined to make their long distance relationship work. Karen would call when she could

11

and she would write him while she was in English class. He would call and write her poetry, sending her something new every week, which of course she kept in a trunk in her closet. He gave her love and a new hunger for life. But she was especially happy at that time because he was there with her. They were the perfect couple. Karen and Aaron. Aaron and Karen. Their names even sounded alike.

Aaron had driven up from Atlanta with three of his friends: Tim, Temple, and Jeff. Brook and Dawn were in the living room playing spades with Temple and Jeff. Cicely, on the other hand, was upstairs with Tim playing a totally different game.

"You know I'm getting four of your books for reneging, right?" Temple asked Dawn as she smiled at her sister.

"I don't have any more hearts, sweetie. I don't have a reason to cheat. You aren't that good."

Jeff fidgeted in his chair. He looked around the living room. And then he looked up the stairs.

"Where is everybody?" he asked. "Where are Aaron and your cousin?"

"I believe she's taking him to Paris Mountain so that they can look over Greenville," Dawn answered.

Temple looked over to his friend with a smile and said, "The better question is what's going on upstairs with Tim and old girl."

He said this speaking of Cicely.

"True that," Jeff replied. "They have been up there a while. What do y'all think they're doing?"

Brook shook her head and said, "I don't know. And I don't want to know."

***

"How much higher are we going?" Aaron asked Karen. "I'm getting dizzy going round and round like this."

12

"Hush, boy! We're almost there." She tilted her seat back, enjoying the ride. "Pull in right there."

When Aaron pulled up into the clearing, the sight left him speechless.

"This is Greenville," she said as he switched off the ignition of his Jeep Cherokee. "What do you know about that?"

She removed her seat belt, kicked off her sandals, and propped her feet up on the dashboard.

"It's beautiful," he said. "I've never been this high up before. Everybody looks like ants from up here." He undid his seatbelt and reclined his seat. Rubbing his short, wavy hair, he said, "Yeah, we're going to build a house up here when we get married."

"Marriage?" She smirked. "You haven't proposed to me. You haven't given me a ring. Besides don't think you're in there like that." She jokingly snapped her fingers with attitude.

"Well are you going to Spelman after graduation so you can be closer to me in Atlanta? At least give me that."

She rested her arm on her freshly permed hair and replied, "If you're good to me, I'll give you anything you want."

Then they stared at each other for a moment. However, it seemed as if they were gazing at each other for days.

Karen could not lie; she had thought about what it would be like to be married to him. She would write her new name down to see how it would look. Mrs. Karen Williamson. Or Mrs. Karen Cole-Williamson. Either way sounded fine to her.

If he *did* ask her to marry him, she had made up in her mind that she would definitely say yes. She could see them now. Their children would probably look like him, with the cleft in his chin, his dimples and his brown eyes. They would be so adorable.

She could see them vacationing in the Bahamas, riding his and her bikes through the city, going by the shops, taking in all the sights. She could see herself growing old with him, babysitting their grandchildren, traveling cross country in an RV on a whim.

Of course she would go to Spelman. She had applied there already, and with just a final year of high school ahead of her, and with a 3.8 grade point average, she felt that she was a shoo-in to get accepted.

She wondered where they would make their home as newlyweds. Would they live in Atlanta or come back to the Greenville area? Would Aaron go to law school, or would he follow in his father's footsteps and become a pastor? He was already a junior pastor, so it would not be farfetched for Aaron to go into the ministry.

Aaron often talked to Karen about how tough it was being a preacher's kid. All the pressure placed on his shoulders. The lofty expectations. But that was one of the things that drew Karen to him. With his Godly upbringing, she felt safe knowing that she and Aaron were in agreement on many of the issues that befall young people.

"I got you something," he said, breaking the silence.

He reached in his pocket and pulled out a black suede box.

"Is that what I think it is?" Karen asked, her eyes growing wide.

"Now, now, before you get all excited..." He opened the box and presented her with a gold ring that had a little heart shaped diamond on it. "This is a promise ring. I know we aren't going to get married right now, but I wanted you to know how much I love you."

He slipped the ring on her left ring finger. It was little too big but Karen didn't care. To her the ring was perfect in every way.

"Well, are you going to say something?" he asked as she sat silently gazing at the ring. Then without warning she lunged towards him and into his embrace. And she kissed him fervently.

"I love you so much," she said wiping tears from her eyes.

Then Aaron pulled her feet away from their resting place on the dashboard and draped her legs over his. They kissed again with heat and passion. He rubbed his fingers through her reddish brown hair. He massaged her neck. He held her close to him and she enjoyed every minute of it. He rested his hand on her knee and then moved to her thigh, to the inside of her thigh, up her leg. Seemingly in one move he began working the hem of her sun dress up her thighs. Then he started tugging at her panties, and...

"Whoa!" Karen pulled herself away from him. She sat motionless for a minute, just staring out at the city, puzzled in a way.

"What's wrong? Are you worried about getting pregnant? Don't sweat it. I have protection."

"Protection? We won't need any protection."

Aaron sat silently for a moment. "Okay, I'm confused. Do you want to do it raw dawg?"

"*Raw dawg*?!"

"It means bareback...you know...without a rubber."

"We're not *doing* anything," Karen replied. "There's no need for a rubber."

"Whoa, whoa, whoa, wait a minute! You mean to tell me that we aren't about to have sex?!"

"No we're not having sex because we are not married. You know how I feel about that."

"But hold up, you said in your letters that you couldn't wait to get me up here so that we can be together. You said you had something to show me."

"I did have something to show you." Karen pointed out towards the view of Greenville from the mountain. "This! We came up here for a class trip and I thought it would be something cool to share with you." She put her sandals back on and looked over at Aaron, who

15

was now extremely quiet. His whole demeanor had changed before her very eyes. "I'm sorry if you got the wrong idea, but we need to wait until we're married before we make love. It's the right thing to do and you know that, baby."

"I drove all the way up here for nothing."

He started the ignition.

"What did you say?!" Karen's eyes were saucers. Her brow wrinkled.

When he didn't answer, she turned around and folded her arms in her seat. Anger filled her. She couldn't believe he would say something so crass. But believe it or not, they were on their way back down the mountain and the future of their relationship became more and more uncertain.

***

"Nah, shawty! Don't try to run off," Jeff said to Brook as he rearranged his cards. "I'm not done spanking you yet!"

"I'm not running. I'm going to get something to drink and I was going to get you something until you started running your mouth."

"Proceed." He shooed her along.

They all heard the old staircase creaking. Cicely and Tim were making their descent down to the living room to join them. Brook just shook her head.

"We'll talk later, girl!" Cicely said with a grin.

The clearly spent couple made their way to the loveseat and reclined. Jeff looked over at Temple and smiled as Brook returned to the card table and gave him a glass of lemonade.

"Um, you want to go upstairs?" he asked Brook with raised brows as he received his glass.

She sat down beside him, smiled, patted his slightly round belly and said, "You're not my type."

16

"Oh, you got jokes. But I'm cute, though. You can't deny that I'm cute."

Brook gave him a half smile, curving the corner of her mouth.

"You're alright," she said. "You'll do in a pinch."

"See I told you." Jeff sipped his drink as Brook looked at him, still smiling. Then he said, "The next time we come up here it's going to be me and you upstairs doing the do. Mark my words. Do a couple crunches, a few push-ups, you'll see."

She playfully hit Jeff's arm and said, "Shut up, boy and throw out your card. It's your turn."

They continued their game while Cicely snuggled up to Tim.

Dawn threw out a card and Temple immediately jumped out of his chair.

"You see her now, Jeff!" Temple shouted after she threw out a ten of hearts. "Shawty just reneged! Yes she did!"

"Hold on, hold on, my comrade," Jeff answered with a Russian accent. "I do believe you are right."

"What are y'all talking about?" Dawn looked over at Brook with guilt. Brook just shook her head.

"Nah, shawty!" Jeff said, now beginning to go through their books. "See you started cutting hearts right there. And now you mysteriously came up with a heart!"

Temple extended his cupped hand and said, "Give 'em over." He took four of their books, leaving them with only one.

"I'm sorry, Brook," Dawn said as her sister watched Jeff and Temple collect the books and begin to tally the score with glee. "I didn't see it."

"And that's five hundred!" Temple shouted, slamming the pen on the table.

"Come on! You have to be more careful," Brook said to her sister, who now pouted and gave fake sobs.

17

"Don't stress it, shawty," Jeff said to Dawn. "It was inevitable."

"What do y'all keep calling us?" Brook asked.

"Huh?" Temple replied, with a look of unawareness.

"Yeah, what are y'all saying? Shout? Are we shouting or something?" Dawn asked.

"Oh, you mean *shawty*," Jeff answered. "It's not shouting. It's shawty or shorty if you want to be proper."

"But what does it mean?" Brook asked.

Then Jeff settled in like a college professor about to embark on one of his finest lectures.

"You see in the ATL we call fine young sisters, *shawties*. It's a term of endearment, if you will. A sort of nickname if you won't."

He instructed Brook to stand in front of him with her back towards him.

"Now I see you, and I definitely see what you're working with. And I want to approach you."

He tapped on her shoulder and she turned around and looked up at him, smiling and batting her eyes. No one was sure if she was just playing along or if she really liked what she saw. Girth or not, Jeff stood over her, standing 6 feet, 4 inches. And Brook looked at him attentively.

He popped the collar of his Polo shirt and said with a manly, southern drawl, "What up, shawty? How are you? You are INDEED the finest thing I've seen in MANY moons. So I want to know what's good for a shawty like yourself, and a player like me."

She softly said to him, "Come here." And she tugged at his shirt, bringing his face down to hers as she tiptoed.

Playtime was over. Jeff closed his eyes as she brought herself closer to him. He puckered his lips and the room fell silent. But Brook playfully tiptoed and tiptoed as if she couldn't reach his lips. And finally she said, "I give up. I guess I'm just too short."

The room exploded with laughter.

"Did I get you? I got you right?" Brook asked with a playful smile, as she straightened his shirt.

"You got me," Jeff nodded as everyone continued to enjoy the laugh.

"But you still think I'm cute though, right?"

Brook smiled and replied, "You'll do in a pinch." And they both hugged like old friends.

"Now what if the girl is as tall as the guy?" Cicely asked, draping her long chocolate thighs over Tim. "Would she still be a shawty?"

Tim was very muscular, but at 5 feet, 7 inches he was about an inch shorter than Cicely. There was a moment of silence in which Temple and Jeff stared longingly as Cicely displayed her stallion like legs. Temple was about to answer Cicely's question when Jeff beat him to the punch.

"Now first of all, Tim, you're a lucky boy! That said, even if the guy is 5 feet tall and the girl is 6 feet five, she still would be a shawty. It has nothing to do with height."

"That doesn't make any sense," Brook replied.

"I know. It would make more sense if you and I could go upstairs!"

"What's that got to do with making sense of the word *shawty?*"

"Absolutely nothing! I'm just trying to get you to go upstairs!"

The room erupted with laughter once again. But their banter was interrupted by the sounds of screeching brakes and slamming doors. Karen hastily exited the Jeep and stomped up the front porch. She stormed into the living room, and then made an abrupt turn to look at Aaron who was hard on her heels.

"So you're just going to leave like this?" she asked, staring at Aaron intensely.

"What do you think?" Without even looking at her, he yelled to his friends,

"Let's be out!"

But Tim continued to lounge on the couch next to Cicely. He smiled and asked his angry friend, "What's wrong with you, church boy? Your girlfriend didn't give you any loving?"

"What?" Aaron responded with a slightly raised voice. "I will leave your little swollen behind up here and make you bench press your way back to Atlanta!"

"Hey Brook, I'll check you later," Jeff said gathering his things quickly. "Football practice starts tomorrow and this dude doesn't look like he's playing."

Jeff darted out the front door followed by Temple and a much reluctant Tim.

"Call me when you get back to the ATL, shawty," he said to Cicely.

"No doubt," she answered, as she lay back on the couch, completely oblivious to the stare down that commenced between Aaron and Karen.

"Here's your ring back," Karen said, as she pulled it off of her finger and began to give it to him.

Aaron took it.

Karen was shocked.

Everything she believed about him was a lie. She watched him as he stormed out of the house and into his Jeep. But she could not bear to watch him drive away. He was driving out of her life and all of a sudden feelings of fear and loneliness began to overflow her heart. She couldn't take it. The tears were falling down her face like waterfalls. Her hands shook uncontrollably. She couldn't even hear Brook and Dawn's questions of 'what happened?' and 'are you alright?' It became hard for her to breathe.

With a dash she went to the kitchen, poured a tall glass of water, and removed her prescription medicine from the top cabinet. She dispensed two pills into the palm of her hand and then she popped them into her mouth. Sobbing and weeping, she swallowed the water and slammed the glass down on the counter. It became clear to her. She was destined to be alone. It would not be long before she would have absolutely no one to love her.

Even though she felt that the contents of the bottle from the top cabinet had taken their effect and that she wouldn't be passing out, she felt the need to go out to the back porch and lay down across the swing. She closed her eyes and as the tears made tracks down her cheeks, she fell asleep thinking to herself, "If I want to keep Aaron, I'm going to have to break down and give him what he wants."

***

Many years had passed and Aaron stood tall behind the pulpit of Spirit and Truth Worship Center for the whole world to see and hear. He waved to a crowd of thousands with television cameras zooming in on him so that the nations could see him.

He cleared his throat, placing his left hand over his mouth. Now everyone could see his platinum and diamond wedding band as it sparkled in the spotlight. And then after moments of silence, he began to address the audience.

"I first give honor to God, the great Elohim of Israel. I give honor to my many distinguished guests who take their places with me on the rostrum. To all the saints that are in this building and to all who view this program via television, I greet you in the name of the Most High God.

"I can't go any further without giving honor to my lovely wife. Please stand, darling. Come stand beside me and show everyone how beautiful you are."

Karen rose from her seat and straightened her dress as the audience gave a round of applause. She began walking slowly toward the front of the room. She increased her speed as the applause grew louder and louder. Then she sped up a bit more—

—so she could turn the channel on the television before her five-year-old son walked into the room.

"Mommy, is that my daddy on TV again?" her son asked.

She sighed. "Yes, that's your father."

Then her son hung his head and asked, "Why doesn't he come to see me?"

Karen bolted from her slumber when she heard Ma Geneva scream, "Girls! Get up here, NOW!"

Karen gathered herself and ran into the house and up the stairs to see the rest of the girls waiting at the doorway of her bedroom. Ma Geneva stood beside Karen's bed and she was fuming, far angrier than the girls had ever seen her. Her brown skin seemed as if it had turned red. She wore yellow dish gloves and in her left hand was a used condom.

"Whose is it?!" she asked. It was her habit to place the girls' dry cleaning on their beds when she had picked it up. But it was clear that it wasn't a white dress wrapped in plastic that had ruffled the sheets on Karen's bed and had indented her throw pillows. "Answer me!" But everyone stood stiff as the condom dangled from Ma Geneva's hand. Karen looked at her bed in disbelief. "Say something!" Tears moistened her eyes. "I am so disappointed in you!" She stormed out, went into her bedroom across the hall, and slammed the door. Brook, Dawn and Cicely exited the room as well. But Karen just crouched down on the floor, buried her head in her hands, and began crying.

"Tell me you didn't have sex on Karen's bed," Brook said to Cicely when they reached the bottom of the stairs.

"Well I have that little twin bed in my room and y'all have those bunk beds. It was the only logical choice. I wasn't about to do it on Ma Geneva's."

"You are scandalous!" Brook said as she turned and walked away.

"That bed isn't getting any real use anyway!"

"Tramp!" was Brook's only reply.

Dawn raised her eyebrows and shrugged her shoulders as if to say, 'It was wrong what you did, but how was it though?'

All the while Karen remained on her bedroom floor all alone, sad because she didn't even have a place to lay her head.

***

In the middle of the night, Ma Geneva rose from her bed. She hadn't slept at all. There was something that needed to be said and this was the time to do it.

She quietly opened her door and tip-toed to Karen's room. She didn't want to wake anyone.

She opened the door and saw Karen on the floor by the bed, her arms wrapped around her lifted knees. The lights were still on. Karen sat in the same spot that she had crouched down to earlier. She rocked back and forth, and stared into space. Ma Geneva slowly lowered herself down to her side.

"Dearest, I know that you had nothing to do with that condom." She rubbed Karen's reddish brown hair. "I know whose it was."

"I can't sleep in that bed."

"I—I know, sweetheart. We'll get you another comforter set, or another mattress if you like." Then Ma Geneva took a deep breath and began to speak softly and sweetly to her youngest granddaughter. "Look, I know this situation has no doubt upset you, but we have to put it aside for now because I have some important things to discuss with you. I'm not always going to be around and there are some things that you need to know, some truths I need to tell you before I leave this earth."

"Don't you speak of dying, Ma Geneva. Don't talk about leaving me!"

"Now hush! Everybody has to die eventually." She stroked Karen's reddish-brown hair with its blonde streaks and gazed upon her skin's light sandy complexion. "You don't look anything like us." She looked at her granddaughter with wonderment.

"You're scaring me," Karen said, as she observed her grandmother's intense inspection of her.

Ma Geneva ceased from gazing and began to speak again.

"I need for you to prepare yourself for what you are about to hear." Karen wiped the tears from her eyes, which were now bloodshot red, and began to listen attentively as the old woman spoke. "You, Cicely, Brook and Dawn are all precious flowers to me. As beautiful as those orchids in my living room. More so! And strong. Each one of you are so strong. But believe it or not, of all the girls, you are the strongest." Ma Geneva spoke hurriedly, not that this information wasn't important, but because there was something else that she desperately needed to say. "Now here's what we really need to talk about. Your mother was very smart. Did you know that she started playing piano at the age of four? Well she was beautiful and intelligent and if your grandfather had a favorite, it was probably her. She was always his little baby.

"Well she took music all through school; she marched and played in all of the school bands. Your mother was leading the choir down at the church at the age of fourteen, and I mean the adult choir."

Karen took all of it in. These were facts about her mother that she was hearing for the first time.

"Now your mother, though she was smart, she was also very rebellious. She and your grandfather used to butt heads all the time. But one of the things they definitely went to war over was where Adele would attend college. She wanted to go to a school in

24

Charleston and your granddaddy wanted her to go to Furman, right down the way, so that she could be close to home. They fussed and argued about that thing for all of Adele's senior year. But in the end, she ended up going to Charleston. Her grades were so good and she had plenty of recommendations so she didn't need our money at all. She just left and went down there on her own.

"Well a year later, your mother had to come home. Apparently she went down to Charleston, had an affair with a married man and ended up getting pregnant. Both of your aunties were married with kids on the way, and your granddaddy was old school. 'You get pregnant, you get married'. Your momma knew how he was, so she wouldn't tell him who the father was. She knew he was going to go down there and find the man and make him take care of his responsibility. That's how your grandfather was. So Adele never gave him a name or an address. That made your grandfather so mad that he stopped speaking to her."

Ma Geneva paused as if she was about to shed tears, but she quickly regained her emotions and continued.

"Well your mother gave birth to you. And your grandfather never even came to the hospital. He wasn't even there for your first birthday. It really wasn't that he was being mean, it's just that he was hurting inside and didn't quite know how to deal with it."

Again there was a pause.

"Well he never got the chance to speak to her. Adele moved away, and—you know the rest.

"I don't exactly know why she got into drugs, why she would go so far as to overdose. Honestly, there was no sign of it. And to keep from being unmercifully angry with your grandfather, I tried not to think about it. But he never forgave himself for acting so foolishly. I really believe that he began working so hard so that he could get his mind off of it all."

Then Ma Geneva reached into her housecoat pocket and retrieved a long white envelope that was folded in half.

"When you were two-years-old, your mother gave me this and made me promise that I wouldn't tell your grandfather."

Ma Geneva opened the envelope. "This is information about your father. He was a music professor at The College of Charleston. His name is Dennis Jordan."

She smiled and gave the envelope to her granddaughter. Karen held it in her hands for a moment. She never thought in a million years that she would ever have a chance of meeting her father, of seeing what family she might have elsewhere.

"You might not be ready to go down to Charleston to meet your father now. But when you feel that you are, let me know and we'll go down there together."

Karen smiled and embraced Ma Geneva.

"I love you!" she said.

"I love you more. Now come on let's get some sleep. You can stay in my room for tonight until we get your bed squared away."

Karen rose from the floor and helped Ma Geneva to stand to her feet. And then they both walked out of Karen's bedroom hand in hand, stepping quietly so that they wouldn't wake the others. And indeed the twins were fast asleep. But Cicely was wide awake. She had been listening outside of Karen's room the entire time.

When she heard that they were coming out, she quickly removed her ear from the wall and scurried back into her room, resting against the door after she closed it. Her breaths were rapid and rigid and her face produced a scowl, as if to say that her archenemy had triumphed once again.

***

The next morning the house was extremely quiet, but not in a good way. No television. No radio. It seemed as if the birds were not even singing that morning. The quietness came at the instruction of Ma Geneva, who had demanded that she didn't want to hear a peep out of anyone.

She had the girls folding laundry and she specifically requested that the sound of folding clothes was all that she wanted to hear. But Karen just couldn't ignore what Cicely did in her room, on her bed.

"Don't go in my bedroom anymore," she said to Cicely as she folded a shirt.

Brook had told Karen earlier that she and Dawn had nothing to do with it. But Karen already knew who the culprit was.

"What did you say?" Cicely stopped folding clothes.

"You heard me! Don't go in my—"

Before Karen could finish her sentence, Cicely charged at her and slapped her across the face, sending the shirt that Karen was folding across the room.

Karen was stunned as she hunched over on the couch and held her face. She and Cicely had arguments before. They had gone back and forth many times. But things had never gotten physical.

"Go get her medicine, Brook!" Cicely snarled. "She's about to spaz out again!"

"Leave her alone, Cicely!" Brook shouted to no avail.

Cicely slapped Karen again, this time making her buckle to the floor between the couch and the coffee table. Karen was frozen. Her ears were ringing. She couldn't hear Cicely cursing at her while her cousins tried to pull her away.

She was stunned by the attack but she wasn't about to be smacked in the head again. So she lunged at Cicely, grabbing her around the waist in an attempt

27

to take her down. But Cicely was just too strong and too mean for her. She raised both of her hands above her head and brought them down with a mighty blow on the small of Karen's back.

Karen collapsed on the floor, exposed to a volley of blows that Cicely delivered with pinpoint accuracy. She was being pummeled. The faint taste of blood filled her mouth and she could do nothing but cover up her face as Cicely wailed away.

"I HATE YOU! I HATE YOU!" Cicely shouted as she swung. It seemed like there was no hope for Karen until—

"CICELY, GET OFF OF HER!" Ma Geneva yelled.

Cicely dare not go against Ma Geneva. Everyone knew that old woman didn't play. So she slowly got off of Karen, breathing hard. Her hair ruffled. Continuing to stare harshly at Karen, she slowly backed away. But the speed at which she was doing things wasn't fast enough for Ma Geneva.

"I SAID GET OFF OF HER!" she screamed as she pulled Cicely out of the way to see scratches on Karen's face and blood streaming from her mouth. "What has gotten into you, Cicely?"

At that time all respect for Ma Geneva vanished from Cicely. She stormed past her grandmother, picked up a vase, and threw it against the wall as she ran out of the living room, through the kitchen and out the back door.

Flames grew in Ma Geneva's eyes and smoke seemed to billow from her nostrils as she began to go after Cicely.

"Ma Geneva!" Dawn yelled. "Karen is going to need some help!"

She said this because Karen's face was in pretty bad shape. Her lip was swollen and white muscle could be seen on her cheeks and forehead. She also said this to save Cicely's life. Both Brook and Dawn knew that if Ma Geneva could have gotten to Cicely, that she would have looked far worse than Karen did.

***

Later on that day a terrible storm rolled in. Cicely's mother had come up to Greenville at the command of Ma Geneva and their heated battle could be heard in every room of the house.

"Your daughter is out of control, and you need to start talking to her!" Ma Geneva yelled.

"Cicely IS NOT out of control. You're just playing favorites just like daddy did!" Susan screamed as they started going back and forth with each other.

"That condom has absolutely nothing to do with playing favorites!"

"Well, why does it have to be Cicely's condom? Why couldn't it be your precious Karen's? It was in her bedroom!"

"That's because Cicely had sex in Karen's room, on Karen's bed!"

"That's BULL, and you know it!"

"I will not have you or your daughter disrespecting my house. And you will watch the way you talk to me too, or I will slap the taste out of your mouth and give your daughter what she's needed for a long time: A BEATING!"

"You are not touching me or my daughter!" Susan retreated from her mother's room and down to the living room where Cicely and the twins sat.

"Get your things, Cicely! We are leaving!" Then she darted out the door.

Cicely quietly gathered her things and gave the twins a look of good-bye. No words were exchanged between them though.

"I said move it!" Susan bawled.

With that Cicely left the house and got into the car. The door wasn't even closed when her mother hit the gas and flew up Willard Street, leaving behind a cloud of white smoke from screeching tires.

Just as she did at the end of every summer, Cicely looked into her side-view mirror and watched as the house got smaller and smaller. But this time no one hugged good-bye, and no one waved farewell from the front porch. That was the last summer the girls spent together at Ma Geneva's house.

Chapter 3

Cicely had survived four years of college and was about to get her degree in business and management. In spite of the events that transpired just five years before, she decided to go to Furman University, not very far from Ma Geneva's house. Even though she apologized for what she did, their grandmother/granddaughter relationship never fully recovered. But if she wasn't anything else, she was a trooper.

"Please come in and have a seat," Cicely said to her extremely tall visitor.

His name was Derrick Smalls and his reputation in the bedroom preceded him. But Cicely Shaw had a reputation of her own.

"Wow, this room is a whole lot bigger than some of the other girls' rooms I've seen in this dorm." He lowered his head to enter the room.

"I'm an RA. That's one of the perks we get: a bigger room all to ourselves, privacy."

Derrick sat on the bed and watched his hostess' chocolate frame as she sashayed across the room lighting candles and incense. He definitely liked what he saw. "I can't believe we haven't hooked up yet."

"Well you're always surrounded by your little groupies. And I don't usually kick it with campus guys."

"So you're making an exception for me?"

She gave him elevator eyes and replied, "Yes I am, just this once."

They both laughed as she sat down beside him, wearing nothing but a tank top and Umbro shorts. She moved in closer, measuring her prey, preparing for the kill.

Derrick said, "Can I get a drink, or something?"

Cicely raised her eyebrows and shifted her mouth to one side. "I've got some wine coolers. Is that cool?"

"Yeah, toss me one of them!"

She filled his request then sat down beside him and began to massage his thigh while kissing him on his neck.

"Um, what kind of music do you have in here?" He lifted himself from the bed and away from Cicely's clutches.

Clearly perturbed, she rolled her eyes and went to her CD changer. "I got some R. Kelly, some Guy, some Luke. What do you want to hear?"

"Put on that R. Kelly." He took a swig from his bottle and sat back down. "Yeah that will set the mood off right!"

Once she had filled his request, she took a deep breath, walked over to Derrick, and began working his wife-beater off of him. But then he took her by the hand and began singing to her, very loudly, and in the wrong key.

Cicely could not take anymore. She took the wine cooler out of his hand and said, "Are you scared or something?"

"Nah I'm not scared. But you sure are forward."

"Forward *and* shocked."

"Shocked?"

"I'm standing in front of you wearing practically nothing and you aren't getting the message. So let me be frank." She removed her tank top, took his right hand, placed it on her bare left breast and said, "My cousins will be here in an hour to pick me up. We haven't got much time. You need to stop playing around so I can get mine!"

***

"I'm here to see Cicely Shaw," Dawn said to the front desk attendant in the lobby of AD Hall.

About five minutes after the attendant called her room, Cicely came around the corner with her tall visitor.

"If you're ever in the ATL, call me." She handed him a piece of paper with her number on it.

"You know I will," he said. "No matter where I'm drafted, when we play the Hawks, I will definitely come see you!"

They hugged and he made his exit, walking by Dawn as she turned and looked him up and down.

"Cicely, please tell me that you didn't just—"

"You know good girls never tell."

"So you can go ahead and tell me what happened!"

"You aren't funny." Cicely playfully punched her cousin in the arm. "You know I'm going to fill you in."

Dawn said, "Let's get going so we can pick up Brook."

"Pick her up? You can't drive. How'd you get here?"

"That's our ride over there." Dawn pointing to the jet black, stretch Hummer parked up the street. It rested on twenty-six inch chrome rims and had chrome trim on the door handles, wheel wells, grill and bumpers.

"How in the world did you hook this up?" Cicely asked in amazement. She was so awe struck by the vehicle that she didn't notice the driver, who had long since gotten out of the Hummer and was standing by the opened back door.

"Let's roll!" Dawn said as she pulled Cicely into the limo. "You know I'm going to fill you in!"

***

Brook heard the car horn and rushed by the many boxes that were stacked neatly in the living room. She hurried out of the door and ran down the steps to see Cicely and Dawn waiting outside of the stretch Hummer.

33

She said, "This is nice, how did you hook this up, Cicely? Which one of your parents gave you the cash for this limo?"

Cicely's parents were well off. Her father was a prominent surgeon in Atlanta, Georgia and her mother was the vice-chair of Ophthalmology-Research at Emory. Both easily bringing in six figures and everyone knew that she, being the only child, received anything she wanted.

Cicely smiled and shook her head no to Brook's question. Then she pointed at Dawn.

Now Brook and Dawn's financial situation was a *little* different. Their mother worked at a manufacturing plant in Fountain Inn, South Carolina. She often worked double shifts to provide for her girls. Their father didn't work at all.

"How did you get the money for this limo, Dawn?"

"Get in the car! We're late as is!" Dawn hurried her sister and cousin into the Hummer.

Cicely poured Brook some champagne as they whisked off down the street.

"Whose limo is this?" Brook asked quietly as she received her glass.

But Dawn looked ahead, not really wanting to divulge the information.

"Go on and tell her, girl!"

"Cory Mack," Dawn said softly.

"Cory Mack?! Cory Mack from Southern Side?!"

"The one and only!" Cicely responded as Dawn gave her a cold glare.

Immediately, Brook banged on the driver's window and shouted, "Driver! Stop this car immediately!"

The driver stopped and opened his rear window to see what was going on.

Dawn reached out to restrain her sister as Cicely instructed the driver that everything was fine.

"Let me explain!" Dawn said.

"I'm not going to jail!" Brook exclaimed. "I'm getting married in a week and I'm not going to jail!"

"Nobody's going to jail!"

"Tell her the story," Cicely said.

So Dawn explained how she met Cory Mack at a club in Greenville one Sunday night.

"He stopped me as I was leaving the club. We talked for a while and after I told him that I was in school for accounting, he offered me a job keeping his books. We went to lunch a couple of times. And the next thing you know, we were a couple."

"Do you know what he does for a living?"

"He owns Mack Custom Automobiles on Laurens Road."

"No that's the front business! Do you know what he *really* does?"

"Listen, I've heard the rumors and I can attest that they are all lies."

"So he's not a drug dealer?"

"I have been working with Cory for about three months now, doing all of his accounting, and I haven't seen one shady thing about his business," Dawn said. "But that's one of the reasons that I haven't mentioned it to you, Brook!"

"And why is that?"

"Because I knew that you would jump to conclusions."

"So Cory Mack is not a drug dealer?" Brook asked softly.

"No, he is not."

Of course that was a lie and Dawn knew it. Cory Mack, the Southern Side kingpin, supplied many of the tristate dealers with cocaine. Dawn knew that from day one.

"He's a really cool guy and I want you to meet him," she said. "When I told him about tonight, he suggested that we use the stretch Hummer. He also got us the VIP passes for the hair show from some connections

35

he has at the radio station. So just kick back, relax, and enjoy one of the last evenings you have left as a single woman."

"Yeah, chill!" Cicely said, now drinking the champagne straight from the bottle. "Because for a minute, you were starting to sound like—"

Then she paused, and became very quiet.

"Go on and say it!" Brook exclaimed, poking her cousin in the arm. "Say her name. Say *Karen*. You can't even say her name, can you? You didn't even say a word to her at Ma Geneva's funeral!"

The limo slowed down as the driver pulled into the front of the coliseum.

"There's the radio station van," Dawn said as she got out of the limo. "I'm going to go get the passes."

"What is up with you and Karen?" Brook asked. "Why is there always so much strife between the two of you?"

Cicely took a swig from her champagne bottle and sat back in her seat. "You know how she is. And I just don't like her, that's all."

"How is she? Why don't you like her?"

"She's a spoiled brat!" Cicely took another swig of champagne.

"If anyone is spoiled, you are. Your parents give you everything you want. You haven't worked one day in your life! You're rich!"

"I'm not talking about anything like that." Cicely put the bottle down. "I mean those anxiety attacks. You and I both know there's nothing wrong with her!"

"But how would you feel if your mom killed herself and you had to move in with two old people?"

"Her mom overdosed. BIG DEAL! You know what? For some, that would be a blessing in disguise!"

"What are you talking about?"

"She used to pull that anxiety stuff just to get attention!"

36

Brook moved closer to Cicely and asked, "Attention from who?"

"I got the passes y'all," Dawn said after she hopped back into the limo. "Let's go on inside."

Dawn saw that Cicely was sitting quietly in her seat and that Brook was staring at her. So she asked, "What's up?"

A silent moment passed between them.

"I get it," Brook said. "I honestly don't know why I never noticed it before."

"Let's just go!" Cicely said as she quickly exited the limo.

"What's with her?" Dawn asked Brook as they followed.

Brook raised her brows and sighed. She had stumbled onto a dark family secret.

***

The hair show was over. Happy with the connections she made, Brook looked forward to the post-show festivities at Embassy Suites. But she was startled when the stretch Hummer arrived at Dawn's apartment.

"What are we doing here?" she asked. "I thought we were going to an after party."

Instead of responding to Brook's question, Dawn fumbled for her keys and then opened her front door, revealing a room full of young women with drinks in their hands and filth in their eyes.

"Surprise!" they all yelled.

"This *is* the after party," Dawn added.

The music of Snoop Dog blared through the house speakers.

"I told you that I didn't want a bachelorette party!" Brook said with a smile.

"I'm your twin sister. I know what you really want even if you deny it. And guess what? I have another surprise for you."

Dawn took Brook to her guest bedroom.

"Surprise!" Karen screamed as she ran to embrace Brook.

They hadn't seen each other since their grandmother's funeral over a year ago. Dawn beamed and joined in the embrace. Cicely's reaction was much different.

Who invited her? she thought.

"I can't believe you made it up here, Karen!" Brook shouted.

"My last exam is not until Tuesday. So I had plenty of time to drive up."

Brook, Dawn and Karen were catching up while Cicely was drinking Crown Royal straight from the bottle and staring at Karen with contempt.

"You have been down there grinding, cousin!" Dawn exclaimed.

"I have been in school for four years. So I am definitely ready to get out and go to work."

Karen caught sight of Cicely, who was staring in their direction at first. But she quickly turned away when Karen made eye contact with her.

"How is Cicely doing?" she asked.

"She's still Cicely if you know what I mean," Dawn answered. "You should go over there and talk to her."

"No, I don't think that's a good idea," Brook said.

"I think I *will* go and say hello."

When Karen walked away, Brook gave Dawn the stank eye.

"What I do?" Dawn asked.

Brook just shook her head.

"Hey, cuz!" Karen said over the music. "Congratulations on graduating!"

Cicely gave a half smile and said nothing but, "Thanks."

Karen thought to herself, Be the bigger person. Be the bigger person.

"Look, Cicely, I'm going to get straight to the point. We haven't really been the same since that incident about five years ago. You didn't even speak to me at Ma Geneva's funeral."

Karen moved closer to her, measuring her words carefully.

"Listen, I know that you and I have some bad blood between us, and at this point I really don't care to know why that is. I want to know if we could just wipe the slate clean and become friends again, maybe even cousins."

Karen smiled with sincerity as she stretched forth her right hand toward Cicely's.

"Yeah, we can be friends," Cicely replied as she loosely shook Karen's hand.

Then the doorbell rang.

"OH YEAH! It's time for the festivities!" Dawn shouted as she opened the front door revealing three male strippers. Everyone gathered around Brook, who was smiling from ear to ear.

"Excuse me," Cicely said coldly as she slid past Karen.

Knowing that nothing had changed between the two of them, Karen watched with a raised brow as Cicely brushed past her as if she wasn't there to join the other ladies. In making her plea, she lied about one thing. She did care to know why there was bad blood between them. She desperately wanted to know why Cicely hated her so much.

***

The alcohol levels lowered rapidly in every bottle. The party had matured into a hedonistic ritual where ladies stuffed singles in garters and underwear elastic and we're rewarded with lap dances and lewd acts.

Laline, one of Brook's friends from Atlanta, had also called some female strippers to come to the party. Laline worked for a fashion magazine. She was very beautiful, with a caramel complexion and short, silky jet-black hair that bounced on her shoulders when she walked.

Laline and Brook had become close friends while Brook lived in Atlanta in spite of how they met. When they met at a hair show Laline was covering, it wasn't because Brook wanted some contacts in the hair industry media. It was because Laline wanted to take Brook out for a date.

"My, my, my. Females get just as wild with male strippers as the guys get with us," said Trixie, one of the female strippers that Laline and her friends had called up.

"Yeah, yeah women are dogs too!" Laline said. "But never mind that. Get naked for mommy!"

The stripper happily obliged.

Everyone became wild animals but no one was more untamed than Cicely. She had lifted the hem of her skirt up to her waist. And she was grinding her backside against one of the male strippers as he leaned against the wall.

She was obviously drunk. Her speech, slurred. Her eyes, half-closed. Through her eyelashes she must have caught a glimpse at Karen, who sat across the room, bopping to the music, but clearly not involved in any of the foolishness.

Cicely passed the liquor bottle to the stripper. He was pretty drunk himself because his eyes were also half-closed and bloodshot. Cicely held his bikini shorts in her hand. The stripper was completely naked.

She reached down into her bra, retrieved two one hundred dollar bills, and asked the stripper, "Do you want to make some real money, daddy?"

He nodded yes. Then she whispered into his ear and shortly afterwards they began to make their way over to where Karen sat alone. Karen stared at him dumfounded. She wondered why Cicely was bringing him over to her, him naked, Cicely half-naked. But she would soon find out the answer.

"My friend here says that I'm yours for the rest of the evening," the stripper said. Then he began dancing in front of Karen and waving his manhood in her face.

"No thank you, I'm fine."

"Nah, I'm trying to do you a favor," Cicely said. "I'm going to teach you how to get *and* keep a man."

Then Cicely pushed the stripper closer to Karen, spun him around, dropped to her knees, and began performing oral sex on him. Karen's eyes widened. Both Brook and Dawn, who were across the room, were stunned as well. But Cicely continued with gusto as the rest of the ladies in the room began cheering her on.

Cicely stopped, looked longingly at the stripper, and licked her lips. And then she changed her facial expression into one of a serious instructor.

"And that's how it's done," she said to Karen. "Now you try."

Cicely pushed the stripper closer to Karen's face, but she quickly moved him out of the way.

"You didn't get it!" Cicely said sharply. "Now look closely and I will show you again!"

She went back to work, getting oohs and aahs from the crowd. Brook and Dawn couldn't believe what they were seeing. Again Cicely pushed the stripper close to Karen's face, but Karen got up this time and backed away.

"Well you're never going to get it if you keep running away from it!" Cicely shouted with laughter as the stripper smiled and nodded in agreement.

"That's enough!" Brook shouted as she pushed the stripper out of the way and got in her cousins face.

Karen screamed, "NOT EVERYBODY IS A WHORE LIKE YOU!"

Cicely saw red. She rushed toward Karen and would have gotten to her if Brook, Dawn and Laline hadn't restrained her.

"LET ME GO SO I CAN KILL HER!" Then she lifted her hands, gesturing she was cool. "On second thought, I don't have time for beating Karen down again. I'm late for a bootie call."

She pulled her car keys from her purse and began stumbling towards the front door.

With Cicely inebriated and off balance, Karen easily pushed her to the floor and took the car keys out of her hands.

"YOU'RE NOT GOING ANYWHERE!" Karen yelled with passion.

"YOU ARE NOT MY MOMMA!" Cicely screamed, her skirt still riding up on her backside.

"I don't care what beef we have between us! I'm not letting you leave this apartment. You're too drunk to drive!"

"Leave me alone, Karen! ALONE! You do know what ALONE means, don't you?"

The music had stopped and so had the party. Karen dropped the keys on the floor and threw up her hands. Then she gathered her things and walked to the front door. But before she opened the door, she turned around to face Cicely.

"What did I do to you?" she cried. "Why do you hate me so much?"

Then she dashed out of the door with Brook chasing behind her.

"Karen wait!"

Brook finally caught her as she was getting into her car.

"Cicely can't go anywhere because she rode here with us in the limo."

Karen fumbled to put her keys in the ignition. She had not drank an ounce of alcohol but her hands still shook. The simple task of starting a car had become nearly impossible for her. Finally, she stopped fighting with the keys. And then, with tears streaming down her face, she asked, "Why does she hate me so much, Brook? What did I do to her?"

With tears in their eyes, they stared at each other silently for a few seconds. Then Brook backed away as Karen finally started her car, closed the door, and sped down the dark street—alone.

Chapter 4

For miles and miles around, Dawn could see nothing but water. The cool breeze tickled her bare back and gently lifted the hem of her fringe dress. A gentle spray of water kissed her cheeks as she stood by the railing of the cruise ship, Queen Majestic. It was all so beautiful.

Dawn looked out into the ocean and thought of how lucky she was to be on her way to the Bahamas with the man she treasured. Cory and Dawn had been together for two years. To the outside observer, everything seemed right in Dawn's world. But upon closer inspection, one would recognize that there were changes in the air, and that she was uncertain now of how those changes would affect her relationship with Cory.

"Guess who?" Cory said as he placed his huge palms over her eyes.

"I know it's you. I know your voice."

She removed his hands and pulled him close to her. She flat out loved that man. She adored his broad shoulders and his thick neck. She craved his broad chest and huge arms. Even his bald head, which he usually covered with some type of hat. But on that cool Friday evening, he wore formal attire: a Michael Jordan tuxedo and a pair of Mezlan Platinum alligator dress shoes.

"It's beautiful out here," she said.

"I have never seen anything like it."

They watched the sun retire below the horizon.

"I'm buying us one of these boats," Cory said.

"You don't have the money for a cruise ship."

He pulled out two folds of one hundred dollar bills encased in platinum money clips and waved it in front of Dawn.

"You don't know how much money I have, baby-girl!" He cracked a wide smile, revealing his platinum bicuspid.

"Ooh, give me that!" Dawn playfully attempted to get at the stash.

"No, no, no. This money is only for good girls!" He put the cash back in his pocket.

Money was never an issue with Cory. He had a lot of it and he amassed it quickly. On a daily basis, Dawn would count more money than most people made in a year. But she was beginning to wonder if the money was worth all of the worry.

***

Later that evening, Dawn and Cory attended the customary Captain's dinner. Cory was a people person. So it was easy for him to strike up a conversation with the middle-aged gentleman that sat next to him at the round table.

"I sell medical equipment up in Boston," the gentleman said. "I do about $2.5 million in sales a year. What do you do for a living?"

"Well, I sell people dreams," Cory replied. "Tell me this. What was your dream car growing up?"

The man scratched his forehead right below his receding hairline.

"A 1957 Ford Thunderbird," he answered, snapping his fingers and widening his eyes.

"Is that it? Nothing else to it but that?"

"Well of course I wanted it to be candy apple red, with cream interior."

"Go on."

"I wanted it to have a chrome tail pipe and white wall tires."

"Is there anything else?"

"Well, there was this one thing."

"What's that?" Cory asked.

"Well—you'll probably think this is stupid."

"Try me!"

"Okay." The man looked away. A boyish smile slowly broke across his face. He chuckled and then said, "I wanted the dash and door paneling to be lined with fur, expensive white fur."

"You've got it!" Cory leaned back into his chair.

"I've got what?"

"Your dream car! I'll make a few calls and it should be ready for you in a couple of weeks, a month tops."

"Are you serious?" the man asked, his face lighting up.

Cory began with his sales pitch.

"You see, I sell dreams. You come to me and tell me what kind of vehicle you want. And this is my guarantee: I'll find it for you or I will build it for you. Period!"

"Is he serious?" the man asked Dawn.

"I saw how your face lit up when you were talking about your dream car," Cory replied. "I can get that car for you. Nothing is impossible when it comes to Cory Mack Custom Automobiles!"

***

The long and short arms of Cory's Rolex rested over a diamond encrusted 12 by the time they returned to their state room. They were to dock at Nassau in the morning, so Dawn reclined on the bed. She wanted to get some rest before her shopping spree the next day. Cory had other plans. He had already hung his tuxedo neatly in the closet and was putting on some shorts and a polo shirt. He had intentions of hitting the casino with a vengeance.

"Did you see how I had that guy eating out the palm of my hand?" he asked. "I probably made about two hundred grand tonight just sitting at that dinner table."

46

"You're not going to get any sleep?"

"You know I don't sleep. Besides, I'm going to join 'Mr. Thunderbird' at the poker table."

Dawn rolled over on her side and sighed softly. Cory noticed the somberness of her mood, so he sat beside her and began rubbing her braids.

"What's the matter?" he asked.

"Well, you've been doing pretty well down at the dealership."

"Yeah."

"And you said yourself that you made two hundred thousand tonight at dinner."

"At least that much."

"So here is my question: do you think you'll always be in the game?"

"Oh, I get it." Cory's hand explored the curvature of Dawn's waist. Then his palm found the softness of her bottom. He gave it a firm squeeze which made her giggle. Then he sighed and said, "No one wants to deal dope forever; at least I don't. A rag business is where it is right now. That's my goal: to get out of the game and concentrate on building up my business."

Hearing those words made Dawn breathe a sigh of relief.

"That sounds good to me, because I wouldn't want to raise a child while living that lifestyle."

"Me either. Raise a child? Are you trying to tell me something?"

"Yes, Cory. We are having a baby!"

"Stop playing!"

"I'm serious. I am two months pregnant."

That news made him jump for joy. He raced out to the balcony of their state room and began shouting for the whole cruise ship to hear.

"I'M GOING TO BE A DADDY!"

"Cory, get back in here!"

"I want the whole world to know it! I'm going to be a daddy!"

47

He held her close. She felt safe with him in every sense of the word. He was an excellent provider and he was definitely an ominous protector. She wanted for nothing when she was with him and feared nothing when he was by her side.

"I should've known you were pregnant. Look at you. You're glowing. You look so beautiful right now that I don't know what I'm going to do with you!"

"I'm sure you'll think of something."

Dawn said as she melted into his arms. And Cory never made it to the casino that night.

Chapter 5

Brook sat in her office in the back of Co-Ed Greenville, speaking to her husband about their long distance marriage: how she stayed in Greenville to run the shop there while he ran the shop in Atlanta. He would only come up to Greenville one weekend a month and every holiday. That was what they agreed upon when they first got married. But Brook found herself regretting that agreement more and more. And she didn't hesitate to voice her opinion to Walter about it. She was very unhappy.

"I really can't take this anymore," she said.

"You knew the deal when we got married. You know that we have to grind to get these shops off the ground."

"They *are* off the ground. All I'm asking is for you to be reasonable. You can let someone else run the Atlanta shop!"

"No I can't do that. I don't trust anyone enough to leave them in charge down here."

"Well then I'll let Miss Mattie take charge of things up here and I'll move to Atlanta. I just want to be with you!"

"NO!" Walter exclaimed almost instantaneously. "I need you to stay up there! The shop in Greenville is doing so well, better than we're doing in Atlanta. We're going to need those profits to spring board the Co-Eds in Charlotte and Augusta."

Brook's tender sobs could be heard over the phone.

"Don't do that, baby. Don't cry."

"It's our anniversary this weekend and you're not even going to be here."

"I'm really sorry about that. You know I have that thing this weekend. But I'm going to be up there Monday; I promise."

Brook and Walter had this conversation many times. She just genuinely loved her man and the long distance relationship was starting to wear on her.

***

"Where is Brook? Time is money!" Calvin, one of her clients bellowed.

"She'll be up in a minute," Miss Mattie replied. "I think she's on the phone with Walter."

Now Miss Mattie was the glue that kept Co-Ed Greenville together. She served as mother, aunt, and spiritual advisor all rolled in one. She was a little old, but after their interview, Brook didn't hesitate to hire her.

"On the phone with that tired brother," Calvin said with a sneer. "She needs to drop him and get with me!"

Calvin Bass was a pimp. Most people would say that he had genuine game about himself. He wore his hair long and straight. But sometimes he would ask Brook to curl his ends. People knew him for the large diamond ring he wore on his pinky as well as the beautiful ladies he wore on his arm.

"She is married to him!" Miss Mattie said with attitude. "Do not bring that drama up in here, Calvin!"

"Alright. But that dude is a loser. She needs to be with a winner, like Calvin Bass." He pointed to himself. His pinky ring glistened in the light.

"Calvin, I don't want to have to throw you out again!" Miss Mattie warned.

"Besides," Stacy interjected, "Brook wouldn't be your only woman!"

Stacy's chair was right next to Miss Mattie's. Brook placed her there so she would learn a thing or two from the seasoned matron, like how to keep her mouth closed. Stacy loved to talk and was often reprimanded for butting into other people's conversations.

50

"This has nothing to do with you!" Calvin said to her. "Don't get mad because you tried out for my varsity squad and didn't make the cut!"

Everyone gave a simultaneous "ooh" to that comment. Stacy had nothing else to say to Calvin after that.

"Shut up, Calvin!" Miss Mattie reached over to Brook's chair and popped him on the arm with a styling comb. "You know you couldn't handle a woman like Brook!"

"What do you mean?"

"I mean she is an entrepreneur. She's intellectual, cultured, and stylish; she's nothing like the women you usually date. No offense, Stacy."

"None taken." Stacy patted her burgundy hair which was gelled tightly to the side of her head.

"What are you talking about?" Calvin asked, raising his brow. "If anybody can handle a woman like that, it's Calvin." Calvin the Pimp had perfected the art of speaking of himself in the third person. He continued without missing a beat. "She needs a real man. You know what I'm talking about, Miss Mattie? A *real* man."

"What are you trying to say?"

"I'm just going to put it on out there. Brook is the only person too stuck on stupid to see that her man's door opens both ways!"

Everyone in the shop became extremely quiet, even Miss Mattie. Sade, who sat in the last chair of the salon, broke the silence. "Just because a man carries himself a certain way doesn't mean that he's gay!" she said.

Sade's chair was last for a reason. She was the best stylist in the shop even though she was the youngest. She also had a very sweet personality. She tried to see the good in every body and very rarely would you see her without a smile on her face.

51

"I don't know baby," Miss Mattie said. "My daddy always told me that if it walks like a duck and talks like a duck—well—Quack, Quack!"

"Not you too, Miss Mattie."

"Honey, I just call them like I see them."

They then began to get into a lengthy discussion about the matter, which was fairly normal around the shop. Whether they discussed politics, world affairs, neighborhood affairs, relationships or general gossip, the discussions were always lengthy and usually ended with Brook having to instruct them to get back to work and consider the customers, even though the customers were usually more into the conversation than the hairdressers.

"Okay, what about men who don't have feminine tendencies but sleep with other men just the same?" Sade inquired.

"Oh you mean the down low," Miss Mattie replied.

"Yeah," Stacy chimed in. "It's a lot of guys out there like that!"

"I mean look at Trap." Sade pointed to one of the barbers across from her.

Trap, who came down from New York to work at the shop, was a tall guy with thick muscles who didn't mind flaunting them either; he usually wore a wife beater and jeans with fresh Timberland boots just about every day. It was no secret that Sade and Trap had a connection, though they had never acted on it. As the barbers were on one side of the room and the hair stylists were on the other, Trap and Sade playfully went back and forth everyday about one thing or another. Brook and Miss Mattie would often tell them to stop fooling themselves, break down, and get a room.

"Don't bring that over here, shorty," he said to her with a swagger. "I only have love for the ladies."

"That could be a front," she replied, batting her eyelids at him.

"I don't find anything attractive about the male frame. But the female frame on the other hand, now that's a different story. See a woman is soft, and hairless, well most of them, anyway. A woman smells sweet and has a genuine sweet way about her. Her body is curved and inviting. Like take you for instance, Sade."

"What about me?"

"You are banging! I'll tell you the truth. And since you opened up this can of worms with me, I'll take it there with you without hesitation."

"Make it plain then!"

"I'm just saying, if I had my way, I'd take you in the locker room right now."

"And do what?"

"You know what." He looked directly at Sade and then returning to his work. "I'd sweat that perm right out of your hair!"

The whole shop went wild as Trap gave the barber on his left a fist bump.

Sade just smiled, continued styling her client's hair, and said, "We'll talk later."

"What's going on out here?" Brook asked as she came walking down the back hallway and into the shop.

"Nothing much," Miss Mattie replied. "Just Trap and Sade going at it again."

Brook did not reply with a funny comment. As a matter of fact there was sadness on her face and her eyes were still red from crying. Everyone knew what ailed her. So they just returned to business as usual.

"Finally!" Calvin exclaimed as Brook walked over to her chair.

"I'm not in the mood for it today. What do you need?"

"I respect that. I just need you to shape me up around the edges."

Brook didn't smile. She just began to lather the edges of Calvin's laid-back hair. She took out her straight razor. That act alone almost brought her to tears.

Walter gave the razor to her not long after they started dating. He said that he wanted to give her something that was special to him: the straight razor given to him by his grandfather. The fact that he gave her that beautiful instrument let her know that he truly loved her. Seeing it used to bring her joy. Using it once made her smile. But now there was only pain.

"You know, Calvin would never make you cry," he said to her softly.

"Don't start with me!"

"I mean, I respect what you and Walter have. But you know you're unhappy. Why be with someone that makes you unhappy?"

"And you would make me happy?"

"All day, every day!"

"And what about all of your other women? Would you give all of them up for me?"

"No I wouldn't!" Calvin quickly replied. "But I would make you my number one lady, though. And being my number one would be a whole lot better than being Walter's only one!"

Calvin's statement made Brook giggle. A smile began to show. Even though Calvin repulsed her in every way, one thing that she liked about him was that he was very honest. And extremely silly. Even though Brook would never entertain the thought of leaving Walter for a man like him, he was still good for a laugh every now and again.

Before Brook started to trim his edges he reached back, touched her hand and said, "See I made you laugh."

"I'm laughing because you're silly."

"Oh I'm silly, huh?"

"You couldn't be serious if you tried. That's why you can't make up your mind about what girl you want to be with. Because you can't be serious."

"So you're calling me a joke?"

"I didn't say that."

Calvin quickly grabbed Brook's hand and gripped it tightly in his own. Brook was frozen.

"Do you want me to be serious? Here it is. Your man is a FRUIT CAKE!"

The room fell silent. All emotion left from Brook's face as she stared at Calvin. They had gone back and forth playfully before, but he had never put his hands on her. And he was never mean to her.

"Let her go, Calvin!" Miss Mattie shouted to no avail.

"No! She has to know that Walter sleeps with men!"

The bell on the front door chimed as it opened and closed. Miss Mattie gasped and Sade hurried across the room to Trap as Calvin continued with his tirade.

"I may be a clown!" Calvin yelled. "But I'm not a fairy like your man!"

Walter smoothly took the straight razor away from Brook's free hand, slid her out of the way, and took position behind the chair that Calvin was sitting in. Calvin and Brook didn't even see him come in.

All eyes were on Walter, as he stood tall behind Calvin with a straight razor. They watched as the pimp began trembling with fear.

"I got this, baby," Walter said calmly.

Then he rested the razor on Calvin's neck as he looked at him savagely through the mirror.

"I don't want any trouble, boss man." Calvin lips trembled.

"There's no trouble, playboy. You didn't do anything but disrespect the man of the house. But we will take care of that!"

Walter grabbed a handful of Calvin's straight black hair and yanked his head back. Every one gasped as he began slowly digging the razor into Calvin's flesh causing a small stream of blood to run down his neck.

"You think I'm a punk, don't you?"

"No man! I—I don't think you're a—"

"Shut up!" Walter said, yanking his head back even more.

This caused everyone to gasp again. Sade wanted to call the police, but Miss Mattie nodded against it.

"Don't freeze up on me, playboy! Am I a punk or what?"

Calvin didn't respond. He couldn't respond.

"HUH? AM I?"

"Walter that's enough!" Brook yelled.

Luckily for Calvin, Brook had come out of her trance and began rubbing Walter's shoulders calming him down.

"Come on in the back." She led him down the hallway to her office.

Calvin was still in the chair, frozen. And he would have stayed there if Miss Mattie hadn't gotten him up and walked him out of the front door.

"Everybody back to business," she said calmly, comforting the customers.

"Why didn't you want Sade to call the police?" Stacy asked.

"Because Calvin put his hands on Brook. And Walter was only protecting his woman. That's the rules there, honey. That's old school!"

Everyone agreed with her. Trap even said that he was about to check Calvin himself. Everyone in the shop supported what Walter did that day. He was holding it down for his woman.

"I'm sorry for what happened out there, Brook," Walter said as he sat down in Brook's chair. "I saw him with his hands on you and I just snapped."

Brook wasn't focused on that.

"What are you doing here?" she asked. "You said that you weren't coming until Monday!"

"Well you should've known that I was just pulling your leg. You know I wouldn't miss our anniversary!"

Brook swallowed him in her embrace. She cried tears of joy because she was able to feel his skin against hers.

"I know, I know. I love you too!" he said. "I bought you something." He reached in his pocket and pulled out a set of keys. "You remember that candy-apple red Benz you were looking at the last time you were in Atlanta?"

"You didn't!"

He led her out of the office and out the back door. He had parked a brand new Mercedes Benz right outside in the back.

"You said that we should wait to get it!"

"Honey I love you. Anything you want, I'll get it for you. You just name it," he said as he held her in his arms.

"I want you to take me home, right now!" she answered.

She went back in and told Miss Mattie to close up for her. And they went whisking down the road. She held his hand as he drove and they said nothing the whole way home. They said nothing when they entered the front door. But as soon as the door closed, Brook began ravishing Walter. They never made it to the bedroom.

***

After making passionate love to each other, Brook and Walter both lay on the living room floor, holding each other.

"Just be patient, baby," he said as he stroked her arm. "If we keep grinding like this, we should be able to retire in ten years, and then we can be together twenty-four/seven."

"I'd like that," she replied, "I'd like that very much!"

57

Brook felt secure with Walter. He protected her. He kept coming up with new ideas for them to increase profits. So money was never an issue. They had everything that they wanted. They owned two homes that would both be paid for in seven years. They now had four vehicles between the two of them, all of which were paid for with cash. But more importantly, they had each other. At that moment she realized that even though one hundred and forty miles separated them, Walter was always right there with her. She held on to him tightly in their living room and they fell asleep in each other's arms.

Chapter 6

Cicely drove down Interstate-85 on her way to work in downtown Charlotte, North Carolina. The song Brick House blared through the speakers of her new Toyota Land Cruiser. She let the windows down so that she could enjoy the cool summer morning air. Just about every guy she passed did a double take. Some even waved at her, trying to get her attention. She was beautiful from head to toe and every man around her took notice, even if he was with someone else.

The dash clock read nine a.m. when Cicely pulled her SUV into the parking garage located on One Mann Way.

"Don't drive my truck all fast," she said to the valet. "When you went to park it yesterday, I heard tires screeching."

"Sorry about that," he replied, his eyes carefully watching her backside as she walked to the building entrance.

Cicely had accepted a position in sales and marketing at Mann Information Systems, an IT firm that specialized in procurement software. She started as a sales rep and became a regional sales manager in just two years. It took her a lot of hard work, late nights and early mornings. But she managed to boost sales and attract new customers; so much so, that upper-level management had to put her in a leadership position.

"Good morning, Ms. Shaw," a security guard said as he opened the front door for her.

"Good morning," she replied with a smile.

"Man, you're looking good today!" he said, shaking his head and licking his lips.

Cicely only smiled and walked toward the elevators.

He was right. Cicely worked out every day so her five-foot-eight frame was tight where it needed to be and supple where it wanted to be. Her chocolate skin glistened and carried the scent of Chanel and cocoa butter. Like the song she loved listening to every morning, Cicely was a brick house in every way.

Cicely liked to walk through sales floor every morning, not for the response that she received from the male reps, but to be close to the action. She wanted to see how her people were doing, to make sure that there were no problems. She wanted her presence to be felt.

She didn't view sex in the same way anymore. She had by no means become an angel, but now she had priorities. She looked out for her best interests now more so than ever and handled herself with discretion. When she did make time for anything extracurricular, it was always on her terms. She felt like she was in control from the boardroom, to the bedroom. She was proud of herself for that.

"Any messages for me," she asked her assistant, Camille as she passed by her desk on her way into her office.

"Let's see, Atlanta called. Mr. Harrison said that everything is on for next week. You got a call from the radio station. The program manager said that he'd agree to increase the length of the spot if you'd agree to go out to dinner with him."

"Of course. Is that all?"

"No there's one more—what did I do with—oh here it is. Mr. Inman will be flying back into town today and requests that you meet him at his house tonight."

That message stopped Cicely in her tracks.

"Are you okay, Ms. Shaw?"

It was a few seconds before she answered.

"I'm okay. You know how I just space out sometimes?"

"I guess," Camille replied as she began typing at her workstation.

Cicely closed her office door and leaned against it. She breathed heavily and decided that she better get off of her feet. She sat at her desk, turned her chair around, and stared out of the window, thinking about all the changes she had made in her life. She liked the way things were. They were on her terms. She didn't want to backpedal.

Todd Inman supervised Cicely as well as all of the whole southeastern division of Mann Information Systems. So she did not have a problem meeting with him. However, she *did* have a problem with the location of the meeting: his home. Cicely was bothered by the request to meet him at his home because that is where they used to have sex.

The affair began at Cicely's job interview with Mr. Inman. She flirted excessively because she wanted to make sure her résumé didn't get shuffled to the bottom of the pile. She did the only thing she knew how to do at the time: use what she had to get what she wanted.

On her second interview she wore a blouse she could barely button over her ample bosom. After she was hired, she let Inman fondle her ample bosom. Their affair escalated when his wife was out of town one weekend. He requested that Cicely meet him at his house to "go over some figures." Hers was the only figure he had in mind and all he really wanted was to be on top of it.

Todd Inman began making up excuses to send his wife away: cruises with her friends, trips to her mother's. It didn't matter. He had to get his wife out and Cicely in. They made love like wild animals; she definitely had him whipped.

Then one day it all stopped, as if nothing had ever happened. Inman started giving Cicely more assignments of which she completed to perfection. She began moving up the ranks and neither of them ever spoke of their illicit past. She understood things to be over. She thought maybe he couldn't get his wife to go out of town any more.

Though the affair lasted only a year she matured a lot during that time. She realized sex might have gotten her in the door with Mr. Inman, but he may not always be around. Hard work is what she needed to master if she was going to survive and succeed in business. She liked her current position. And she was extremely happy until she got that message. Mr. Inman's wife must be out of town again.

***

Cicely returned to her condo that evening in the same funk that she had been in the entire day. She tossed her keys on the counter and proceeded upstairs to her bedroom. Without checking the messages on her answering service, without turning on the TV, or switching on her CD player, she slowly got undressed in the silence that engulfed the entire condo.

She turned on the shower and at a snail's pace pulled herself in. She stayed in the shower for so long that steam filled the entire bathroom. She couldn't see her hand in front of her. She decided that she had better get out of the shower before her skin began to shrivel up. So she got out of the tub, and walked out of the bathroom into her bedroom.

A cloud of steam vigorously dispersed as soon as she opened the door. She didn't even bother to towel herself dry, which resulted in wet foot prints on the carpet as she walked over to her vanity mirror. She looked at herself as she stood naked in front of the mirror. A spark of energy filled her and she quickly put her hands on her hips.

"This is MY body!" she said. "No one gets inside of me unless I want them there! I am in control!"

62

With that she began to dry herself quickly. And then she hurried over to her Chester drawer and pulled out an old pair of jeans and an old tee shirt. She reached down and opened the bottom drawer and retrieved some old bloomers and put them on, pulling the waist elastic way over her navel. She threw on the rest of her clothes and then she put on a pair of athletic socks and some track shoes. She put her hair in a ponytail and looked at herself in the mirror.

"This should send a message to him. No more sex for you, Mr. Inman."

She raced down the stairs, grabbed her keys from the counter, exited out of the front door and closed it shut. She was about to lock the door when she stopped.

Who am I kidding, she thought.

Her positive energy abandoned her. She slowly opened the door and proceeded up the steps to her bedroom. Then she stripped back down to nakedness. She replaced her large plain white underwear with a lace thong with matching bra and garter; her athletic socks with silk stockings; her tee-shirt and jeans with a cotton pant suit that fit her every curve. She let her hair hang freely over her shoulders. Sprinkled Chanel on her neck and her wrist. A frown replaced her smile; she swapped that spark in her eye with the sudden darkness of a blown out candle. She faced the facts. She had started the affair and to deny Inman now would be like committing professional suicide. She was *not* in control.

As she got into her SUV and pulled out of her driveway, tears begin to well in her eyes. She was going to have sex with Mr. Inman again, a married man.

***

A seven-foot, metal gate guarded Mr. Inman's subdivision. All visitors had to check in before entering. The houses were huge, the lawns, immaculately kept, and the streets looked as if they had been paved just the day before. Many pro-football and basketball players lived in that neighborhood as well as many other wealthy business owners and entrepreneurs. All of this fascinated Cicely when their affair began. But now, she just wanted to go to his house, drop her draws, and get over with it.

After she parked in the large circular driveway, she unhurriedly got out of her Land Cruiser and went to the front door of Mr. Inman's large mansion. She didn't want to ring the doorbell.

You can still leave, she thought. With the experience you have you can always find another job. But then she started questioning herself and doubting her abilities. Did sex alone open doors for her professionally? Did her thick hips and bedroom tricks alone sustain her position? Finally, she managed to ring the doorbell. Mr. Inman promptly answered the door.

"Do come in!" he said with a huge smile on his face. "I hope you didn't have any trouble finding the place."

Of course I didn't have any trouble finding the place, she thought. I've been here hundreds of times.

"No. I didn't," she replied with a puzzled look on her face.

"So you must be Ms. Cicely Shaw. I've heard so much about you!"

That was Todd Inman's wife. Mrs. Inman walked into the room, wearing a long summer dress and donning an apron that said World's Greatest Cook. She gave Cicely a huge hug and kissed her on her cheek.

Cicely was now extremely puzzled. Mr. Inman just looked at her as if nothing were wrong with this situation at all.

"I thank you for coming out at such short notice," Mrs. Inman said. "But I just had to meet the woman that made it possible for my husband to finally retire and spend some quality time with me!"

Cicely couldn't find the words to say.

"My wife cannot keep a secret to save her life."

"I'm sorry, darling. You did say that you were going to tell Cicely yourself. Let me just go and finish up dinner. You show Cicely the house."

And then Mrs. Inman returned to the kitchen, humming a gospel tune that Cicely could not quite make out.

Cicely furrowed her brow and tucked the right side of her lips into her cheeks to show her confusion. Inman was actually showing her their house as if she had never set foot in it before in her life. Her instincts told her to play along, so that's what she did.

"I'm going to show Cicely the pool and the tennis courts now, honey!" he shouted to his wife.

"Okay. Dinner shouldn't be ready for another thirty minutes so take your time!"

Both Cicely and Mr. Inman exited out of the Italian doors into the backyard. They began walking down the freshly treated wooden steps down to the pool house. Mr. Inman whistled all the while. Cicely said nothing.

They arrived at the pool house which was a good ways from the main house. And then Inman stopped whistling.

"This is awkward isn't it?" he asked.

"I don't know what to say."

"Have a seat. I'm just going to get right into it. About a year ago I arranged for my wife to go on a cruise to the Bahamas with some of her friends. I dropped her off at the airport and quickly returned home so that I could get in touch with you so we could do our thing.

"But when I got back to the house, I had a sudden, uncontrollable urge to go the bathroom. I mean it felt like I was about to explode. I began using the bathroom and I noticed that there was blood in my urine: lots of blood.

"I made an emergency doctor's appointment for the following day. Then my wife called. Somehow she knew something was wrong. Finally I broke down and told her what was happening. How did she know? She was so far away, she couldn't see me. How could she tell that I feared for my life?

"My wife left her luggage on the cruise ship and got on the next thing smoking back to Charlotte. She wouldn't eat. She said that she was fasting for my healing. Where did all of that come from? I never knew her to be spiritual. But that night as I lay down to sleep, she began rubbing oil on my head and on my groin area. And she prayed for me.

"We received the test results a few days later. The doctor said that strenuous exercise may have caused the blood in my urine. But there was no sign of cancer. My wife and I rejoiced. We held each other and we cried tears of joy together.

"During that ordeal, I saw another side of my wife. I saw her spirituality. Her desire to nurture. I saw *her*. And I realized then that I honestly didn't deserve her. When I told her that I had done her wrong, she just hushed me. She said that she didn't want to hear me say it.

"So I asked her what she wanted from me. No matter what it was, I would give it to her. She told me that she wanted me to retire. She wanted to sell this big house. And she wanted to travel around the world with me. And so the house has been sold. We move out next week. And yes, I am retiring, effective immediately!"

Cicely took all of this in, still at a loss for words. She wanted to be careful. She had never seen a man be so sincere about his feelings. She had never seen a man cry.

"I'm very happy for you," she said as she handed him a tissue from her purse. "I always wondered why we just came to a halt. But to tell you the truth, I was glad."

"Believe me," Mr. Inman said. "It was all for the best."

"Wow! You're retiring. I can't believe it. Who are they sending down to head the division?"

"No one."

"But who's taking your place?"

"You!"

Cicely gasped for air. She couldn't believe what she was hearing.

"Me? I've only been with Mann for two years!"

"Yeah and nobody has worked harder and brought in more business than you. It is my recommendation that you be the new head of the south-eastern division. I've spoken with Mr. Mann about it. He already has your CV. Of course he'll want to speak with you personally, probably at the company meeting at the end of the month. But you are a shoo-in!"

Flabbergasted, she never imagined that at the age of twenty-four, she would be given such a charge.

"Cicely, there's one more thing I'd like to tell you. Our affair should never have happened. I took advantage of the situation and I'm sure that you had your reasons. You are about to be given an important charge. And you got here not because of our past illicit relationship, but because of your work ethic, your insight, and your leadership qualities. That being said, you should NEVER have to resort to using sex as a tool for promotion. Let your work speak for itself." Then he kissed Cicely on her forehead, like a proud father who had just given his daughter some vital advice on life. "Let's get back up to the house, before my wife suspects that we're down here having sex or something!"

They both returned up the wooden staircase and back into the house.

Cicely enjoyed everything about dinner: the conversation, the way that Mr. And Mrs. Inman went back and forth with each other, the way that Mrs. Inman spoke wisely, and how Mr. Inman listened so attentively to her. It made her appreciate love in a whole new way.

The evening finally neared a conclusion and the Inmans said their good-byes to Cicely. She received a warm hug from Mrs. Inman and a firm handshake from her former boss. As she drove away, she looked in her rearview mirror and saw them still waving good-bye from the front porch. She smiled and happiness began to overcome her. It was almost as if they were her parents, standing on the front porch, sending their little girl off with love.

Chapter 7

"Burning the midnight oil again," Tamara, Karen's co-worker and good friend, asked her as she passed her office on her way out. Tamara was a medium height sister with brown skin and a thick build. She was very pretty. She could have easily been a plus size model.

She entered the office.

"Please, come right on in," Karen said sarcastically as she typed away at her PC.

"Do you sleep here? When I come in, you're here. When I leave you're still here."

Karen continued typing, explaining that she was trying to wrap up a case. But she was always trying to wrap up a case. Never in a hurry to get home.

"Why don't you get out more?" Tamara asked.

"Too busy to date."

That was a lie.

"What happened to that guy I hooked you up with?"

"The minister?"

"Yeah. I know you're into the church thing. When I met him at the youth center, I just knew that the two of you would hit it off, the two of you being spiritual and all."

It's true that the minister and Karen had gone on a couple of dates. But when sex entered the conversation, like sex always did, she told the minister that she was a virgin and that she intended on remaining so until she was married. He never called her again.

"It didn't work out between us," Karen replied.

"Well, I'll catch you later. I have a date with Maxwell again."

"The researcher?"

"Yeah. This is the second date. So it's almost time to put it on him."

Tamara spoke of her three date rule. She would not have sex with a man until after their third date.

"There is no shame in your game," Karen said as she waved her off.

***

Later that evening, Karen entered the house and papers were everywhere. The smell of cat urine was strong in the air and the living room looked like it had not been cleaned in weeks. She slid a large stack of sales papers from off of the dining room table and put the bag of groceries down. She surveyed the room. It looked like a hurricane had hit, left and then doubled back for seconds.

"Let me get to work."

She rolled up her sleeves and started cleaning the house.

"Oh Sister Karen, I'm sorry my place is such a mess," Mother Wayne said as she rolled her wheel chair into the dining room from the back of the house. She was one of the old widows that went to Karen's church. "I was looking for some pictures of my Henry. You know I think someone stole them."

"I'll find them for you."

"You are so sweet. Child you don't have to keep coming around here. Go out and have some fun for a change!"

Go out. Get out more. Meet somebody nice. If Karen had a nickel for every time she heard those words, she might not be a millionaire; but she *would* have a *gang* of nickels.

Frankly she grew tired of it. Why should she go out, get out, meet somebody nice when no one shared her views on abstinence. She felt strongly about her virginity and she wanted a man who was willing to respect her and the relationship that they could have.

70

So far, no one fit that bill. She decided that it may be her fate to walk alone.

So she visited Mother Wayne three nights a week and then volunteered at a group home in Downtown Charleston the other four nights. She kept herself busy that way. Kept her mind off not having a social life.

***

Karen threw her things on her couch and settled into her nightly routine. She turned the TV on the 10 o'clock news. She went to the freezer, retrieved a frozen dinner and popped it in the microwave. After eating and watching stories of gunshots and stolen money, she took a long, hot shower. She let the hot water hit her olive skin and soothe her ills, let the drops hit her face and run down her cheeks, filling her dimples. She couldn't differentiate between water and tears.

Her medicine was nearby in the medicine cabinet. So she quickly hopped out of the shower, retrieved the bottle and popped two tablets. She didn't need water to wash them down. She was a pro at taking those pills.

She looked at herself in the mirror. She had gotten in the habit of running every day, mostly because it calmed her. But the running also kept her nice and trim. She surveyed her body, her lean shoulders, and her firm breasts. Her tiny waist, her curved hips, her thick thighs, her round calves, and her tiny feet. She looked at her hazel eyes, how they curved at the edges. She gazed at her full lips, her reddish brown hair with natural blonde streaks. When she smiled, her dimples lit up the mirror. She was saving herself for a man that didn't exist. This saddened her deeply and made her ask herself if it was worth it.

When she placed the bottle of pills back in the medicine cabinet, she noticed she had taken the last of them. Frantically she called to refill her prescription. But she was over her refill limit.

She *had* to see her doctor the next day. Her job, her visits to Mother Wayne's, her going to church, all of those things kept her busy and occupied her mind. But the moments she spent alone in her apartment broke her down. She would not be able to sleep the next night without her medication. She HAD to see her doctor.

Chapter 8

Karen sat in a room filled with pretty normal looking people: no coughers, no sneezers, no bleeders, and no pregnant ladies. But each patient of the Institute of Psychiatry had their own issues. And all of them needed to be healed, no matter how well they appeared.

Karen had become quite fond of her appointments with Dr. Arthur Malone. They were quick visits that usually ended with him renewing her prescription. She needed nothing else. She had never truly opened up to him or anyone else for that matter about her problem. Why should she? She had been riding on her prescription for almost ten years. There was no need to fix something that was not broken.

"How are you, Karen?" Dr. Malone said as he came around the corner.

"I'm doing well. And you?"

"Child support. Vindictive ex-wife. But what else is new? Come on in my office."

Dr. Malone was an average-height Caucasian with red hair which was slightly thinning at the top. As always, he presented a generous smile that really warmed Karen's heart. And as always, he spoke fast. He was known for being direct. That was why Karen enjoyed her visits with him. She knew that she would have her prescription and be on her way in a matter of minutes.

"Please have a seat."

He opened up a file folder and began thumbing through some papers. He usually complained about his ex-wife and his ungrateful children extensively. But that day, he slowly thumbed through crumpled pages. He took his time reading through the file. That made Karen quite nervous.

"So how's the wife and kids?" she asked, but she was thinking, renew my prescription and be done with it!

"Oh they're fine, I guess. As long as the checks are sent on time, I have no problem with them whatsoever. But if that money's a minute late, then I'm in big trouble!"

Good. Same ole normal gripes about the ex. Now on with the prescription.

"Listen, Karen. You've been on Anxinon for quite some time. I think that we need to consider sort of weaning you off of those meds slowly."

"Um, I don't know about that. I'm doing quite well. I really don't see the need to—um—if it's not broken, why fix it?"

Dr. Malone presented his generous smile. Karen's heart was not warmed at all.

"You've been my patient for about two years. I've never really pushed it before. But I think that it may be time to explore other treatment options."

"Other treatment options?"

"Well yes. Perhaps a series of sessions that will target the root of your anxiety. You see, in some cases anxiety is actually brought on by a psychological stimulus as opposed to a physiological stimulus."

"I'm sorry Doc. I'm not following you."

He took a deep breath. Karen did not like where their conversation was going at all.

"Here's what I'm saying. If we are able to get to the root of your anxiety, what you fear, we may be able to start psychological treatment that would lessen your dependency on your medication."

There was a long pause while he allowed her to digest everything he had said. She never gave much thought to being free from her medication. Nor did she give much thought to discussing the root of her anxiety.

Karen looked around nervously because she honestly had no response to give the man aside from begging him to renew the prescription. She would look extremely silly and desperate, but during that brief silence, while Dr. Malone waited patiently for her reply, groveling was a very real option for her.

"Alright, Karen. All I'm asking you to do is think about it. Get back to me when you're ready."

He then wrote out a script for her renewal. Silently, she breathed a sigh of relief. Happy she didn't have to beg.

Chapter 9

Karen stepped off of the elevator and hurried to her office at the end of the hall. She needed to pick up a few files to review that evening before she headed to the group home. With any luck, she could beat the rush hour traffic.

She unlocked her office door and moved quickly to her desk. She wanted to avoid anyone that might hold her up; especially Tamara, who was asking very often about her dating life, or lack thereof. After her scare at Dr. Malone's office, Karen wasn't in the mood for the usual questions.

"Oh good! You're still here."

That was Tamara.

Shoot, Karen thought.

"Your door was closed earlier and I thought you were gone for the day." Tamara plopped down into the chair in front of the desk.

Karen did not want to be there long, and she was initially annoyed by Tamara's sitting down. But then she noticed a worried look on her friend's face, a look that said that she needed someone to talk to. So she took a seat.

"Okay, girl. What's bothering you?" she asked.

"Oh, nothing."

Karen's hazel eyes peered deeply into Tamara's.

"You might as well spill it."

"Okay! Since you dragged it out of me. Well I'm at date three with Maxwell."

"Yes. I know. We've had this conversation. You're going to put it on him. Blah. Blah. Blah."

"Um, I'm not so sure about that. I think I want to take this one slow."

"Excuse me?"

"I don't know. I really, really like my Maxi."

"Okay. He's your Maxi now?"

"Yeah. I think he may be the one."

"The one to what?"

Tamara was more of a love them and leave them type of girl. She always complained that she bored easily.

"You know. The *one*."

Karen got up from her chair and placed the back of her hand against Tamara's forehead.

"Are you okay?" she asked.

Tamara playfully bit at her hand as she pulled it away.

"Yeah. As crazy as it may sound, I think Maxwell is the one for me."

There was a brief silence. And then Karen embraced Tamara and smiled.

"Aw! I'm so happy for you!"

"Thank you, Kay! It's like he gets me. He really gets me. He sent me roses the other day for no reason at all. He opens doors for me. I'm saying. What guy does that anymore?"

"True."

"I think about him all the time. And when I know I'm going to see him, I get all excited and nervous. Woo!"

"Tamara...you sound like you're in love."

"I think I am."

Another silent space passed between them as they smiled at each other.

"Tamara is finally in love!" Karen exclaimed. "You think he feels the same way?"

"I believe he does. But neither of us has used the L-word yet."

"Well just don't tell him first. My Ma Geneva always told us to let the man be the first to say it."

"Wise words from Ma Geneva," Tamara replied. She loved hearing Karen speak of her grandmother, sharing the wisdom that she passed down to her.

77

"Well, what you've told me is good news. Why did you look all concerned earlier?"

Tamara looked away sheepishly. Then she said, "Well there's always a thing, right?"

"Tell me what's up."

"Well Maxwell has invited me over his house tomorrow night to meet some of his friends. A little get together, you know? And I was wondering if you'd come with me."

"Sure, I'll come. Just casual attire, or more dressy?"

Tamara looked away again. "Um—dressy would probably be better."

"Cool. Tomorrow night it is. See that wasn't so hard, was it?"

Tamara smiled and stood to her feet. "Great. I'll swing by your place and pick you up. I really appreciate this, Karen."

"Hey! That's what friends are for. I couldn't have you going to his place all alone with all those strangers gawking at you."

And all of a sudden, Tamara was overwhelmed with guilt. She turned around and stood by the office door, watching Karen gather things. She was so unassuming.

"I have a confession to make," she said. "There won't be that many people there."

Karen continued packing up. "Okay. Well...how many people will be there?"

"Besides you, me, and Maxwell? Just one other person."

Karen stopped shuffling through her papers, looked up at Tamara and asked, "What's his name?"

***

Dr. William Ward pulled into the driveway that he shared with his best friend, Maxwell Broadus. He had a long and tiring day and wanted nothing more than to kick up his feet and watch Sports Center. But his friend Maxwell had other plans.

"Hey, buddy! What's the deal?" Maxwell asked as he waited in the drive way. William pulled in, put his Lexus in park and shook his head. Maxwell was at his car door as soon as he parked and would have opened the door for William if his hands weren't already full.

"Yo! Will! I've got that new Madden. Come hang with your boy."

"What's the occasion?"

"Man you don't need an occasion to get smashed in some Madden. But if you must know, I got a great score on my grant!"

"Awesome, but I really just want to chill out tonight."

"Come on, big dog! Besides there's some other things we need to discuss."

William reluctantly agreed to go down to Maxwell's condo as soon as he put his bags away. He thought that the camaraderie would do him some good.

***

William and Maxwell had settled into their game of Madden. In between plays and hefty gulps of Red Bull, Maxwell told William about his grant being funded and how excited he was.

"That's great, Max. Maybe you can give me a job if I don't get funding soon."

"Don't speak negatively! Your blessing is right around the corner."

William and Maxwell were scientists and two of the few in their Department that professed faith in God. That was one of the reasons they got along so well.

Maxwell put his X-Box controller on the table next to him and said, "But there's some other things going on in my life. I think I may have found the one."

"The what?"

"The one."

William looked surprised.

"You, Mr. love them and leave them, have found the one?"

"Yeah! I was just as shocked as you. But she's the one, no doubt about it."

"What's her name?"

"Tamara. I told you about her. She works for D.S.S."

"Oh! The thick one."

"Yeah, boy! Thick just like my Momma!"

William initially found that statement a bit odd. But he later had to admit that he'd heard it before.

"She's all that, Will: beautiful, funny, *and* she can cook."

"Yeah, knowing how to cook *is* important."

William noticed that his sarcasm went right over Maxwell's head and that his friend owned a serious look on his face, a look he never recalled seeing before.

"I can't believe I'm saying this. I think I love her, Will."

William paused and thought about what Maxwell had just said. He professed his love for his woman. He had to admit that it was a beautiful thing.

He grabbed his Red Bull can from the table and lifted it towards Maxwell.

"To finding the one," he toasted.

"To finding the one."

After the toast, Maxwell took a generous swig and placed his empty can on the coffee table.

"Yeah, it's like I'd do anything for Tamara," Maxwell said. "That brings me to why you're really here. You see, Tamara has this friend, a co-worker."

William raised his right brow. He was starting to catch on.

"Aw man," he replied. "I should've known."

"Hear me out. I'm out with Tamara and she asked me if I had any cute friends. I said, 'I don't know. I don't judge other men.' Then she goes into this whole thing about wanting to fix her girl up with someone. Before I knew it, I agreed to the four of us having dinner at my place Thursday night."

"You did what? Come on, man. I just got out of a relationship. Tiffany and I may get back together."

"You and Tiffany will not and *should* not get back together."

William thought briefly about Tiffany, his college sweetheart. They were each other's first. Tiffany was the woman he was going to marry. Then he thought about how she flipped on him in the end.

"Okay, you're right about Tiffany," he said.

"So come on man. Do this one thing for me."

"How does she look?"

"Huh?"

"How...does...the friend of Tamara's...look?"

"Don't know. I've never seen her."

"Never seen—she's probably not good looking."

"Come on, dude. How do you know that?"

"Max, how many good looking women need their friends to hook them up with someone?"

Maxwell thought about it for a second and replied, "Yeah. You're right. She's probably busted, disgusted and can't be trusted."

"Aw, man!"

"Will, buddy. I need you on this one."

William hesitated. But then he realized that doing this for Tamara was a big deal for Maxwell.

"Alright!" he said. "I'll do it."

***

Karen sighed in desperation.

"I hate when you try to play matchmaker, Tamara."

"I just want you to be happy."

"I'd be happy just being alone. Besides, I believe that's my lot anyway."

81

"Oh, Karen." Tamara reached into her shoulder purse and pulled out her compact mirror. "Look at yourself. You are beautiful, girl."

She looked into the mirror and saw a strikingly beautiful young woman with smooth sand colored skin, hazel eyes, and brown hair with natural blonde streaks. She never doubted that she was attractive.

Karen took the mirror from Tamara and gently placed it on her desk. Then she circled the contour of her face and said, "All of this doesn't matter. I'm not having sex before I'm married. No man, not even a church going man, has wanted to deal with that."

Tamara looked defeated.

"Okay. I'll tell Maxwell that our double date is a no go."

"I didn't necessarily say that."

Tamara beamed and hugged Karen tightly. "So you'll meet him?"

"I guess so," Karen replied and playfully bit at Tamara, making her jump back.

"This is good!" Tamara exclaimed. "I've got a good feeling about this."

"By the way. You never gave me the guy's name."

Tamara smiled and replied, "His name is William."

Chapter 10

Dr. William Ward zoomed past all of his defenders as he raced to the baseline on the cracked asphalt basketball court. He flashed like lightening. He was young again, dribbling through his legs, crossing over and making his way to the hoop. He jumped into the air and somehow the ball slipped out of his hands and flew into a crowd of young girls standing nearby. One of them caught the ball and held it up towards him.

The girl looked odd, like no other girl that he had seen before. Quite frankly he was frightened by the way that she stared at him, batting her eyes.

As he approached her the girl asked, "You want your ball back?"

"Yeah!"

"Well you have to kiss me for it!"

"And then you'll give it back?"

"Sure."

He reached down to get the ball. She handed it to him, simultaneously tip-toeing up toward his face. And then they kissed. His lips touched her soft, tender lips. His hand caressed her soft face and—

William jolted out of the bed, breathing heavily. He wasn't on a basketball court. He was in his bedroom. But the dream felt so real.

***

Karen put the finishing touches on her hair and then went over her face with Oil of Olay. She had the toughest time trying to decide whether she would wear her hair up or let it rest on her shoulders. She finally concluded that it didn't matter. This would be the first and only time that she would see this William guy anyway.

83

Tamara arrived to pick up her just as she had finished getting dressed. As soon as she stepped out of the house Tamara exclaimed, "Oh my goodness, girl! You look gorgeous."

She spoke of the black form fitting dress, patterned stockings, and quarter inch heels Karen wore.

"You're looking mighty busty, I mean beautiful yourself," Karen replied, making jokes about how Tamara's bosom was on full display.

"You know I have to make Maxwell's mouth water."

"Girl you are too much! Let's go!"

They were nearing Isle of Palms when Karen said, "It's nice out here. I live right here in the Charleston area and hardly ever go to the beach."

"Yeah, I guess I'll be spending a whole lot of time out here, of course until we get married."

It still sounded strange to hear Tamara talk about being in love and marriage. But she had to admit that it was a beautiful thing. She wished she could be at that point with someone. But it didn't look like it was going to ever happen.

"Tamara, you told me yesterday that you were going to take your time with Maxwell. What if he doesn't want to wait for you? What will you do then?" Tamara gulped and looked at Karen with guilt. "You didn't!"

Tamara nodded her head up and down. "Oh yes I did!"

"You are a bad girl!"

"I'm sorry. I don't know what happened." Tamara looked ahead and raised her brow, shrugged in an attempt to claim innocence. "And here's the bad part. I'm the one that started it."

"Bad girl!"

"It was incredible. It was like my first time. I mean we made love! And after we were done, I felt so bad about it that I started crying."

"Oh no."

"Yes. I mean boo-hoo crying. I must've looked like a fool lying in his bed, crying like it was the end of the world. I was all, 'Oh no! You're going to think I'm a slut for sleeping with you so soon.' But he held me in his arms and he told me that he loved me."

"He did?"

"Yes he did. Like I said. He's the one."

They were crossing the Isle of Palms Connector and the water and beaches came into view. It was a truly romantic site, a place where lovers walked hand in hand and let time slip away from them as the sand tickled their feet and the full moon lit their path. The beach was a place to spend time with your true love. Karen wondered if she would ever find her true love.

***

"Oh good, Will! You're here! I feared you'd be late."

Maxwell nervously ushered him into the house.

"Why are you so uptight?" William asked.

"I don't know. Am I acting nervous?"

William watched as Maxwell raced around his spotless living room moving items around.

"The place looks fine," he told him. "Chill out. I have never seen you act this way about any woman."

"I can't deny it; I've got it bad, bro. But that's a good thing. I just want to make sure everything's right for her. Am I really acting nervous?"

"Just a little bit."

Maxwell took a seat at his bar. He raised his brow and looked at William with a shy grin. Then he said, "We took it there last night."

"*There*?" William asked.

"Yep! There!"

"You sly old dog you!"

Maxwell waved it off and said, "No. It's nothing like that. It was spiritual, man. We connected on a level that's hard to explain for me. She took me back to the

85

Mother Land, had me chanting. I was dizzy, Doc! I really believe that I had an out of body experience; I *did* it and *watched* it at the same time. I felt high or drunk...or maybe high and drunk. It got to one point that I thought I would black out!"

"Wow!"

"Wow, for real! I told her that I loved her and everything."

"What?"

"Sure did."

"Well do you?"

"Of course I do. She's the one! I am officially out of the game. And I've never ever been there with anyone like that. I guess that's why I'm nervous."

"You sure you're not scared?"

"I might be." Maxwell laughed. "But really Will, I want to thank you from the bottom of my heart for agreeing to this double date."

"That's what friends are for. And don't worry. I'll be witty and suave. I promise I'll say all the right things. I'll be Mr. GQ smooth. Hey! It's no pressure on me."

Just then the doorbell rang.

"Cool. That's them," Maxwell said. "How do I look?"

"Are you serious?"

"Answer the door for me, man."

"No! This is your house. What's gotten into you?"

When he saw that Maxwell was sincere about it, William walked to the front door and opened it. And that's when he saw her for the first time.

"Hello I'm Tamara and this is my friend Karen. You must be William."

But William was speechless. He just stood there in the doorway, staring at Karen.

"Well don't just stand there," Maxwell said as he walked to the door. "Let them in for Pete's sake."

Maxwell gave Tamara a hug and kiss. Then he said to Karen, "So nice to meet you. Tamara has told me nothing but good things about you."

86

"Good to meet you, too," Karen said. "And you must be William."

Karen extended her hand. William just looked at it for a second. And then he snapped out of his trance and took her hand.

"Hello. My name is William."

"I know," Karen said with a smile.

"Okay. Come on in," Maxwell said. "I set up a table on the patio where we can all eat and—talk."

The last portion of Maxwell's statement was for William. He had been acting strange since he opened the front door.

"So what do you do for a living, William?" Karen asked.

At first he said nothing. Just stood there with his mouth slightly ajar. Finally he replied, "M.U.S.C."

Karen looked confused because she asked him what he did for a living and not where he worked.

"Excuse me a minute," he said. Then he walked back into the house.

"I'm sorry," Maxwell said. "He probably has to use the bathroom or something."

"MAXWELL!" William yelled his name from the back of the house.

"Excuse me, ladies."

Maxwell found William in his home office, leaning against his desk. He said to him, "Hey, I told you that I owe you one for doing this double date thing. But *you* actually owe *me*. Karen is beautiful!"

William said nothing. He just continued leaning against Maxwell's desk deep in thought.

"You okay, Will? I thought you were going to be Mr. GQ smooth. But you are really bombing out there."

"I dreamed about her last night."

"Dreamed about who?"

"Her—the woman sitting on your patio. Karen. I dreamed about her last night."

"But you've never seen her before, have you?"

"Never. But it was her in the dream. I'm sure of it."

"You must be mistaken. Maybe it's like Déjà vu. And you know dreams are fuzzy sometimes."

"No this dream is clear, down to the very detail of her skin color, her hazel eyes, her red hair, those blonde streaks."

"Okay," Maxwell said, taking a seat behind his desk. "Tell me about the dream."

"Well I'm at this playground playing basketball with my brothers. Of course in the dream I was me at a younger age, fifteen or sixteen I guess. There's a crowd around us. There's a group of young girls standing around. One of them stands out, she's literally glowing. Well, I'm going strong to the hoop and then somehow I lose the ball. It goes straight to her. She picks it up and tells me that I have to kiss her before she gives the ball back. So I kissed her."

"That dream doesn't sound so bad."

"No I guess it's not as bad as I'm making it out to be. It's just that the young girl that's in the dream, the one that I kissed, is out there on your patio right now! A full grown woman!"

Silence settled between them. And then William continued.

"That's not all."

"What else is there?" Maxwell asked.

"As soon as I saw Karen, I felt love."

"Whoa, whoa, whoa. Hold on there, buddy." Maxwell pulled his chair around the desk so that he was sitting right beside William.

"It's not like I don't believe in love at first sight," Maxwell said. "I do. But you have to be careful, man. Take it slow. Talk to her. Please go out there and talk to her. Strike up conversation and see what happens."

"You're right."

"Of course I'm right. Just go back out there, have a good time, see if there's any chemistry there. But definitely don't tell her that you dreamed about her last night. That may freak her out."

"You're right."

William and Maxwell walked back out to the patio where Karen and Tamara waited.

"Are you okay?" Karen asked William.

"Yes. I'm good."

And they all sat at the patio table as the waves crashed against the nearby shore. Maxwell broke out his brand new gas grill, serving grilled steak tacos with a grilled vegetable medley of mushrooms, onions, and peppers. And because Tamara was a chocoholic, Maxwell rounded out their meal with a chocolate decadence cake topped with fresh raspberries.

William marveled at Maxwell's evolution. Tamara had turned him into a master chef. Of course William gave him much grief over this and he shared many laughs about it with Karen. As they enjoyed dinner, dessert, and the accompanying group conversation, William slowly learned how to respond to simple questions in a timely manner and give answers that actually made sense.

***

As the sun started easing below the horizon, Maxwell and Tamara decided to take a walk down the beach, leaving Karen and William alone.

"William, I expect you to be on your best behavior while we're gone," Tamara said with a wink.

"I'll be a perfect gentleman," he replied.

As soon as they left, William asked Karen, "Do you want to go upstairs to my place?"

She tilted her head to the side and smiled. "I thought you said you were going to be a perfect gentleman."

"Oh and I will."

Karen thought about it for a few seconds and then she replied, "Okay, sure."

As they walked up the steps to his apartment, William spied Karen's backside. He really liked what he saw. Her beautiful face, her stunning body. But he had to admit that there was something else there, way beyond things physical. Maxwell told him to ignore it. But it was still there.

"This is my place," William said as he opened the door for Karen.

"Okay, okay, I hear you. This is really nice." She marveled at his décor. "I love the open space. Your place isn't like Maxwell's at all."

"No. The previous owners of this unit made some serious upgrades."

She admired the African statuettes as well as the life size mahogany framed poster of John Coltrane.

"What do you know about Giant Steps?" She rubbed her fingers over the elegant frame and looked at the late great tenor sax man in his element.

"Aw, that's my favorite jazz record right there."

"This portrait is autographed," Karen noticed.

"Yes. My dad got that when he and my mom were overseas visiting some friends. My parents travelled a lot. They have college friends all over the place: Peru, Europe, Japan, all over the U.S. Sometimes they'd take me and my brothers along when they visited their friends. So I've literally been around the world."

Karen toured the rest of the living room, admiring the tan Berber carpet and the suede couch and loveseat with oil-finished oval drum end tables. Then she made her way to the kitchen and dining room, complimenting William on his stainless steel appliances and marble counter tops. "Look at me," she said. "I'm just making myself at home."

That made William smile.

Then she asked, "I'm not going to find any of your girlfriend's panties lying around here, am I?"

He laughed. "No, no, no. There are no panties because there is no girlfriend."

"I find that hard to believe."

"What about you? Do you have a boyfriend?"

"Nope. I am single."

"I find that *really* hard to believe."

Karen took a seat on one of the Cierra bar stools. "Why is that?" she asked.

"You're too beautiful to not have a man."

That made her smile. "Aw shucks. But wouldn't you know that I get that all of the time."

William and Karen just looked at each other for a moment, beaming. A part of him wanted to scream, I'm in love with you! I dreamed about you last night!

But instead he asked, "Do you want something to drink?"

"Bottled water's fine."

"Coming up."

William retrieved two bottles of Dasani from his pantry and handed one to Karen along with a paper towel.

"It must be nice living right on the beach," she said as she looked out onto the balcony. By then the sky was lit with thousands of stars.

"It has its perks, until a hurricane comes. Um—do you want to go out to the balcony?"

"Sure."

They quietly sat on the balcony, enjoying the night sky and the sounds of the ocean's waves crashing against the sandy shore.

"I have a balcony in my bedroom, too." Why did I just say that, William thought.

"Oh yeah? If I lived out here, and I had a balcony in my bedroom, I'd sleep with the door open every night so I can hear the ocean. It's magical."

Karen glanced over at William, who caught her looking. She quickly looked away.

"I'm glad that Tamara asked me to come with her tonight. I was really getting tired of her trying to fix me up with guys." Oh goodness! Why did I just say that, Karen thought.

"Yeah, Tamara's nice. Maxwell is head over heels for her. And he doesn't usually do head over heels, believe it or not. He was very nervous before y'all showed up."

"Nervous isn't always bad. Sometime nervous is a good thing."

Karen giggled.

"What's so funny?"

"Oh nothing."

"Nothing in woman-speak means something."

"Woman-speak?"

He gave a shy smile and said, "Never mind."

"What? Don't be scared. Tell me what woman-speak means."

He turned to face her. She gave him her full attention.

"Woman-speak is when you say one thing but mean another."

"Elaborate."

"Oh boy, I'm in trouble now."

"You're not in trouble." She brushed her hand against his arm. "Continue."

"Like when something's on a woman's mind and her man asks, 'What's wrong?' And she says 'Nothing.' But in reality something is really wrong. And her man has to keep on asking her what's wrong until she finally tells him. Woman-speak. You ladies have your own language."

"So are you an expert on women?"

"By no stretch. But I have a great appreciation for women. My mother's a woman."

Karen chuckled again. "That's nice. You know, William, I was worried about you earlier. You were all quiet. I didn't know what was wrong with you."

"I guess I was just nervous."

"It's like I said earlier; sometimes nervous is a good thing."

They looked at each other briefly, Karen admiring William's handsome smile, he marveling her beautiful eyes.

Then he asked, "So Tamara is trying to set you up with someone, huh?"

"I cannot believe I told you that."

"So let's not disappoint her. We should go out."

"You mean like on a date?"

"Yes. Dinner, a movie perhaps."

"You're a nice enough guy. I guess that will be fine."

"I *am* a nice enough guy," he replied. "And I promise. I will be a perfect gentleman."

Chapter 11

Cicely sipped champagne and gazed around the ball room of the Key Largo Grande Resort and Beach Club where Mann Information Systems held its quarterly manager's meeting. Inspecting the crowd, she saw the corporate higher-ups, all deeply engaged in their separate conversations. She learned quickly that they were all fast and cut throat. She thought to herself, maybe you had to be that way in business.

"Oh there you are, Ms. Shaw. I've been looking for you."

It was Vincent Mann, the CEO of the firm. He stood 6 feet tall, had brown skinned with short wavy hair. His face was clean shaven and he wore thin rimmed glasses with a slight tint on the lenses. He looked athletic, like he played point guard once upon a time.

Vincent Mann interviewed Cicely a few weeks before the meeting. The interview went extremely well. But like Mr. Inman said, Cicely was already a shoo-in. Vincent Mann already knew a lot about her from her performance history. She remembers him saying to her the first time they met, "I've heard so much about you, Ms. Shaw."

What was that, she wondered. How much of a freak I was in the bed?

"You doubled our sales last quarter, Ms. Shaw. I heard that you made new contacts and got us into advertising niches that we didn't even know existed." She remembers Vincent Mann saying that when they first met.

She found out that he was a family man. That he was married with two kids. In fact she was looking at the company pamphlet when he walked up to her.

"How do you like everything?" he asked her.

"Everything's wonderful, Mr. Mann. This resort is beautiful, the food is magnificent. I haven't gone on any excursions yet, but I plan on doing so tomorrow."

"That sounds good; maybe you can join us tomorrow. We're going jet skiing in the morning."

"Sounds like a plan."

"Great. Oh yeah, here they come. There are some people I'd like for you to meet. Ms. Debra Waller, the head of the Pacific Division and Ms. Gladys Springs, the North Western head."

Vincent Mann waved the two ladies over and then he said, "I'll let the three of you get acquainted. It's almost time for my address."

And just like that, he marched off, greeting people as he walked by, receiving love and positive energy from all he passed along the way to the podium.

Cicely, Debra and Gladys found some seats and spoke with each other briefly before the speech began.

"Congratulations on your promotion, Ms. Shaw," Gladys said with smile. "If you ever have any questions about the politics that go on within the corporate ranks then just call me up any time."

Then Debra chimed in.

"If you have any questions about the filth that goes on then—"

"Debra!!"

Gladys interrupted her in mid-speech. Debra smiled, took a sip of her drink and said, "Yeah. Congratulations."

All eyes were on Mr. Mann as he began to address all of the corporate heads and all of the heads of the various divisions of the company. He spoke calmly yet with bravado. Like a general encouraging his troops for battle. He smiled and made it a point to make eye contact with everyone in the room.

"The state of the company is strong. Five years ago we were just a small outfit out of Charlotte, North

Carolina. Now we're nationwide. In five years we will be global!"

The crowd gave him a standing ovation as he smiled, waved, and pumped his fist in the air in victory.

Dinner had ended and the ball room had lost nearly all its diners, except for a few gung-ho members of the corporate elite. Cicely's company retired for the night, but she was too wired to go to bed. She saw Vincent Mann standing alone on the balcony and wanted to go over and thank him for the opportunity.

"No, no, no. You made it all possible when you doubled sales for the last two consecutive quarters," he said.

"You have a beautiful family, Mr. Mann. The way that you talked about them in your speech, it moved me; the way you said that you try to spend time with them amid your busy schedule."

"Well it's hard, but I've got to do that. Having all of this would be a waste if I had no one to share it with."

"Your wife must really love that."

Cicely really didn't know why she mentioned his wife. The reason why she went out to that balcony started to become fuzzy to her as well.

"My wife and I are together, but we aren't happy. I'll just say that we married too soon, started a family too fast."

"I'm sorry to hear that."

She wondered if she was really sorry to hear that.

"Don't be. I have two beautiful boys and they love me. I love them. I still love their mother. I always will."

"It sounds so sad though, you not being happy and all."

"It is what it is," he replied matter-of-factly. "Besides, my wife and I respect each other. And even though the relationship may not be what I want it to be, we said 'I do' before God. We will be married 'til

96

death do us part. That, my dear, is bible. You of all people should understand that."

Cicely wondered what he meant by that.

Just then, Rex Felder came out onto the balcony and greeted the two of them. Rex Felder was Vincent Mann's right hand, second in command. His face possessed a sly grin. He was shorter than Mr. Mann. His balding head made him look older than his boss as well. He reminded Cicely of an older version of Ron Johnson from A Different World.

"You don't mind if I interrupt this little rendezvous, do you?" he said, his face refusing to release the grin. It almost seemed sinister to Cicely.

"No, no, no. It's nothing like that," Mr. Mann said as he patted him on the shoulder. "Ms. Shaw, if you'll excuse us."

"Sure. You two have a good evening."

"Remember, jet skis in the morning."

"Wouldn't miss it for the world," she said as she walked off.

She glanced back when she entered the ball room. Felder's sinister grin was on his face to stay. Maybe he had something to do with the filth that Debra had alluded to earlier. As for Mr. Mann, he looked all business, smiling occasionally, but for the most part always the professional.

She left the ballroom and entered the luxurious hallway that led to the lobby of the hotel. She found the elevators that went to her floor. There were two sets of elevators: one for the second through the sixteenth floor and one for the seventeenth through thirty-first floor. She got on the elevator and pressed the number 15. Her mission: go to her room and get some rest. Her colleagues had the energy of teenagers and she did not want to be the slow poke.

***

97

Cicely lay on her queen sized bed alone in her room. Indeed proud of herself. She wanted to be here. In a place that didn't even feel like work anymore. And she had made it on her own terms.

She thought about who she could call to celebrate her accomplishments. Her dad? Their past conversations only consisted of Cicely asking for money and him agreeing to give it to her. Her mother? Their conversations usually consisted of her mother's harsh chidings and disapproval. Brook or Dawn? She hadn't spoken with either of them in about six months. With Brook being married and running her shop, Dawn practically married and raising her daughter, their words had been few and far between. And then there was Karen. Cicely admitted to herself that she thought about her often. But what was done was done.

Cicely shifted her thoughts.

"I'll get married, have kids, and then I can share all of my accomplishments with my children," she said to herself.

But there were no prospects for her as far as husbands go. Her work would have to become her family for the time being.

Her thoughts shifted to Mr. Mann. She remembered what he said about his family. She admired the fact that he was a family man. He spent time that he really didn't have with his sons. She honestly admired the fact that he stayed with his wife even though they weren't happy. His words stuck with her, made her respect his manhood. It made her value him.

It actually made her want him.

Cicely was on auto-pilot. Primal desire had taken over. Cunningness was in charge.

Call the front desk and see what room he's staying in. Lie if you have to! Put on your two-piece and wrap that see-through sarong around your waist. Remember your Chanel pheromones. Not too much.

Get on the elevator; go down to the first floor. Get off the elevator. Go to the elevators that go to the thirty-first floor, the pent house floor. Get on the elevator. Press 31.

Check your hair. Don't worry about how fast your heart is beating.

Get off the elevator. Go to the left. His room is to the left. Quickly now! We don't want to be seen.

There's his door. You remember what to say. You remember what to do.

She knocked on the door, gently rapping twice.

Knock again. He can't hear that!

Cicely knocked again, three strong knocks this time. She looked down at her watch. It was two o'clock in the morning.

"What am I doing here?"

You remember what to say. You remember what to do.

Surprisingly he answered the door right away. It was almost as if he was expecting her to come. "Ms. Shaw?"

Cicely pushed her way into the door and said, "If you don't want me to stay then tell me so and I'll leave."

He didn't answer.

She closed the door.

She wasted no time in seducing Vincent Mann. He began walking her back toward the bathroom. This startled Cicely and at that moment she noticed that there were candles burning in the room. But she kept walking backwards.

The bathroom was filled with candles. The Jacuzzi was going strong, bubbling a tune all its own. None of this raised a red flag for Cicely.

As they made love, Cicely could swear she heard knocking.

Knock! Knock! Knock!

Someone knocked hard on the front door.

"Ignore it! They probably have the wrong room!" Vincent Mann commanded.

Cicely and Vincent Mann were oblivious to all else. Eventually the knocking stopped.

***

Cicely never made it to the jet skis the next morning and neither did Vincent. They had just finished their room service and were holding each other in a king-size bed with white satin sheets. The large French doors were open, letting the cool morning breeze come over the balcony and into the room.

They had spent the entire night making love. She was impressed with his stamina. He was impressed with her flexibility.

"You're amazing" he said as he fed her grapes.

"Where do you hide that Energizer battery of yours?" she asked in jest.

He laughed.

"I'm just shocked. Mr. Inman told me that you were a church going, Christian girl. I would never have thought that we'd be here, like this."

She quietly wondered why Mr. Inman would tell him something like that.

"At some point in time you and I are going to have to talk about what just happened, Cicely."

"I know. I know. I can't really explain it, Mr. Mann."

"Please. Now I think that we are way pass formalities. Call me Vincent."

"Well, Vincent—" she liked the way his name rolled off her tongue. "I don't know what came over me really. It's like I have this voice in my head and it encourages me to do the things that I know are wrong."

"And last night that voice told you to come up here and ravish me?" Cicely had no answer for him. "I'm married. I don't usually do things like this. I don't want you to get the wrong idea."

"I understand. I'll get my stuff and go. And don't worry. It doesn't have to be awkward for us. Believe me; I have practice with this sort of thing."

"Hold up. Wait a minute." He stopped her from getting out of the bed. "There is a connection between us. I can't deny it and you can't either. I felt it the first time that we met."

"Really?"

"Yes. I just feel that this is something that we are going to have to be careful about, you know. But I definitely don't want it to end."

She agreed. She told him that she was on the same page with him. She showed him by ravishing him again. She was obeying the voice in her head.

***

Cicely and Vincent spent the rest of the weekend together. They were very discreet in public; so much so that no one would have guessed that they had become lovers, that they had made love numerous times over the course of a few days. They had to be careful. He was married after all.

The meeting came to a close and it was time to check out of the hotel. Cicely had turned in her room key and was walking toward the front door when she saw Vincent Mann.

"Thanks for everything, Mr. Mann," she said as he walked by.

He didn't respond.

He was talking to Debra and the conversation didn't seem to be a friendly one. His tone, firm. His look, deadly serious. Debra's face displayed a mixture anger and fear.

As Cicely continued walking, all that she could make out of the conversation was this.

"You know what I expect from you, Debra! You knew the requirements before you took your position! We will talk about this when I come out to California!"

Wow, she thought to herself. She didn't know what Debra had done, but whatever it was, Mr. Mann wasn't happy at all.

She didn't want to get that speech. So her mission was to out-perform every other division. She wanted to make Mr. Mann happy. Her mission was also to turn her condo into a love nest. She wanted to make Vincent happy.

Chapter 12

Brook entered the shop very early on a Tuesday morning. Miss Mattie was the only person there, as she normally opened the shop.

"You're here early, boss."

Brook didn't respond. She only dropped her bag on the black and white tile floor and plopped herself into the chair next to Miss Mattie's.

"Well, how was your weekend?"

Brook remained silent. Her eyes were swollen from crying. The skin on her face was so tight that her cheek bones protruded. Her hair was tied into a pony-tail, barely combed down. She looked like a zombie to Miss Mattie who was determined to get her to say something.

"How much more weight are you going to lose? You're going to fly away soon. You and Dawn don't even look alike anymore."

"He's cheating on me."

"What?"

Miss Mattie pulled her comb off of her counter, walked over to Brook, took her pony-tail out and began to comb through her hair.

"Say that again."

"You heard me. That low life is cheating on me. And I am a fool for not seeing it."

"How do you know that Walter is cheating? Did you catch him or something?"

Brook began gazing at her wedding ring, playing with it. She wiggled her finger so that the light could hit the diamond and make it sparkle. Then with a sob, she covered it up.

"I don't feel like a married woman. I don't live with my husband. I don't go to bed with my husband every night and I don't wake up beside him every morning.

He used to come up one weekend a month but now even that's stopped. You can't be too busy to be a husband."

Miss Mattie let the comb slowly work out the kinks in Brook's jet black hair. She said nothing. Instead she listened as Brook began pouring her heart out to her.

"I was tired of it all. I was tired of not having my man with me. I was tired of living alone. I was tired of the rumors that I was hearing."

Brook's voice began to crack. She fought the tears away, beginning to be relaxed by Miss Mattie's soft, motherly touch.

"What rumors have you heard, baby?"

Brook looked at Miss Mattie through the mirror. Her look said it all. If she had not said another word, Miss Mattie knew exactly where her head was. Brook sensed that her eyes were being read by her mother figure. So she closed them tight. She felt that Walter was being unfaithful. That was all Miss Mattie needed to know.

"Do you know who he's cheating with?"

Brook's eyes remained closed. She remained silent.

"Okay. Do you think it's another woman?"

All Miss Mattie saw was Brook's eye lids.

"Do you think it's a man?"

Brook's eyes popped open.

A week earlier, Brook received a phone call from Laline, one of her old friends that lived in Atlanta. They talked for a minute, Laline telling her about the artists that she had interviewed for the fashion magazine. Brook told her about how well the shops were doing. How Walter was such a hustler and how he was on top of his game. That's when Laline dropped the bomb.

"That's why I called you," she said.

"What's up?"

"I saw Walter at this bar off of Peachtree."

"What? Was some hoochies all on him or something? You know Walter is fine as all get out so I'm used to ladies throwing themselves at the brother."

"Well the brother was there with some other brothers."

"Okay. So what?"

Brook was confused and Laline could tell in her tone.

"You really don't know, do you? I mean you don't have a clue at all?"

"Don't know what?"

Laline took a deep breath.

"It was a gay bar. I saw Walter there with some other men."

Brook was silent at first. Then she searched her mind for some response to the accusation.

"He was probably bar hopping with some of the guys from the shop," she replied. "They probably didn't even realize that they had walked into a gay bar. They probably left as soon as they realized it."

There was a long pause in the conversation. Millions of things could have been said in that space. Millions of ideas ran through Brook's mind. She hoped with all of her heart that Laline agreed with her.

"You're probably right. I mean he did leave as soon as he saw me."

There was another bout of silence. Brook twirled the phone cord around her finger, wrapping it very tight.

"Listen I didn't mean to start any trouble," Laline said. "I saw him there and I just thought I'd call because we sisters have to stick together. Most of the men that hang out around that bar are on the down low. Some of them are so scandalous that they're not using protection. If Walter is caught up in that, you need to take measures to protect yourself."

"Thanks. But I know Walter. His being there was a mistake."

Brook was tired of hearing things. She was so tired that she found herself racing down Interstate-85 on a Saturday afternoon to their townhouse in downtown Atlanta. She got there, unpacked her things and jumped straight into a bubble bath. She lit incense and put on some Gerald Albright. After dressing in nothing but a matching black bra and thong set, she lay down on the couch so she would be the first thing that Walter saw when he finally came home from the shop. She was comfortable on that leather sofa; so comfortable that she fell asleep.

Hours later, Brook thought that she heard the front door open and then close quickly. But she dismissed it thinking that she must have been dreaming. A few moments later, looking through her thick eye lashes, she focused on her handsome husband. His eyes sparkled to her. His scent was inviting. His frown was clearly evident.

"WHAT THE HECK ARE YOU DOING DOWN HERE?"

Brook was still half asleep. She thought that she may be still dreaming. But Walter's voice got louder. His frown grew more menacing.

"WHAT ARE YOU DOING HERE?" he shouted.

Brook fought past her drowsiness.

"What's going on? Why are you yelling at me?"

"Who's at the shop?"

"Why?"

"BROOK RIGGINS, ANSWER ME NOW!"

"Miss Mattie! You know she can run that shop without me! Why are you worried about that? Aren't you glad to see me?"

"Why didn't you call me and tell me that you were coming down here?"

That question floored Brook. She sat up on the sofa and covered herself with one of the large throw pillows.

"Why should I have to call you? This is my house too. I am your wife. Why do I have to call you? Do you have something to hide?"

Walter was silent. The only sound that was heard for the next few minutes was the jingling of his car keys.

"You know I have nothing to hide. It's just that you abandoned the shop. I wasn't expecting you."

"Like I said, Miss Mattie is handling everything."

Again there was an awkward silence. He stopped jingling his keys and went for the front door.

"I'll be back in a few."

That was all that he said before he left.

Brook looked at the living room, all decked with candles, the blinds drawn, the soft music playing. She looked down at her caramel skin barely covered by lace lingerie and said, "He came in here, saw me dressed like this, and walked out because I didn't call before I came down?"

About thirty minutes later Walter returned to the house with some flowers. He had turned his frown in for a bright cheery smile that lit up the room when he entered.

"I'm sorry, Brook."

He gave the flowers to Brook and sat down beside her on the couch. She looked at him with confusion. She loved him. But she didn't know how to take him right then.

"I just got so wound up about you leaving the shop on one of our busiest days."

Brook said nothing. Walter took the flowers from her and began rubbing her hair from the crown of her head to her shoulders. He closed his eyes and kissed her. Brook returned the kiss.

But she kept her eyes open.

"Do you think it's a man?" Miss Mattie asked again. Brook didn't answer. She was still in a daze, reliving the memory of what happened the weekend before. "Well, do you?"

"Does it matter?"

Brook finally came out of her coma to speak those three words.

Of course it mattered. But she wasn't ready to admit that. Not to herself and definitely not to anyone else.

Miss Mattie walked to her counter and started going through her purse. She retrieved a small tan business card, looked at it for a moment, and then handed it to Brook.

"I was married before." She rubbed Brook's cheek lightly and said, "For your peace of mind."

Brook took the card and inspected it closely. Then she looked back at Miss Mattie. Tears were trying their best to get pass the barrier that Brook had put up, but they couldn't. Brook would remain strong. She didn't want anyone to see her cry anymore.

"Go on, get out of here and handle your business. I'll take care of the shop today."

Brook gathered her things and headed for the front door. Before she made her exit she stopped short and said, "Just tell everyone that I'm sick."

Miss Mattie gave a nod and a look that said that she had Brook's back no matter what.

As soon as Brook got home she wasted no time. She pulled out the business card and dialed the number.

"Law Detective Agency. This is Detective Terry Law. How may I help you?"

Brook paused.

"Hello. Is anyone there?" Terry Law asked.

"Hi, my name is Brook Riggins."

"Hello Ms. Riggins. How may I help you?"

Brook cleared her throat and answered, "I need peace of mind."

Chapter 13

Karen was a nervous wreck and Tamara could sense it. So she decided to treat her to a day of mani-pedis in an attempt to settle her a bit. She had a date with William that evening.

"So where is he taking you?" Tamara asked.

"I don't know. He's being all secretive. But he said that it was somewhere very nice. I'm so nervous. No. Nervous isn't the word. I'm scared."

"Scared of what?"

Karen wiggled her toes, displaying their clear polish with slight touches of glitter.

"What are you afraid of, Kay?"

"Oh nothing," Karen replied. Then she thought about something that William said. Woman-speak. She had to laugh.

"What's so funny?"

Karen took a deep breath and said, "This will be our third date."

"Oh."

"Do you think that William and Maxwell talk about each other's sex life? What I mean to say is this. Do you think that Maxwell told William about the two of you sleeping together on your third date?"

"William and Maxwell are best friends," Tamara replied. "I'm positive that Maxwell has told him."

"Shoot!"

"What's the big deal?"

"They're best friends," Karen replied. "We're best friends."

"Aw! That's right. You are my B.F.F!"

"So William may think that the same thing applies to us. He may think since you gave it up on date three, that tonight is his lucky night." Karen leaned back and exhaled in desperation. "I really like him. It would

109

break my heart if he stopped seeing me because I won't—"

"Because you won't give him any?"

"Well, yeah."

"Listen, Karen. If William is the one for you, then your celibacy shouldn't be an issue for him. If he's the one, he'll wait for you."

Karen felt a little bit better.

"Now I can't promise you that he's going to wait alone," Tamara added.

"What?"

"A man has needs, girl!"

"Gee thanks. I was feeling so much better about tonight."

Tamara rested her hand on Karen's shoulder.

"Trust me, Kay. He'll wait."

"What if he doesn't? What if he pressures me?"

"If he doesn't wait, then he's not the one for you."

Karen was right back where she started before her conversation with Tamara. Afraid. She was really starting to like William. She didn't want to lose him.

***

William picked Karen up at six p.m. When she opened the door, she saw that he was wearing a black three-piece suit, a light blue dress shirt and a jet black neck tie with tiny light blue stripes.

"Wow, don't you look dapper," she said. "I'll just go and get my shawl and purse."

As she turned and sashayed to her bedroom, she heard him say under his breath, "Mm, Mm, Mm." She grinned initially. But afterwards felt the same fear she felt earlier at the nail salon.

"So where are we going?" she asked when she returned to the living room.

"It's a surprise. You said that I could surprise you."

"I did. But now I don't know if that's such a good idea," Karen said with a smile.

"You look beautiful," William said, admiring Karen's gray wrap dress, black tights, and black and gray stiletto heels. He curved his right arm toward her and said, "Shall we?"

"We shall."

And so William and Karen were off, down Sangaree Parkway and then to Main Street. Karen was a little surprised to see William take the I-26 West entrance ramp, because it actually took them away from the city.

"Are you taking me to some new night spot in the boonies or something?" Karen said half-jokingly.

"No. We're going to Columbia."

"Columbia? But that's a hundred miles away? What's in Columbia?"

"When I asked you where you wanted to go on our third date, you said to surprise you."

"You're right. I *did* say that."

"So just sit back and enjoy the ride."

"Okay. But you just watch your speed, buddy!"

William smiled and said, "I promise not to go too fast."

***

They made it to Columbia in an hour and a half. But Karen didn't mind the drive because it gave them time to talk. She loved talking with William and he felt the same way about her. He told her about how things had gotten better for him at work and that he had two Foundation grants lined up. She told him about some of the things she had to deal with on the job. Without going into details, she told him about one of her cases, a neglect case. She told him that helping children deal with their hurts helped her to deal with her past. She found William to be an excellent listener and that was truly important to her.

Before Karen knew it, they were cruising around downtown Columbia.

"This is my old stomping ground right here," she said with pride. "I had an apartment not far from where we are now."

"Is that so?"

"Oh, so that is. Gamecocks for life!"

"Well don't get too rowdy over there, okay? My friends around M.U.S.C. tell me that Clemson is the real undergraduate school in South Carolina."

"You watch your mouth, Dr. Ward. Don't get spanked, alright? I don't want to have to put it on you and it's just our third date."

Why in the world did I just say that? Karen thought.

"Well call me Bruh Rabbit, because I might like that," William replied.

"Bruh Rabbit?"

"Yeah. The story of Bruh Rabbit and the Tar baby. Bruh Rabbit asked Bruh Fox to throw him in the briar patch but—" William saw that Karen clearly had no idea what he was talking about. "Never mind. We're here."

Their destination was The Blue Martini: a jazz night club on Lady Street. Karen could hear the smooth hum of the double bass before they even entered the club.

"Coltrane?" Karen asked as she read the marquee.

"Yes. Well, Ravi Coltrane. John Coltrane's son. That was the surprise. Let's go on in."

Their table was right beside the stage. Coltrane's quartet had just started their first set. Karen marveled because she didn't even know that John Coltrane had a son that played tenor saxophone.

"May I get you guys something to drink?" the waitress asked.

"Iced tea for me," Karen replied.

"Make that two iced teas," William added.

"Great!" the waitress exclaimed. "I'll be back with your drinks in a jiff."

"Tea? I figured you would have something a little stronger," Karen said.

"No. I'm driving. Plus I noticed that you don't drink."

Karen smiled.

"This is very nice, William. I love bop. I guess I inherited my love for music from my mother."

"Tell me about her."

He already knew that her mother had passed away, but Karen had yet to give him the gory details.

"Well, from what I was told, she was very talented, very beautiful."

"I imagine that you also inherited your red hair and blonde streaks from your mother."

Karen played with the rim of her glass and then her mood began to match the musician's melancholy tune.

"No. I didn't get that from my mother."

She had no idea where she got it from. There was a part of her that she didn't even know.

William decided to lighten the mood.

"So we know a good bit about each other. And we'll learn more and more as time progresses." Karen loved William's statement about their time with each other progressing. "So tell me. What was your most embarrassing moment?"

"Are you serious?"

"Sure I am. And afterwards, I'll tell you mine."

She thought about it for a moment.

"Okay. Here it goes. It was my senior year in high school. I was in a Cotillion Ball that was held at the Greenville Memorial Auditorium and the place was packed. I had on this beautiful white ball gown. My hair was up, my shoulders were bare. Everybody said I looked like a princess."

"I bet you did."

"Brownie points! Anyway, I was on stage and my escort was on the floor waiting for me. There was a beautiful orchestral arrangement playing in the background and the spotlight was right on me. I guess the light was a little too bright because as I was walking down to the floor, I missed like three steps. The whole crowd was like ooh! So there I was in this beautiful gown on the floor."

"Wow! You hit the floor?"

"Oh yes! Even my escort was laughing. But I had to be honest with myself. It was pretty funny. Okay your turn."

"Okay. And mine was a little more recent. I had just gotten the position at M.U.S.C. I was walking down Ashley Avenue on my way to Wickliffe House to get some lunch. I saw one of the senior faculty members, Dr. Malone."

William noticed that Karen raised her brow and widened her eyes. She thought about her last visit with Dr. Malone.

"What?" he asked.

"Oh, it's nothing. Go ahead."

"So I waved to Dr. Malone and said hello. Well you know how the sidewalks are in Charleston. You really have to pay attention to where you're walking because of all the bricks that stick up from the sidewalk. I wasn't paying attention. I tripped over one of those bricks and went crashing to the ground. I tore that sidewalk up! Well, Malone raced across the street and helped me up. There wasn't anything hurt on me except my pride. Malone and I still have a good laugh about that." William chuckled and then he added, "Why do the most embarrassing moments in someone's life often involve falling?"

Karen gave a smile but no reply.

"Did I say something wrong?" he asked.

"No. It's just—it's nothing."

114

William took a sip of his iced tea and replied, "Woman-speak."

"Shut up!" Karen said jokingly as she playfully hit William's arm.

She took a sip of her iced tea and placed the glass back on the coaster. She circled the rim of her glass with her index finger.

"William, I'm starting to think that our meeting each other was not coincidental."

"Tell me about it. Because the night before we met, I—"

William had gotten carried away with himself. Telling Karen that he dreamed about her before they had even met was not a good idea. So after a brief pause he replied, "Nothing."

Karen chuckled and said, "I see that you're fluent in woman-speak as well."

"Whatever!" William retorted jovially.

"I have a question for you," she said.

"Fire away!"

"When you picked me up at my house earlier, I went to get my purse and overheard you say, 'Mm, Mm, Mm!' under your breath."

"Oh, you heard that?"

"Yes, I did. Why did you say it?"

He gave a nervous smile.

"Do you really want to know why? Because I'm afraid it's probably a little worse than what you're thinking."

"I honestly want to know."

"Okay," he said. "I worked for a construction company the summer of my freshman year of college. I was out on a job with one of the foremen, this dirty old guy. And we were just downtown, woman watching. The old guy told me—and I'll have to clean this up for you—but he told me that you can tell how good a woman is in bed by the direction her dress sways when she walks."

Karen's jaw dropped.

"No lie!" William added. "The old guy said that if a woman's dress sways in and out when she walks, then she's horrible in bed. But if her dress sways from left to right, then she's pretty much amazing in the sack! There I've said it."

"That is incredible," Karen said as she blushed.

"I know. I've had some pretty bad influences growing up."

"So how did my dress sway?"

"Excuse me?"

"My dress. How did it sway when I walked off?"

William looked away to hide his sinister grin and embarrassed eyes.

"Are you guys ready to order?" the waitress asked.

"Sure! What are you having, dear?" William asked Karen, eager for the subject to be changed.

Karen shook her head and smiled at William as if to say that he was not off of the hook.

"I'll have the Chilean Sea Bass," Karen replied.

"Excellent. And for you, sir?"

"I'll have the Australian Rack."

The waitress collected their menus and headed off. Karen just smiled at William and said under her breath, "Mm, Mm, Mm!"

William had to laugh.

***

After dinner, William and Karen found themselves at a Royal Z's Bowling Alley for Moonlight Bowling. Perhaps it was William's constant bragging about his bowling skills that made Karen suggest that they settle it once and for all. People probably thought they looked crazy, William wearing a three-piece suit, Karen wearing a dress and stockings, both of their outfits rounded off with glow in the dark bowling shoes. But they didn't care. A score had to be settled.

Royal Z's was packed and every lane was full of bowlers. Loud music blared through the subwoofers as strobe lights, runway lights and lasers lit up the darkness. Glow in the dark bowling balls added a special touch that further electrified the atmosphere. Karen was all smiles. William was enjoying himself as well, even though he was losing horribly.

"My arm is tired," William said, making excuses as he took off his jacket and rolled up his sleeves.

"There's nothing wrong with your arm. You just suck! I'm whipping you and I'm wearing stockings and footies!"

"Okay, let's play again. I'm not going to let you win this time."

They bowled another ten frames. William lost again.

"Best of five!" he shouted over the music.

William was competitive by nature, but he really didn't mind that he was losing. He was having so much fun with Karen that he lost track of time.

"No! I'm tired of beating you," Karen said. "Swallow your pride and admit that I'm the boss."

"Yeah! Yeah! Yeah!" he replied.

William paid for the games and returned their bowling shoes.

"Ooh look! A photo booth!" Karen exclaimed. "Let's go take some pictures! My treat!"

She pulled William by the hand to the photo booth and guided him inside. Then she eased beside him really close. Their hips touched and William felt a pulse of energy run up his leg. He loved being close to Karen and apparently she felt the same way as she smiled at him and asked, "Are you ready?"

"I'm ready," he replied.

And as the flash went off, Karen reached over and kissed William on the cheek. Electricity surged up and down his neck. He didn't remember the last time that he had so much fun just laughing, smiling, and joking around. He really liked Karen and he could only hope that she felt the same way.

It was three o'clock in the morning when they walked out the front door of the bowling alley and headed for William's Lexus. They walked with each other arm in arm. With the music of Ravi Coltrane still playing in her mind, Karen rested her head on William's shoulder and said, "I've had so much fun tonight, William. It's a shame the night has to end."

"Well it doesn't necessarily have to end," he replied. "We could check into a hotel."

And then the music stopped playing for Karen.

"It's after three in the morning and we're both tired," he added. "What do you say? You want to go and get a room?"

Karen kept her arm locked tight in William's. She tried very hard to hide her apprehension. But she really didn't know quite how to answer him. It was true that they had fun. And she honestly wanted the night to last. But now she was at a crossroads. They were nearly at his Lexus and the question was still in the air.

"If you don't want to its cool," he said. "It's just that it's late and it's a ninety minute drive back to Charleston."

"Okay."

Karen couldn't believe that she had just said that.

"Cool."

In Karen's mind, William's new ear to ear smile was like that of a little kid who was about to get some ice-cream. She was definitely in a pickle.

Before she knew it, they were pulling into the parking lot of the Embassy Suites. It was early in the morning and a hotel was the last place that she thought they'd be. As they entered the automatic doors, Karen's heart dropped. She clearly didn't want to go through with it. They walked into the lobby and Karen's conscience was pounding her.

118

Tell him no. Tell him that you don't want to do this.

But another part of Karen didn't want to lose William, didn't want to lose another relationship. She was tired of being alone. But her virginity was important to her. It was one of the few constants in her life.

"I'm going to wait over by these chairs," she said.

"Okay. I'll get us checked in."

What am I doing here, Karen thought to herself. She thought about the conversation that she had with Tamara the previous day.

If he doesn't wait, then he's not the one for you.

Tamara's words were playing over and over again in Karen's mind.

William jolted her from those thoughts with an eager, "We're all set."

They took the glass elevators to the fourth floor. William led the way around the corner and along the balcony that overlooked the grand courtyard. Karen's heart beat harder and harder with each step. She didn't want to do it, but she had to.

She said softly, "I can't go through with this."

But she whispered those words so William never heard her. He stopped at room 434 and said, "I wasn't able to get our rooms right next to each other. So, I'm down the way in room 417. Here's your room key."

Karen looked shocked as she took the key card from him. She covered her heart with her hand and then wiped her brow.

"What?" William asked. "Did you think that we were staying in a single room together?"

"I don't know. Yes."

"Well I'm sorry, Ms. Cole, but I am just not that easy," he replied with a smile. "You are going to have to woo me."

Karen giggled with relief.

"But seriously, Karen. I've learned that it's best to take things slow."

119

"Slow is good."

"If you need me, I'll be right down the way."

"Okay."

And then they told each other good night.

Several minutes later, Karen pulled the duvet covers back and lay down on the bed sheets. She looked at the photo of her kissing William on the cheek. She enjoyed that kiss. She loved the way his skin tasted on her lips. And she couldn't lie to herself about that fact that she really did want to be with him intimately. But she also had to admit that she was relieved that William was such a gentleman. Maybe he *was* the one for her.

Karen's cell phone rang. Of course it was William.

Karen answered with a soft, "Hello."

"Left to right," he said.

"What was that?"

"Your dress. When I watched you walk away, your dress was swaying from left to right."

After they bid each other good night, Karen held their photo close to her heart and she thought about William. She wanted him to be the one to find out whether or not the old construction foreman was correct.

Chapter 14

As soon as Cory got up and started getting dressed, Dawn lit into him.

"So are you just going to come here, sleep with me, and leave like I'm one of your chicken heads?"

"Dawn, I don't have time for this."

"Cory you never have time for this. You stay in Greenville more than you do your own house!"

"You're the one who wanted to buy a house out here in the boonies. I was fine with the house we had in Nicholtown. But you wanted it, so I bought it. But don't expect me to be out here twenty-four/ seven. I have a business to run and I can't run it from way out here."

They lived in a two story mini-mansion in Easley. In a new subdivision where amazingly not every house was on top of each other. Cory bought the house after Dawn begged and pleaded with him to do so. She was tired of the city and all of its drama, the girls showing up at their door claiming to have children by Cory. But the last straw for Dawn was the big fight she got into with a girl named Nina. Nina was pregnant at the time.

Dawn began putting on her robe and fixing her hair. She cleared her throat and sat on the edge of the bed.

"I see what this is about," she said. "You're still mad about the cruise."

"I'm not tripping about that. It just taught me a lesson, that's all. But it won't ever happen again."

That statement made Dawn very quiet for a moment. After she digested what he had just said, she took a deep breath and continued.

"You don't even sleep here anymore. You barely see your daughter. Do you even remember her name?"

"Why are you asking me stupid questions, Dawn?"

"Stupid questions? You want me to ask you some questions? Okay, did you have a baby by that ugly tramp?"

"Dawn, what are you talking about?"

"What am I talking about? I'm talking about the girl that lives off of Washington Street, the girl who ran up on me at the club, the one I beat down!"

Cory put on his shirt and picked his cell phone up from the night stand. Then he walked over to the stand-up mirror and began fixing his clothes.

"Dawn, you're the one acting like a tramp right now."

"I hate you!" Dawn yelled. Then she picked up a brush from her night stand and threw it at him. It missed him by an inch, shattering the mirror he was looking into.

"Woman! If you would have hit me, I would—"

"You would what? Dope me up and burn the house down with me in it like you did Ricky and Tonya?"

There was a silence in the room and a chill in the air. They both stared at each other. Cory's was a stare of anger, Dawn's was a stare of fear. She couldn't believe that those words had escaped her lips.

He began walking slowly toward her. He quickly grabbed her by the arm and jerked her closer.

"Be careful what you say in my house," he whispered sternly.

Dawn gathered courage and broke away from his grasp.

"Get your hands off of me," she said softly.

She was deathly scared of him at that time because of the look in his eye, because of what she knew he had done shortly after they returned from their cruise.

Cory found out that Ricky and Tonya stole some money from him while they were away. One week later, they were found in the smoldering ruins of their home in Cleveland Park. It was made to look like an

122

accident, but everyone knew what happened. The whole situation made Dawn uncomfortable.

"I'm going to go check on Tarsha, and then I'm out. If you need me, hit me on my hip."

And with that, Cory walked out of their spacious master bedroom and into the hallway that led to their daughter's bedroom. Dawn decided that she wouldn't bring up the other girls. She definitely would not ask him to leave the game. The game, and all of its intricacies, was a part of him.

He could not quit now.

He would not quit.

***

It was late afternoon. The sun stood alone in the light blue sky. It was the kind of day that made ladies come out in their short shorts and loose sundresses to show off their soft flesh in the bright sunshine. Dawn and Brook were two of those ladies.

They dubbed it twin sisters' day out. The both of them had just arrived at Applebee's in the mall. Brook had on a tight fitting Fly Girl tee shirt, some snug Capri's, and a pair of Air Force One's. Dawn sported a thin sundress that swayed with her every movement and a pair of brown and cream sandals that showed off her platinum toe ring and freshly painted toe-nails.

"Afternoon, ladies," a sharply dressed young man with a dark complexion said as they were walking by. "Would the two of you like to join me and my colleague for a drink?" he asked boldly.

Both Brook and Dawn smiled and shook their heads no.

"I'm married," Brook said.

"I'm engaged," Dawn added.

"It's just a drink," the sharply dressed man said, extending his glass to them with his left hand, showing off his Rolex.

123

"No thank you."

Dawn was forceful with her answer. Brook had already left the two young brothers high and dry and was on her way to the table.

"That's a shame," Dawn said parking the stroller right beside their table. "You have a diamond on your finger the size of Mount Rushmore, and here I am rolling a one year old around in a stroller. And dudes still try to holler. I guess we're fine, huh?"

Brook said nothing. It was almost like she had not heard a word Dawn said.

Dawn continued anyway.

"Well I'm fine. But you, you're getting too skinny. How much more weight are you going to lose?"

"I'm trying to get down to one-ten," Brook answered.

"Well you need to stop trying and start eating."

Dawn picked up her menu, looked over it for only a few seconds and then quickly put it back down on the table.

"You know something that's funny, Brook?"

"What's that?"

"You and I are identical twins. You were born a couple of hours ahead of me."

"Uh huh."

"We grew up sharing the same bedroom."

"Yeah."

"But I can't read your mind. I mean I have never been able to do that."

"I can't read your mind either."

"I feel bad because of that. I mean if something is wrong with you, I should be able to feel it. I should be able to know what's wrong. But I've never been able to do that."

"Don't worry yourself over it, little sis. I think that mind reading stuff is old wives tales. If you think something's wrong with me, then you can just come right out and ask me. No need for the twilight zone, telepathic mumbo-jumbo."

"Well, is there?"

"Is there what?"

"Hello. Where have you been? Is there something wrong with you?"

There was a brief pause.

"No. I'm good. Why do you ask?"

"Because you've been mega quiet since you came and picked us up, that's all."

"I can ask you the same questions," Brook said.

"What questions?"

"Hello. Where have you been? Is there something wrong with you?"

There was another brief pause.

"No. Why do you ask that?" Dawn replied.

"Because you've been extra snappy to everybody today. You snapped at the lady at the dry-cleaners. You gave Stacy much attitude when she asked you about your house at the shop earlier."

"The dry-cleaning lady had it coming," Dawn said. And then she rolled her eyes and added, "Don't get me started on Stacy. You know she's friends with you know who. She just tries to be nice to me so she can get info and run back and tell her friend. But I didn't think I was giving her attitude. Just thought I was keeping it short and sweet."

"So nothing's wrong with you?"

"No. I'm good."

Both were lying. Both had men but were lonely. Both lived in fear and were too much in denial to open up about it.

They ordered their food, ate, talked for a while about meaningless things, paid their checks and then left.

It was about four-thirty p.m. when Brook pulled the Toyota 4-Runner into Dawn's driveway. The temperature was cooler in Easley. The smell of freshly

125

cut grass was in the air. Brook pulled up right beside a forest green Ford F-150 that had a trailer hitched to the back. It was loaded with riding lawnmowers and weed-eaters and the lawn guys parked it right behind Brook's red Mercedes. Dawn was livid when she saw it. So she rolled down her window and began screaming.

"I told y'all to stop parking this truck in my driveway. Do I have to call my man?"

A short, stocky Latino man with a wild scruffy beard and tattoos on his arms replied, "No ma'am. I'll move it right now."

Dawn got out of the 4-Runner and began unbuckling her daughter's car seat strap.

Another Latino man came from the side of the house carrying lawn debris in a black trash bag. His work shirt was drenched in sweat. He wore a New York Yankees fitted baseball cap which was turned to the back. It too was drenched in sweat. He slung the bag of lawn debris on the back of the truck as the stocky lawn guy started the ignition.

"She must be wearing a G-string!" the stocky guy yelled in Spanish. "It's like jelly, man!"

"English in front of the lady!" the lean man snarled. Then he went back to the side of the house to retrieve more bags.

Brook heard the whole thing as she got out of the truck and snickered.

"What's so funny?" Dawn asked.

"Nothing. I'll get Tarsha. You get that heavy Ottoman, the one that you had to get today instead of having it delivered."

"You're dirty, sis." Dawn said as they switched places.

She opened the back hatch, displaying the large wine and cherry wood Ottoman. She tested it, tried to lift it.

"Did this thing get heavier since this morning?" she asked herself.

126

She tried it again. This time she was able to budge it just a little.

"It must've gained weight somehow. Oh that's right. The guy from the store put it in the truck. How am I going to get this thing in the house?"

"Do you need any help with that, ma'am?" the lean Latino asked as he dropped two large trash bags by his feet and wiped his brow with his soiled baseball cap.

Dawn slammed the hatch shut, startling both the man and Brook, who had just finished gathering her things and was taking the baby out of the car. Dawn raced over to Brook, took the baby away, and began walking fast toward the house.

"No thank you. I'll get my man to get it when he gets home," she said as she hurried to the front door. The man shrugged, picked up his bags and proceeded to the truck.

Brook had to double time it to catch up with Dawn, who was walking so fast that the baby bounced in her arms. Dawn opened the front door and hurried inside the foyer. Brook followed.

"You see what I mean?" Brook asked. "Snappy!"

Brook put her things down in the living room. Looking out the front window she noticed that the F-150 was pulling off and riding down the street. She snickered again.

"There you go again with the giggling," Dawn said. "What's so funny?"

Brook had taken Spanish for four years in high school. She was nearly fluent.

"I'm just laughing at what the heavy-set guy said about you."

"What did he say?"

"That you must be wearing a G-string and that your booty shook like jelly."

"Whatever. What did the other guy say?"

Brook raised her brow and smiled.

127

"I think he was cute, Dawn. Did you think he was cute?"

Dawn rolled her eyes and sucked her teeth. But she never answered Brook's question.

***

Dawn put the baby down for a nap and made some sweet iced tea. She carried two tall glasses through the back French doors and found her sister sitting on the patio, enjoying the view as the sun began creeping past the hills. The sounds of New Edition's Greatest Hits poured from the French doors that led to the patio. Dawn handed her sister a perspiring glass of tea and sat down beside her in a huge wicker chair.

"Dawn, you really need to get your license. It's a shame you have that 4-Runner and you can't even drive it.

"I know, I know. I'll get around to it."

They both sipped their tea, enjoying the moment, enjoying the company they rarely had.

"I've enjoyed myself today," Dawn said. "We really should do this more often."

"That would be nice. Miss Mattie is running the shop, so I have a lot more free time to gallivant."

"You know what would be an even better idea?"

"What's that?"

"We could have slumber parties: me, you, and the baby, in our PJs, popping popcorn, watching movies. I know that may sound corny."

"That doesn't sound corny at all. Let's do it. Next Saturday night I'll come down here and we can make a whole weekend of it. I can stay until Monday night."

"That sounds cool. Me and Tarsha could come up to Greenville and kick it with you one weekend. Maybe get our hair done. That is, if Walter's not home. I don't want to intrude on your Walter time."

"Believe me. It's cool. I wouldn't be intruding on your Cory time would I?"

"Nope. It shouldn't be a problem. You're my sister. I should be able to kick it with my sister on the weekend, right?"

"Right. Then it's settled. Next Saturday. Me, you, and Tarsha. PJs, movies, and popcorn."

It was getting darker out so Brook decided she better hit the road. The both of them were excited about their plans. Looking forward to the weekend, looking forward to not being alone.

Chapter 15

"So what's up with you and Karen?" Maxwell asked William.

"We're good friends," he replied.

Maxwell would regularly ask William that question and William would give the same reply.

"Still just friends, huh?"

"Yes. Say, aren't you the man that told me to take it slow?"

"I said take it slow. I didn't say come to a rolling stop."

William laughed and gathered the rest of his tackle gear.

"But I don't buy it," Maxwell protested. "You're not being honest with your boy. And quite frankly, I'm offended."

"Offended by what?"

"You guys went on your third date and conveniently stayed overnight in Columbia in "separate rooms." And now you're taking Karen on a "deep-sea fishing trip." Spill it! You're hitting the skins, aren't you?"

William laughed again.

"Come on, Will. I told you about me and Tamara the very next day!"

"Yeah."

"So why do you have to be so secretive?"

William plopped his hand on Maxwell's shoulder.

"We're just friends," he said. And then he drove to Charleston Pier to meet Karen.

***

William was waiting in the parking lot of the Charleston City Marina when Karen pulled up and parked her Honda Accord. Like always, they greeted each other with a warm hug.

"I would have come to Summerville to pick you up," William said. "You didn't have to drive all the way down here."

"Oh no, it's cool," Karen replied. "Are you ready to get your behind whipped in fishing?"

"See, there you go, talking junk as always. Come on. I've got a surprise for you."

"Humph. You and your surprises."

He took her by the hand and led her to a beautiful white Jems Luxury super yacht that was docked at the end of the pier.

"Oh my goodness. I thought we were going out a little boat. This is fantastic!"

"I know. It belongs to one of our faculty members. He lets us take it out from time to time."

William led Karen into the luxurious living room, complete with open spaces and contemporary décor. The navy blue modern sectional sofa, chairs and jet black end tables gave a great contrast to the charcoal colored plush carpet. Large picture windows looked out into the bay, shading the room with a light blue tint.

"I may leave all of the fishing to you," she said.

"What happened to all of that junk you were talking?"

"Yeah, that was before I knew I was going to cruise the ocean on a yacht."

William smiled and showed her the rest of the ship, which was large enough to accommodate five couples. Karen was so enamored with the beauty of the yacht that she totally overlooked the framed photographs that hung on the walls of nearly every room.

When they were done with their tour, William took Karen to the back deck to meet the crew and check out their fishing platform. He was introducing her to the crew when they heard a voice that was familiar to both of them.

"Hi, William," Dr. Malone said as he extended his hand. "So this is the fishing partner you told me about."

"Hi Arthur. Yes. Her name is Karen Cole."

Karen's heart sunk down to her stomach. She awkwardly shook Dr. Malone's hand. But she really couldn't look him in the eye. William picked up on that.

"I wanted to make sure that everything was just right on the yacht," Malone said. "But I was just leaving. You guys have fun."

Karen awkwardly looked away as Malone left the yacht. William picked up on that too. Then Karen noticed a photo on the wall of Dr. Malone with his children. And she thought to herself, this is definitely not a coincidence.

***

Once they were a few miles from the Charleston harbor, William brought Karen an iced tea from the kitchen and put it right beside her chair. Karen hadn't said much since they shoved off.

"Is everything okay?" he asked.

She looked up at him, shielding the sun with her hand.

"No. Not really," she replied.

"What's wrong?"

"William, please sit down. I have something that I need to tell you."

He sat in the long chair right beside her. He braced himself for the worst as she began to speak.

"Did you notice that I acted sort of strange when I saw Dr. Malone?"

"Yes. I did notice that."

"Well, the reason I acted strange is because I've been seeing him."

"Wow," William said as he furrowed his brow. "Have you slept with him?"

Karen's eyes widened and her jaw dropped. "Goodness, no! I'm sorry. I phrased that all wrong. I've been seeing Dr. Malone because I'm his patient."

"Ohhh! Whew!"

William wiped his forehead and got his rod and reel together to throw out into the sea.

Karen said, "You're not going to ask me to elaborate?"

"No. That's not really any of my business unless you want it to be."

He threw his line out into the water and then reeled it in a little bit. She continued looking at him, wondering if she wanted to say more about it.

"I want it to be your business," she said.

"Okay then." William put his reel in the holder and turned to face her.

"I want to assure you that I'm not crazy or anything like that," she started.

"I know that you aren't crazy."

"Dr. Malone is treating my anxiety disorder. Well, I guess he's not really treating it. I'm not letting him treat it."

Karen took a deep breath. She noticed how attentive William was and at that time she was eternally grateful for his friendship. He was such a good listener.

"On the day before I met you, I visited Dr. Malone. He told me that my anxiety was mild and that I should consider cutting back on my medication. And then he told me that at some point in time, I would have to open up and talk about the root of my anxiety: my fears."

"That sounds like a good idea. And Arthur's a great guy."

133

"You're right. He is a great guy. He didn't even let on that we knew each other."

William nodded. He wanted to say something. But instead he opted to listen.

"I know what I'm afraid of," she said. "I've always known. I just don't know if I'm ready to talk about it. But someone definitely wants me to talk about it."

"Who? Dr. Malone?"

Karen shook her head, looked up into the sky and replied, "No. I'm afraid it's someone else."

***

It was dark when they returned to the marina. William walked Karen to her car and sat his fishing gear down on the ground. Then he embraced Karen and kissed her on the forehead.

"I'm glad that you felt comfortable talking to me," he said.

"I'm glad that you were there to listen."

"What are you going to do now?"

Karen took a deep breath so that her breast rose and fell on William's stomach. This small, unintentional movement sent a thousand sparks up William's spine.

"I don't know," she replied. "I think I'll talk to Dr. Malone. I think that it's time."

As the full moon lit up the night sky, William held Karen in his arms. He burrowed his nose and lips into Karen's flower-scented red hair. He relished in the aroma of her being. He didn't want to let her go, but he knew that he had to. But just as William was pulling away, Karen held his arms tight and looked up into his eyes.

"Thank you, William. You are the sweetest man I've ever known and I'm glad you're in my life."

Then she tip-toed and gave him a gentle kiss on his lips. The kiss was brief, but it was enough to leave the

134

taste on William's lips. Karen smiled and then kissed him again. Then she told him goodnight, got into her car, and headed for the Crosstown. Had she looked in her rearview mirror, she would have seen that William remained in that spot for a long time.

As Karen drove up Interstate-26 toward Summerville, she thought about William and their friendship. She enjoyed the fact that he just listened to her. He didn't rush to give his opinions. In fact, he would not have pursued the matter had she not invited him. She was thankful for having a friend like him, especially since she might soon need a good shoulder to cry on.

Chapter 16

Karen couldn't believe that she had worked up the nerve to try getting off of her medication. But there she was in the office of Dr. Arthur Malone once again.

He gave her a small note pad and an ink pen.

"Making things visible helps us to understand what we're up against. I want you to make your fears visible. What are you afraid of? Write it down on that notepad and then give it back to me."

Karen didn't hesitate. She wrote on the paper and returned it to Dr. Malone.

"Here you are," she said softly. "This is what I am afraid of."

Dr. Malone looked at the paper and saw that Karen wrote three big letters—

G-O-D

Karen took a deep breath so she could explain what she wrote.

"I have three cousins. We all were born around the same time, so of course we sort of grew up together. My cousins weren't like me though. They had their mothers and their fathers in their lives. All I had was my mother at first. I've never meet my father. But I never really gave my mom a hard time about it. She had other problems. She was on drugs.

"I remember living here in Charleston as a child. I was about seven years old, almost eight. My mother came home with this tall dark-skinned guy with dreadlocks and gold teeth. He was a young guy. Had to be no older than sixteen, seventeen. My momma told me to go and sit on the couch and she'd be out in a little while.

"I took my little battery powered radio in the living room, sat on the couch, and continued listening to the quiet storm. My mother and her guest went in the bedroom and closed the door. But even with the door closed, I could hear what she was saying. I never heard the guy, only my mother. It was like he went out of his way to whisper while I guess she really didn't care.

"I turned up the radio. But I guess the batteries were dying. I felt like someone, somewhere, wanted me to hear what was going on in there. I heard my mother moaning and groaning. I heard the box spring, the head board banging against the wall. I heard things that a child should never hear!"

Karen gasped for air. After a minute of complete silence, she continued.

"About a week later, my grandparents came down to Charleston, packed all of my things, and whisked me back up the road with them. When they came and got me, my mother wasn't even there.

"It was about nine o'clock at night when we were finally finished unpacking. I got ready for bed and my grandma, told me to remember to say my prayers, thank God for all of his blessings. But I wanted my momma. I didn't understand why I had to leave my momma! So when my grandmother told me to pray, I began to feel bitterness in my heart. And that night I got down on my knees and I called God every bad thing I knew to call Him."

Karen paused. For a moment she relived that memory of being a scared and angry little girl, screaming, crying, and cursing at the top of her lungs.

"The very next day, we found out that my momma had died of an overdose. That was the beginning of my punishment. He took my mother because of my foolish actions, because of the stupid things that I said to Him. That's why I'm afraid. For cursing God, He has cursed me. Whatever I get out of life, I deserve."

Karen's began sobbing heavily. When her crying subsided, Dr. Malone spoke softly to her.

"You have just broken major ground, Karen. You have invited me to a place in your past that you haven't let anyone else see. We can fix it. We can do it together. We can start the healing now if you work with me."

She agreed to work with him. She wanted to be healed. She wanted to be whole.

When she walked out into the lobby, William was waiting on her with open arms. He embraced her as she rested her head on his chest and cried. She was glad that he was there. And it was at that moment that she had a stunning revelation. If God was truly mad at her, would he have blessed her with such a wonderful friend?

Chapter 17

Dawn had been awake ever since she first heard the sound of the lawnmower that cool Monday morning. She got out of bed and sat on the bench that sat right up against her bedroom window. After pulling her jet black hair behind her shoulders, she watched as the lean, Latino landscaper rode his mower. A sense of shame overcame her because of her voyeurism. She could see his shoulder muscles through his work-shirt as he rode the mower, his sweat glistening in the sun.

"Stop it!!" she said to herself, calming herself down.

She couldn't deny it. She was a red-blooded African-American girl with needs, needs that weren't being met by her boyfriend Cory.

***

Saturday evening rolled around fast. Dawn had cleaned the house, bathed her daughter, and gotten the both of them dressed for the weekend slumber-party. The sun was just setting by the time Brook arrived bearing a grocery bag full of snacks in one hand and large cheese pizza in the other.

"Where's that niece of mine? Auntie Brook is here and we're going to have some fun!"

Dawn brought Tarsha to Brook and they all walked into the den. Tarsha, ever the inquisitive and jolly toddler, was playing with Brook's hair and trying to take off her sunglasses.

"Your yard looks tight, Dawn," Brook said as she tried to take her sunglasses back from Tarsha. "You think your landscaper does yards all the way in Mauldin?"

"I don't know. I can find out for you though."

"Yeah get his business card or something the next time he's up here. My yard is embarrassing to look at."

The twin sisters settled into the evening. Little Tarsha tried to hang with her mother and aunt for as long as she could, but sleep called her. Dawn laid her in her bedroom, turned on the baby monitor and headed back downstairs where Brook was waiting for her with a little surprise in each of her hands.

"I figured we'd break these out when miss ma'am fell asleep," she said holding two cold strawberry wine coolers. She had hid them in the back of the fridge and snuck back into the kitchen to retrieve them when Dawn was upstairs. "We may not get drunk, but we'll definitely get tipsy."

Dawn took one of the bottles from her and put a DVD in the player: old music videos that she had taped over the years. When she got her new computer she transferred all of the VHS tapes to DVD. Their plan was to finish the six-pack of wine coolers and spend the rest of the night looking at BBD, En Vogue and Boys II Men represent the nineties.

Brook was buzzed. She let her hair down and kicked her feet up on the couch. She felt free, relaxed. The videos began watching her as she stared off into space. She had a lot on her mind.

"What's the matter with you?" Dawn asked.

Brook wasted no time and beat around no bushes.

"Walter's cheating on me."

Dawn lowered her bottle.

"Stop playing."

"I'm not playing. He's cheating on me. I have proof."

"What proof? How did you get it?"

"I hired a private detective. Miss Mattie gave me the number."

"Miss Mattie knew before me?"

"It's nothing like that. She was there at the shop when I sort of got the suspicion. She had a similar problem with her ex-husband. Long story short, she

140

gave me the number, I called, they followed him around in Atlanta and they got photos."

There was a brief pause. Brook took a sip from her cooler while Dawn looked at her, wondering how to ask her next question.

"Is it a woman or a man?"

Brook looked at her and narrowed her eyes. A part of her wanted to ask why Dawn would ask that question, but another part of her already knew why. Everyone knew it before her, which made Brook feel like a fool. Now she just held on to hope that it wasn't the latter.

"I don't know any details. The detective told me that she had photos. I told her that I wanted to speak with her in person, to see them for myself. We're meeting Tuesday afternoon. Walter will be up that same day. He doesn't know that I know."

Dawn tucked her shoulder length jet black hair behind her ears. She sighed and looked at Brook, raising her brow and then lowering it.

"Are you okay?" she asked.

"I'll feel better after I know all of the details."

Dawn turned in her seat and looked down into the glass coffee table. She rubbed the back of her neck and a feeling of uneasiness overcame her. Brook remained calm yet quiet as Dawn let out a long sigh.

"We're twins in every sense aren't we?" Dawn asked.

"What do you mean by that?"

"We look alike, so we're both pretty. We both like the same things. We both go through the same things."

Dawn began rubbing the palm of her left hand with her right. Brook gave her a wide-eyed glare, waiting to see where this was going.

"Cory has been cheating on me since day one—with her!"

Brook was confused at first and then a light bulb flashed above her head.

141

"Oh, her. You know that *her* has a name don't you?"

"I can't stand her and I can't stand to hear her name."

"You should really let go of that beef between you and Nina."

Nina was the girl that Dawn had so much trouble with, the pregnant girl that she fought with at the club.

"That baby of hers looks just like Tarsha and I can't stand it. But he's sleeping with both of us. He's probably there right now. He spends about six nights there and one night out here, if that. It makes me sick."

The two sisters sat in silence. The DVD had stopped playing a long time ago.

"Are you going to leave Walter?"

"I honestly don't know. It depends on what I find out. Are you going to leave Cory?"

"I haven't left him yet, so what does that tell you?"

Brook finished her wine cooler and placed it on the coffee table. She took a deep breath, rested her elbows on her knees, and then rested her chin in her hands. Her words were somber when she spoke.

"We're young, smart, and beautiful. Why do we allow ourselves to be mistreated?"

Dawn finished her wine cooler, leaned back on the couch and replied, "Twin sister, I was wondering the same thing."

Chapter 18

Cicely lit candles in her new master bedroom and then stepped right outside of the room to the balcony that overlooked the large foyer. The music of Teddy Pendergrass filled the house by way of the monitors that were in each room. She gazed out of the large window that looked out over the golf course. The sun peaked from the horizon, painting the sky with a golden glow. So beautiful. So romantic.

Cicely surveyed the foyer from the second floor balcony, admiring the Italian marble flooring and Victorian furniture. From that one vantage point alone you could see the beauty of the entire home. Cicely's first home: a three story Colonial with a gabled roof and four huge, white columns. The pride of ownership overcame her.

The movers had delivered all of the furniture a few days earlier. Cicely had finished unpacking all of her boxes the previous day. She spent the entire day putting her special touches on the house: Chanel sprayed here and there, the aroma of filet mignon wafting from the kitchen. She had to prepare her love nest. Vincent would be home soon.

In the middle of her admiration, she noticed a black Jaguar pulling into the circular driveway. Her heart fluttered. Her hands trembled.

The large front door opened. Vincent Mann entered the foyer and dropped his briefcase down at his side.

"Honey, I'm home," he said.

Then he looked up to see Cicely standing at the top of the stairs. Her hair was up, showing off her proud, chocolate shoulders. Her black, silk nightgown gripped her curves and invited him up the stairs.

"Dinner is ready," Cicely said. "But you can have some dessert first if you would like."

Vincent reached the top of the stairs and met his mistress in an embrace.

He said, "Dessert it is."

***

The candles on the nightstands and on the dressers had melted to the holders and Cicely and Vincent lay in the bed under severely ruffled sheets. She pleased him in every sense of the word.

He held her in his arms, comforting her with his embrace. Making her feel like she was his only woman. He was definitely her only man.

It was those times, after long and passionate sessions, when Cicely thought about their situation. She was not his only woman. Happy or not, he had a wife.

Cicely wondered if he made love to his wife the same way, if he made love to her at all. Of course he told her that he hadn't touched his wife in years. But sometimes she wondered if she believed that. She wasn't a fool. Or was she?

She remembered the day that Vincent had her blindfolded, riding down Interstate-77.

"Where are we going?" she asked.

"It's a surprise."

She could tell that they were exiting the freeway. She noticed that they were stopping at lights and making right and left turns here and there. Then they stopped, Vincent rolled down his window and Cicely heard a deep voice.

"Good to see you again, Mr. Mann. Go right on through."

She felt the car turn right then go down a road stopping at what seemed to be a couple of four way stop signs. She felt them make a final turn and then the car stopped. Vincent removed the blindfold.

"Ta da!"

It was magnificent: a large, three-story, brick Colonial home that sat nestled in the middle of a golf course. The lawn was perfectly manicured. There were little crape myrtles that lined the circular driveway in front of the house. The house's entrance was huge—a massive white door with beautiful stain glass in the center of it.

"It's yours," Vincent said. "It's all yours."

Cicely took a minute to breathe everything in. It hadn't fully registered to her that they were parked in front of her new home.

She stuttered out a faint, "Why?"

"Because you are a top executive at Mann Information Systems. And because you are my woman. I want you to have the best."

Those were the memories that gave Cicely a false sense of security when it came to their relationship. When she thought on those things, the things that he did for her, she was convinced that the wife that he left in New York was the other woman, and not her.

Vincent took a long breath. His chest rose and descended and the next thing that he said to Cicely startled her.

"I love you." His tone was matter-of-fact. The words came out of his mouth with no hesitation.

She stroked his face and said, "I love you too."

"Do you really love me?"

That question went unanswered. Nevertheless, Vincent didn't miss a beat.

"When most people use the word love they mean adoration, care. But there's a deeper meaning of love that many people miss. Sometimes loving someone means being hard on them, being tough on them so that they can reach their full potential. Diamonds are produced under extreme pressure. You understand what I'm saying to you?"

She gave a timid nod as she took in all of the things that he said. Vincent continued.

145

"My mother didn't understand my father's deeper meaning of love. Needless to say they weren't happy together. And just like my father, I married someone who doesn't understand that deeper meaning. My father stayed with my mother. He said he did it for me."

He paused for a second, took a deep breath and then said, "I cannot do the same. When my sons are old enough to understand the mistakes that adults make, I am divorcing their mother so that we can be together as husband and wife. Would you like that?"

"I'd like that very much." Cicely snuggled closer to Vincent.

"I just need for you to be patient with me," he said. "This won't be an overnight process. But if you're patient with me I promise I'll make it worth your while. We'll get married and make our company a global entity. We could fill this house with children. Will you be patient with me? Will you give me that promise?"

With sweetness in her voice she told him yes, she would give him that.

After all, he had given her so much.

Chapter 19

Anticipation woke Dawn from sleep several minutes before her alarm clock blared. She didn't stretch because she hadn't truly slept. Her mind raced faster than the pace of her heartbeat. She was about to do something she had never done. Something she thought she would never do.

The clock read six a.m. She hadn't been up that early in a long time. Had she *ever* gotten out of bed that early?

She gathered herself and went to check on Tarsha. She was still sleeping of course. Dawn thought to herself, all normal people are sleep right now... except for landscapers.

Dawn went back into her bedroom for her house coat. She had to hurry if she was going to bake the apple turnovers before he showed up. The landscapers never really kept a defined schedule in terms of what time of day they arrived. So the turnovers had to be ready whenever he came.

It was nine o'clock in the morning when Dawn heard the F-150 pull up to her curve. The truck was as dirty and dusty as ever. Nevertheless, there he was in the driver's seat as always. But he was alone, no stocky helper with him.

He hopped straight to work, starting the lawnmower and rolling it off of the trailer, cutting the front patch of grass first. Then he started on the backyard, which was a lot bigger than the front; edging everything from the edge of the house to flower beds, around the small dogwoods and alongside of the privacy fence that encased her backyard.

Just like always, he'd top off his work by blowing all of the clippings out of the driveway, always leaving his work looking neat. And by the time he was finished with Dawn's yard, he was extremely sweaty. His boots were dyed a brownish-green, his Yankees ball cap was drenched. But that morning, things were different. Dawn wasn't so repulsed by all of the dirt, grass stains, or sweat. It was like she saw it and didn't really see it. That morning she focused on his eyes, which for once weren't covered with shades. They had a beautiful shape to them, his thick eyebrows arched right above the long, thin, slanted traces of his eyes. She couldn't tell if his eyes were black or brown. She'd have to get a closer look for that, which is what she intended to do that day.

Dawn's stride was queenly. Her hair was up, revealing the caramel skin on her neck and shoulders. She wore a tight fitting pink tank top with the word Princess glittered across the front of it and some white soccer shorts. Her hips swayed deliberately as she walked. Her creamy, caramel thighs loosened and tightened as she made her way from the front door to the street where he was strapping his blower in on the back of the truck.

"Good morning," she said. Her tone was soft and friendly. But nevertheless, it startled him.

He jumped.

"Oh! I didn't see you right there. It's Ms. Williams, isn't it?"

His accent was strong.

"Yes, but you can call me Dawn."

"Can I help you, Dawn?"

"I need to write your check. You do want to be paid, right?"

He tapped the side of his head.

"Oh, it is the first Monday of the month. It's just that you usually leave it in the mailbox."

Dawn started writing the check and then blew out a gust of air.

"Silly me. I made this check out to Daniel's Plumbing. I've got plumbing on the brain."

She flipped through the checkbook though she knew there were no more checks in it.

"Oops! No more checks in this book. I'll have to run in the house and get a new book. You can come inside and wait while I find the new checks."

"No thank you. I'm fine out here," he said, worry lines starting to form on his forehead. A fresh bead of sweat formed on his temple.

"Don't be silly. It's almost a hundred degrees out here. I won't be long. I promise."

He looked up and down the street. And then he said reluctantly, "Okay. I guess."

Cool, she thought. Her plan was working. He was following her into the house. She glanced back quickly and caught him watching her backside action. Everything was going according to plan.

When she opened the front door, cool air met them in waves. He took off his Yankees cap. Dawn was impressed by the waviness of his hair. It had a slight brown tint to it. She finally got a good look at his eyes; they were so light brown that they looked like fire burning within his orbs. She could tell that he was enjoying the cool air. Step one was complete: get him in her lair.

Dawn couldn't help but be intrigued by his features. She had to ask him.

"What are you, anyway?"

He chuckled.

"My father is Puerto Rican, my mother is African-American."

He chuckled again at the question.

Dawn led him to the love seat and told him that he could relax while she found the checkbook. She looked at his name tag and tried to sound out what she read.

"An-gul-ee-to? How do you say your name?"

He glanced down to see what she was looking at.

149

"It's Jose Angelito. The "J" in Jose and "G" in Angelito are silent. Jose Angelito Suarez. But everybody calls me Joe, no silent J."

"Okay Joe, no silent J. You sit tight and I'll be right back with the check."

Dawn had never seduced a man and her heart was racing at one-hundred miles per hour. She couldn't believe that she was doing this with her daughter napping upstairs.

She went up to check on Tarsha and saw that she was sleeping soundly. Then she made her way to her bedroom and checked herself out in the mirror. Her tight tank top showed off her curvature just right. Her soccer shorts were sexy in a ten o'clock in the morning sort of way. That was a touch she borrowed from Cicely: easy access when the moment is right.

"What am I doing?" she asked herself. "There is a man down stairs that I don't even know. And I'm about to offer myself to him because I miss the regularity of a man's touch?"

Her head hung low between her shoulders.

"Am I going to do something like this with my own daughter in the house?"

She stared at herself in the mirror, stared at the lips that were seldom kissed, the caramel frame that was seldom caressed.

"Yes I am!" she announced out loud.

It was time for step two. She went back downstairs and checked in on her prey.

"I'm still looking," she said. "Be just a minute. I promise."

He nodded. He had no idea what he was in for.

Dawn went to the kitchen and opened up the oven. The scent of warm apples floated through the dining room and into the living room. Dawn helped the scent travel by turning on the ceiling fans and fanning the air with a large kitchen towel.

"Is that apple pie I smell?" Joe yelled from the living room.

"Apple turnovers. I was in a baking mood this morning. You want one?"

"Might as well."

Shortly afterward, Dawn walked into the living room carrying a tray containing two small saucers of apple turnovers and two cups of cappuccino.

"I hope you like cappuccino."

"I do."

Joe took his turnover and his cup of cappuccino and nodded thank you. Dawn took a seat beside him on the love seat, sitting on top her lower legs, her feet tucked underneath her bottom.

He took a sip from the small porcelain cup and looked around the room but not in admiration. He was making sure that they were alone.

"How old are you?" he asked. "Your dad isn't going to bust in here and get the wrong idea, is he?"

Dawn giggled and put her cup down.

"I'm grown, twenty-five years old. My daddy better not come here unless he calls first. This is my house."

"Oh. Let me rephrase that then. Your husband isn't going to bust in here and get the wrong idea, is he?"

"My man is away on business. He's always away on business."

Joe nodded. He knew what this was all about. Dawn picked up on it.

Move on to step three, she thought. Step three! Step three! Step three!

She wasn't quite ready for that yet. So she decided to further soften the mood by conversation.

"Where's your help, the stocky guy?"

"Oh Charlie? Well let's just say that I'm covering for him today."

He said that with a smile and a chuckle.

Dawn's expression remained serious.

"What does that mean?" she asked.

151

"Well, Charlie has this little chick on the side that he taps from time to time, some rich lady who lives near Clemson. Her husband's always away on business. You know how that is."

That comment offended her. Right then she realized she was not built that way. There would be no step three.

She put down her cup and what was left of her turnover.

"Let me go and get your check," she said and she quickly went to the kitchen where her new checkbook was.

Dawn's mood had totally changed. She couldn't believe that she was going to disrespect herself in that way.

When she returned to the living room, Joe was finishing the last bite of his turnover. She handed him the check and gave a half-smile.

"Thanks for the check, Dawn. You know your checks never bounce. That's a good thing."

That comment went in one of her ears and out of the other. She showed him to the door.

He stopped just short, turned around and gave Dawn a broad smile.

"Thanks for the apple turnovers."

"It was nothing," Dawn replied as she played with the edges of her hair with uneasiness.

Her lair of seduction had turned into a den of awkwardness.

"They kind of remind me of empanadas. My aunt makes the best empanadas down at her restaurant, The Caribbean Queen."

"Oh I think I hear my daughter crying. Have a nice day."

She ushered him out of the door. Nothing was wrong with her daughter. Dawn just came to her senses.

Chapter 20

It was frigidly cold in Brook's office in the back of the Co-Ed Greenville because she had turned her air-conditioning up full blast. The air could be heard rushing out of the overhead vent, flooding the office with arctic winds. Her fingernails had turned light blue. She glanced at them for a second, but mostly, her eyes were fixed on her wedding ring. It still glistened in the light, still sparkled when she wiggled her ring finger. But it didn't give her the same warm feeling that it used to; she didn't get goose-bumps thinking about the man that put that ring on her finger.

She glanced at the styling chair and vanity that sat at the far corner of her office. It was a gift from Walter, fully equipped with everything a barber or hairstylist would need. It was the first set-up that she owned.

She focused on the wedding photo on her desk, the immortal image that signified the love she shared with Walter. She loved him then but did he truly love her? Or was it all lies? How long had he been making her look like a fool? How long had he been cheating on her?

The private investigator had just left Brook's office. Terry Law, PI, was a medium built, brown-skinned woman with short hair. She reminded Brook of a taller version of Toni Braxton. Her voice was soft and soothing, especially when she gave Brook the cream envelope containing pictures of Walter with his lover.

"You're taking this extremely well, Mrs. Riggins," Terry said. "I usually have to deal tissue like playing cards after I deliver the photos."

Brook was doing an excellent job of hiding all of her emotions.

153

"No need to cry," she responded. "I'd rather spend my energy on figuring out my next move."

"That's the spirit. I had no leverage when my ex-husband cheated on me. So he walked away with everything after our divorce. The photos in your hand, Mrs. Riggins, are leverage."

"I never said that divorcing my husband was an option."

"No, you didn't."

Terry Law stood up and gathered her things. "I have another appointment," she said. "So I'll leave you to your thoughts. And again, I'm truly sorry."

Brook stared at her beautiful wedding ring. It made her furious. She did not feel the need to display the binder of their marriage anymore. So she took it off and let it rest in the top drawer of her desk. Maybe she would pull it out again. Maybe she would not.

***

"Hey everybody! It's Jeff Blitzer!"

Brook heard Stacy screaming all the way back in her office. The commotion coming from the front of the salon broke her out of her trance. Her staff got rowdy every now and again. But this time it was different. Several minutes passed by and the commotion had not died down. So Brook hopped out of her leather chair to investigate.

She made her way to the edge of the hall that opened up into the shop and saw a large crowd forming around the front door. Trap, one of the barbers there, even had a poster of a football player in his hand as he tried to maneuver his way around the crowd. Patrons jumped into the mix, with pens and paper in their hands, their aprons still around their necks. Female customers were coming from under the hair driers. Brook heard one of them say to another, "Ooh, he is so fine, child!"

Miss Mattie was the only one in the shop hanging back. She stood beside her chair and shook her head. Brook eased her way next to her. All she could really see was the crowd; she couldn't see who they were surrounding.

"What's going on?" she asked Miss Mattie. "Is the president here or something?"

"Nah, it's some big time NFL star. Jeff Blitzer's his name. You ever heard of him?"

"No I haven't. But I don't really follow sports that much."

"Well he just came in here a few seconds ago. Stacy was the first to see him. Man she almost went crazy when he walked in."

"Well I better break this racket up before the man sues us."

Brook walked over to the edge of the crowd and began working her way through.

"Alright everyone, I'm sure this man didn't come here to be mauled to death."

Everyone cooled off a bit and began to make a hole.

That's when she saw him.

That's when he saw her.

He remembered her the second he laid eyes on her and without ceasing from signing autographs he let out a smooth and deep, "What's up, Shawty?"

Brook couldn't believe it. It was Jeff, the young boy from Atlanta that she had met years ago in her grandmother's house, the boy that she played spades with, the young boy that made her laugh. Jeff was standing right in front of her, a fully grown, six-foot seven inch man.

For a moment they stared at each other. Brook smiled as she looked Jeff up and down. He was still tall, but now his frame looked more muscular; veins popped up from his massive forearms. His calf muscles were round like melons. His dark brown skin was clear and smooth, a big change from the pimples and blemishes he had then. But even then Brook thought that he was cute.

Jeff gave Brook a once over, focusing on her caramel skin and her beautiful brown eyes. Brook wore a black leotard that snuggled against her flesh, accentuating the curvature of her frame. Her tiny waist disappeared into a gray wrap skirt; her feet were wrapped in black sandals whose straps wrapped around the roundness of her lower legs. The ring around her second toe on her right foot screamed sexiness to Jeff. He certainly enjoyed the view.

"Can a player get a hug?" he asked, his voice still possessing that deepness, that richness.

"As long as I get hugged back."

He brought her into his arms, breathing in the sweet scent of her hair.

"You got some explaining to do, Miss Ma'am!" Stacy said, twirling her neck round and round.

"This is an old friend of mine, y'all," Brook said. "His name's Jeff."

"We know who he is," Stacy replied. "But we aren't on a first name basis!"

Jeff continued to sign autographs, but his eyes never left Brook.

"I never thought I'd see you again after we had to leave like that," he said. "How's your cousin, the one that Aaron was talking to?"

"Oh Karen, she's cool. She's the head of juvenile affairs for the Department of Social Services down in Charleston."

"How's your twin sister?"

"She's good. I was just with her this weekend."

"What about your other cousin, the wild one?"

"Oh Cicely? Cicely's the same ole Cicely."

Brook played with her ponytail and then smoothed her wrap skirt. Her hands trembled. Her heart hadn't slowed since the end of their embrace.

"So anyway, what brings you to my shop?"

"I'm speaking at this youth convention here and my barber wasn't able to come down with me. I heard there was a Co-Ed here in Greenville. I used to go to the one in the ATL all the time. Your shop?"

"Yes sir."

Brook and Jeff continued their small talk. For a moment, it was as if no one else was in the shop with them. Stacy interrupted their conversation with her country twang.

"I'll cut your hair, big daddy!" she said as she tugged on his arm.

Without effort, Brook broke him free of her grasp and said, "Park it right here."

Jeff sat down in Brook's chair and then she draped him with an apron.

"Why are you blocking?" Stacy asked. But when Brook gave her the evil eye, she quickly backed off.

"How do you want it?" Brook asked with a little too much sexiness. She noticed how the question rolled off of her lips but she didn't care. She couldn't describe the feeling she possessed. She only knew that it felt ten times better than the feeling that she had when Terry Law left her office.

"A Philly fade. Can you hook that up?"

"For sure." Brook kicked the side lever to raise the chair and began revving up her clippers.

The bells on the front door clanged like never before.

"I told you. Brian said he was in here!" That was a young, skinny little boy who was playing at the arcade next door. He came in with four of his friends, all holding pens and scrap pieces of paper. Jeff handled it gracefully. He smiled and freely gave his autograph to every one of the young boys. Brook was on hold for a second while he did that.

After the boys left, she picked up her brush and began slowly stroking his waves.

"Let me try this again."

The door flung open again.

"Oh snap! Jeff Blitzer! It's Jeff Blitzer!"

That was Calvin Bass, the pimp.

"I have to bring my ladies up here to see you, man. They love you!"

Calvin feverishly shook Jeff's hand. Again Jeff politely signed his autograph, this time on the back of one of Calvin's business card. Brook stood back and shook her head.

"Yeah, just make that out to 'That pimp named Calvin'!"

Jeff did so. Calvin took his card back and slid him another one.

"If you're ever in the market for a good agent, holler at me!"

"Okay, that's enough, Calvin!" Brook said, as she ushered him out the front door.

Without missing a beat, she walked back over to her chair and let it back down.

"Let's go," she said to Jeff. He sat there for a minute with a puzzled look on his face. "Get up and let's go!" Brook began walking back to her office.

Jeff looked around. Miss Mattie gave him a nod that said he better follow. So he did exactly that.

***

Brook and Jeff spent the next hour and a half catching up, or in reality, getting to know one another. It would normally take Brook about ten to twenty minutes to do a fade, but she took her time, savored the conversation they were sharing. She told him that she attended cosmetology school in Atlanta. She went on to tell him about opening the franchise in Greenville. She spoke around Walter though.

Jeff spoke about his first being drafted to the Atlanta Falcons and then being traded to Minnesota his second year in the league.

"That was a very trying time for me then, being traded just my second year in the league," he said.

"Why were you traded?"

"You really don't follow sports, or news for that matter, do you?"

"I really don't watch TV that much. Too busy."

"You never heard anything about the escort service scandal in Atlanta?"

Brook shrugged her shoulders and replied, "Honestly, no."

Jeff told her about his rookie season with the Falcons, about the party that a prominent sports agent threw for one of the players.

Jeff and five of his teammates were in a hotel suite with six exotic dancers. Somehow things got out of hand. Somehow intentions were mistaken. The next thing that he knew, he and the other five players were downtown at the police department.

One of the girls had gone down to the front desk of the hotel and claimed that one of the players in the suite assaulted her. There was really no evidence of assault. It would turn out to be her word against his.

Jeff explained that he did not remember a thing about the incident. He was so drunk that when the police showed up, he was hunched over in the bathroom, sitting on the toilet with his trousers around his ankles and a pool of vomit in his boxers.

"It was a gigantic mess. There I was, a first round draft pick, in a holding cell, drunk out of my mind."

"Well what happened?"

"Money talks. So we walked out of that police department. We all had community service, but that was about it. They just let us off the hook and I was happy and sad at the same time. I found out that one of my teammates really did assault the girl. He was bragging about it to one of the other players in the locker room.

"So I confronted him about it and one thing led to another. Boy we tore that locker room up. After that incident, things weren't the same between us. He was a team leader, and I was a new comer. There was lots of strife aimed at me. Long story short, I was traded to Minnesota the very next season."

Jeff became really quiet. Brook continued with the fade, not really wanting to break the silence. She looked at his expression through the vanity mirror. His face housed memories of pain and emotions that had not completely been washed away by the sea of forgiveness and time. He took a deep breath and continued.

"At that time I was hurt. I mean, I got drafted to my hometown team. I was around family, the friends that I grew up with. It was painful to leave the way that I did. But it's like my dad always said: things happen for a reason.

"Going to Minnesota in my second season was the best thing that ever happened to me. I'm a far better ball player than I ever was. The fans embraced me. I'm involved with a lot of charities and organizations, things I wouldn't be doing if I was still in my comfort zone."

Jeff opened his eyes and smiled at Brook, who had stopped cutting and was looking at him intently. Their eyes began to dance with very slow and deep movements, each trying to search the length and the breadth of the other.

Jeff broke the trance by saying, "So enough about me. You're an entrepreneur. Co-Ed is a big success!"

"Yeah, I'm doing alright. This shop is basically my life."

That statement made Jeff corner his brows. He looked at her bare left ring finger.

"So I assume you're not married," he said still looking in that direction. Brook said nothing to the

160

contrary. "You don't have a man or anything like that?"

"Nope, I'm pretty much single right now."

Brook wondered why she had just lied to Jeff; she wondered why during the whole conversation, Walter's name never came up.

"As fine as you are, I find it hard to believe that you're single," Jeff said.

Brook enjoyed the compliment. She gave a quick smile and continued cutting.

"Well I'll say this. There was someone, but I caught him cheating. So that's over now."

She couldn't believe the ease with which that statement rolled off of her tongue. She wondered again why she wasn't being completely honest with Jeff. Or was she? Walter was beginning to matter less and less to her.

"What about you?" she asked.

"What about me?"

"Do you have a woman? Women? Groupies?"

"No. Not at this time. I'm as single as the number one."

"Liar."

"Why I do I have to be a liar?"

"Because I don't believe you."

"Now I get approached all the time. I date occasionally. But I'm officially single."

Brook raised her brows and mumbled, "If you say so."

She finished trimming his hairline. Then she stepped back and inspected her work. She reached for a hand mirror and gave it to Jeff, who looked at his do from front to back.

"You like?" she asked.

"Sharp. You have skills, Brook. I may have to replace my regular barber for real."

After she removed the apron from his shoulders, Jeff stood up and began reaching into his front pocket.

161

But she reached out and stopped him. Her hand touched his and a spark shot through her body. It felt good to her to have her bare-skin against his. Too good. Brook quickly told her hand to get back to her side and behave.

"Your money's no good here," she said.

"No, I wouldn't think of it. You really hooked me up. I have to at least give you a tip."

"What did I say?" she snarled. He raised his hands up in the air and quickly yielded.

"Let me walk you out," Brook said as she hooked her arm around the inside of his.

They reached the door of her office and Jeff stopped her.

"I never would've thought in a million years that I'd bump into you today," he said. "And I know that you won't take any money for the haircut, but can I at least take you out to dinner tonight?"

Brook's grin grew wide and then she said, "That would be—oh I forgot. I have a prior engagement tonight. How long are you going to be in town?"

"When will you be free?" he asked as he tilted his head and looked upon Brook's mounting beam.

She giggled slightly. "I'm free tomorrow evening."

"No you're not," he replied. "You have a date with me."

She escorted him out the back door to avoid any further commotion. He agreed with the idea, giving her a hug and kiss on her cheek as he walked to the side of the building where his rental car was parked.

Those few hours with Jeff had such a profound effect on Brook that she paid little mind to Walter. It wasn't until she saw Jeff driving off that her mind went back to that place, to that envelope containing the photos, to the business that she had to handle as soon as Walter showed up at their home.

Chapter 21

When Brook finally made it home and hit the automatic switch for the garage door, she saw Walter's Range Rover parked in his temporary spot. He never made himself a permanent fixture in their home. His scent didn't live there. In fact, none of his belongings took up significant space in the house and the realness of the relationship was now becoming clearer to Brook.

She felt the hood of his truck. It was cool, which meant that had to have been there a while. She opened the door from the garage that led to the family room and saw that Walter had lit the gas fireplace. She once loved to hear the romantic crackling noise it produced. But on that day that crackle completely annoyed her.

"Why me?" she whined.

As she made her way to their bedroom she heard the shower going. Walter was bathing with the same gel that used to drive Brook insane for him. A month ago, she would be jumping up and down like a little school girl, anxious for the treat she was in for. But that night she felt contempt for the man in her bathroom; he had betrayed her trust.

"Is that you, baby?" Walter called out. "I'll be out in a minute."

The sound of his voice repulsed her. And indeed her emotions were mixed about confronting him. She wanted to get it over with, but she feared what would happen when she showed the photos to him.

She hurried to the kitchen to get a cold glass of water. She needed to collect her thoughts. The water was doing little for her. A cold Pepsi would probably be better. It burned her chest as she downed the entire 20 ounces. But it wasn't enough. So she chased it with a shot of Crown Royal. The burn in her chest was worse and the speed at which she gulped did not help matters.

Then her heartbeat slowed and she became calm. A small smile began to form. She was ready now. To be on the safe side, she downed one more quick shot of Crown. That was around the time when Walter waltzed into the kitchen.

He walked up wearing a pair of cotton pants and nothing else. He positioned himself behind Brook as she stood facing the counter. He pulled her ponytail to the side and offered her a gentle kiss on the cheek. She offered him the small cream envelope containing the photos.

"Who is she?" Brook asked, short and to the point.

It was a she. It was a woman in the photos. She was tall, thin, and very pretty. Brook felt that she must be some type of model. She thought the fact that it was a woman would make her feel better. But it did not.

"What is this?" Walter asked with confusion.

"Who is she?" Brook folded her arms.

Walter pulled the photos out of the envelope and began flipping through them. He looked up at his wife with wide eyes.

"Where did you get these?"

"Who—is—she?"

Walter's brows raised. He looked at his wife. Then back at the photos.

"What do you know?" he asked softly.

Brook slammed the bottle of Crown onto the counter. The thick glass bottle hit the marble counter top with a loud thud that made the counter shake. Walter looked at the bottle with amazement that it didn't shatter from the force that Brook applied.

"ANSWER THE QUESTION!" she screamed.

"It's nobody!"

"Have you slept with nobody?"

Walter became quiet.

164

"I guess that answers the question," Brook said. "Did you use protection?"

Walter was quiet initially and then he let out a puff of air.

"Baby, how much do you know?"

"Okay, I see that you aren't answering my questions now. I'm going to go hit the treadmill. I'll be in the workout room when you're ready to answer my questions."

She brushed past him, leaving him in the kitchen holding the photos with a blank expression on his face.

***

At first a brisk walk did the trick. Then it was interval training. Brook would run hard for fifteen seconds and then jog for forty-five seconds. Then she came to a steady jog. Her body felt light as a feather, but her heart felt heavier than a cinder block.

She noticed she had been on the treadmill for about two hours when Walter opened the glass door. As he entered the room she asked, "You ready to answer my questions now?"

Walter nodded yes.

Brook stepped off of the treadmill and wiped her forehead with a towel. She took a sip of water and began her interrogation.

"Did you sleep with her?"

"Yes."

That answer came so fast that it stunned her. Nevertheless, she trudged on.

"I figured the answer to that question would be yes. Did you use protection?"

"Honestly, sometimes—we didn't."

Brook wanted to throw something at him: a barbell, a twenty-five pound barbell. But she tried to remain calm.

"That means that you've put me in danger then."

"There's no danger. Both of us were tested recently. We're both trying to be responsible about it."

"Well, dang. I wish you would have let me know. I could have gone with you two to the clinic. Walter, you *did* put me in danger! We have all been having sex together, you know that right?"

"Brook, there's something I have to tell you."

"Do you love her?"

"You see. That's what we have to talk about."

"You've answered my question already."

"Baby, you're not letting me talk!"

"What's her name?"

"Brook, please. Listen to me for one moment."

"I guess names don't really matter now do they?"

Walter grabbed at his hair with frustration. He took a seat on the weight bench and hung his head between his shoulders. He began rocking back and forth with a sporadic rhythm; his hands began to shake slightly.

He said, "Those pictures. I really have to tell you something."

"Why did you betray my trust?" Brook asked softly. She positioned herself right beside her husband and put her hand on his shoulder. Walter stopped rocking and took a deep breath.

"You know we haven't been compatible sexually in a long time."

"Walter, we hardly have sex. You live a hundred and forty miles away!"

"Brook, please listen to me. There are some things that I like to do that you don't really care for."

"Oh give me a break! You are not going to turn this around and make me the bad guy. You are the one that cheated on me!"

"You know how I feel about—you know. I told you that I enjoy that sort of thing."

"And I told you that was nasty. I can't believe you like doing that. I can't believe that your past girlfriends let you do that. It's not natural."

"Oh and oral sex is?"

Brook shook her head and let out a puff of air.

"You are trying to turn this around on me," she said.

"No, I'm just answering your question. You wanted to know why."

"I thought what we had was beautiful and sensual, whether it was oral or intercourse."

"But you never wanted to give other things a shot."

"No I did not. Because I find the idea of anal sex repulsive, not to mention painful, no matter how much lubrication you add. You knew how I felt about that before you asked me to marry you. I can't believe you right now." Brook ran her fingers over her hair. Then she said, "How would you like it if I shoved something up your behind?"

Walter was silent.

"All of that doesn't matter," she added. "What matters is that you cheated on me. You betrayed my trust. And you made me look like a fool."

"What are you talking about?"

"All those times I'd cry on the phone, begging and pleading with you to move here, to let me move there. You always had an excuse and I always fell for it."

"That was about the businesses I *thought* we were trying to build."

"Yeah, right! When I came down to Atlanta last month to surprise you, you were mad because I busted up your little groove. Tell me I'm wrong about that! "

Walter sat on the weight bench and stared off into space. His silence told Brook volumes and the feelings that she had for him slowly began to change.

He inhaled deeply and stood up, fixing his cotton pants around his waist. Ran his hand over his mouth, cleared his throat, and then he said, "Look, I'm tired.

167

I'm sure you're tired. How about we get some sleep and talk about this in the morning."

"Whatever." Brook exhaled and began collecting her water bottle and towel. "I'll see you tomorrow then."

She began walking out of the exercise room.

"Where are you going?" Walter asked.

"I'm not going anywhere." Brook walked down the hallway toward the bedroom. "*You* have a reservation at the Embassy Suites off of Verdae Boulevard."

"You're kidding right?"

"No, I booked it for you. It should be a pretty nice room too. It's costing you a grip."

"Brook, I'm not going anywhere. This is my house too!"

She stopped short, spun around, and gave Walter the evilest glare she could muster. Then she asked, "Do you really want to sleep in this house, with me tonight, after what I found out?"

Walter paused and let it all marinate.

"You said the Embassy Suites off of Verdae?"

Brook only raised her brows and gave a nod. Then she walked into her bedroom with Walter dragging in behind her to collect his bags.

Fifteen minutes passed and Walter was finished getting dressed and gathering all of his things. He asked Brook if she was going to walk him to the front door. She obliged. When they got to the door, he stopped and turned to face her.

"Listen, there are some things that we need to discuss," he said.

"Okay."

"I'm serious. This is pretty important. We might as well get everything out in the open so that we'll know where we stand."

"Okay."

"Could you meet me tomorrow after you're done at the shop?"

"That's cool."

"We can meet at that new club on Main Street? We could get dinner, take in some blues, and talk this thing out?"

"That's cool."

Walter looked into his wife's eyes, hoping to catch a glimpse of softness, of forgiveness. He found nothing of the sort. He lowered his countenance and said, "No matter what, I still love you."

"Good night, Walter."

He walked out of the door and Brook rested her hand where her husband's back had leaned against. She took a deep breath and returned to her bedroom. No tears. No piercing feeling in her heart. No pain in her stomach. Maybe she had prepared herself for this day long before she was sure that it would materialize.

She showered away all the sweat and stress. Then she turned off the lights and rested on her bed, glad that part of the ordeal was over. In spite of the uncertainty of her future with Walter, she possessed a feeling of relief; a feeling of excitement about the unknown. Perhaps it was because of the surprise visitor that she had earlier, the one she would be meeting again the following evening.

Chapter 22

The sun warmed the back of Dawn's neck. There wasn't a cloud in the sky and there was no shade in front of the little restaurant where she and Brook were dining on that hot and humid Wednesday afternoon. The place was called The Caribbean Queen. It was a nice sized eatery in the middle of a newly built strip mall off of Highway 123. Brook had parked far enough away for Dawn to be able to get a good workout going back to the car for her purse. It was her turn to pay for their weekly dining experience.

Dawn hurried back into the restaurant and a cool gust of air from the overhead vent welcomed her. Latin jazz filled the dining room. Waiters and waitresses zoomed from the tables to the kitchen and back, while patrons sat at square tables and in booths enjoying the Caribbean cuisine.

Dawn returned to their table and found Brook bouncing her niece on her lap and humming. She had been humming the whole day. Dawn wondered why she was in such a good mood after her confrontation with Walter.

"Things must have gone better than expected last night," Dawn said.

"No, things didn't go that well at all. Hum, hum, hum." Brook continued to hum and play with her niece.

Dawn cornered her brows and then asked, "Well how did he take it when he saw the photos? Did he deny it or something?"

"Initially he kept trying to get off the subject. But he finally came out and told me that he was sleeping with the woman. He didn't deny a thing. Says he wants to talk later tonight over dinner."

Dawn took it all in. She was amazed at her sister's calm and contentment.

"So is he still at the house?" Dawn asked.

"Nope. I made him stay at a room. I did that for his own safety. I was pretty ticked yesterday. Well that was until—"

"Okay, spill it, big sis. What do you plan to do? Are you going to try to work it out or call it quits?"

Brook stopped bouncing Tarsha and gave her a kiss on the top of her head. Then she looked up at Dawn and said, "You know I came to the realization that we haven't really been married to each other. We've just played that role, or rather I played it. I'm done playing with him." She paused for a second and said, "You know I haven't cried yet, not one tear."

Dawn nodded and Brook began humming again.

The waiter brought them their entrees. They were halfway into their meals when Brook slammed her fork down on her plate.

"Okay. I can't hold it any more. Guess who came into my shop yesterday?"

"Who?"

Brook told Dawn all about Jeff coming to the shop, how they talked for two hours, how fine he was, how he told her that she was fine. She told Dawn that the two of them were going out to dinner that evening.

"But what about Walter?"

"What about him?"

"I mean he's here. You said that he wanted to talk with you this evening. Are you going to have your talk with Walter and then go on your date with Jeff?"

"I have no intention of seeing Walter tonight."

Dawn paused for thought and then said, "It's not that I feel bad for the guy or anything. But are you just going leave him hanging?"

"Yep! Seeing Jeff in that shop was exactly what I needed and it came at the right time. Jeff told me that it was no coincidence that he showed up there. If you

171

add all of the pieces of the puzzle together, me and Walter's situation, Jeff showing up yesterday, I'd go as far as to say that this is fate at work."

Dawn took a sip of water and wiped her mouth. She listened to her sister and understood how she felt. Walter was never there. He never gave Brook quality time and blamed that on the business, even though he was cheating all along.

A light bulb went off in Dawn's head. She looked at her own situation. She knew that Cory was with Nina and that Nina was living in a house that he bought for her in Nicholtown. She knew that Nina's daughter was as much Cory's as Tarsha was. Yet she did nothing about it.

Why did she allow Cory to mistreat her? The answer was simple. She remained with Cory Mack because rain or shine, there was a hefty deposit placed into her checking account at the end of every month. All of her bills were paid. She had a lovely home and even though she had never driven it, she had a brand new Toyota 4-Runner sitting in her driveway. Dawn wanted for nothing. She was still with Cory because she enjoyed living a comfortable, carefree life.

Dawn shifted in her seat and let out a moan. Brook knew that something was on her mind.

"What's up, little sis?" Brook asked.

"Oh, I'm just thinking that—well—" Dawn hesitated for a moment to choose her words carefully. Then she took a deep breath and continued. "Well I'm happy that you're finally doing something about your situation. That makes one of us."

Brook gave her that eye that she was hoping not to get. That was the reason that Dawn chose her words carefully. She did not want to get a lecture, but it was coming whether she liked it or not.

"Dawn, I begged you not to hook up with Cory. I know how his type lives. I was trying to protect you."

"Please don't give me the 'I told you so' speech."

"Why don't you just leave him? I told you that you can come live with me until you get on your feet. You could go back to school."

"What? Give up my house, my lifestyle so that tramp, Nina, can get all the pie? I don't think so."

It was Brook's turn to pause for thought. When she was certain that she had Dawn's undivided attention, she said, "I hate to say this, but that isn't really your house."

"Like heck! I carried his child for ten months: not nine, but ten! I carried her a whole extra month."

"Oh here we go."

"Yes, and I gave birth to his little girl. And he can't deny her because she looks just like him."

"And she looks like Nina's daughter, too. Don't forget that."

"Whatever. I don't care what you say. That house, that money, that everything is mine!"

"Dawn, sweetie. Money isn't everything."

"I guess you're right," she answered as she jingled her ten thousand dollar tennis bracelet in Brook's face.

"What am I going to do with you?" Brook exclaimed.

Dawn put her hands up in truce and said, "Okay. Okay. I'm a fool, alright."

"Humph. I bet you your lawn guy doesn't think you're a fool," Brook whispered.

"My lawn guy?"

Brook pointed over Dawn's right shoulder. She turned around and saw Joe sitting by the bar waving at her with a raised eyebrow. He was wearing his blue work uniform. Dawn wondered were those the same grass stains from a few days ago.

But she couldn't deny that his facial features were striking. He was definitely handsome, even if his attire left much to be desired.

"He's been peeking over here from time to time," Brook said.

Dawn looked nervous.

"Oh yeah?" she asked. "For how long?"

"Oh, ever since you came back in with your purse. As a matter of fact, he's walking over this way right now."

Dawn turned around and saw that Joe was making his way across the crowded room to where they were sitting. She quickly about faced.

"Oh my gosh, Brook! He's walking over this way right now!"

"Um...that's what I just said."

Brook took Tarsha out of the booster seat and gathered her baby bag.

"Where do you think you're going?" Dawn firmly whispered.

By that time Joe had made his way to their table.

Brook smiled, hoisted Tarsha to her waist and said, "I saw the cutest little outfit in the window at Child's Play. It would look great on Tarsha." She greeted Joe who smiled and spoke back. Then Brook quickly left the restaurant.

Awkward did not do justice to the way Dawn felt at that moment.

"Hello again," Joe said as he took a seat right in front of her.

She rolled her eyes, sucked her teeth, and then said sarcastically, "Yeah, go right ahead and have a seat. You're not bothering me."

"Ouch." Joe squinted and grabbed his chest as if his heart hurt. "I guess I had that coming."

Dawn shifted in her chair and looked away; she was ill at ease to be sure, feeling so uncomfortable with Joe sitting across from her that her first inclination was to run out of the restaurant. But for some reason, she remained seated.

"Look, I don't mean to bother you, but I owe you an apology," he said. "The other day I made the mistake of assuming something. I assumed you were trying to seduce me."

Dawn knew full well what he was talking about. She offered a sassy, "Well you know what they say about assuming."

"Yeah, I'm sorry about that. But it wouldn't have been the first time that a lonely housewife or a freaky daughter with the house all to herself has propositioned me. Heck, my cousin Charlie meets most of his ladies like that."

"I was only trying to be nice to you. I see where my niceness got me."

She was lying through her teeth and she knew it.

"Do you accept my apology?" Joe asked sincerely.

"I guess so," Dawn responded, her voice feigning half-heartedness.

One tick later, a short, light-brown skinned woman approached the table where Dawn and Joe were sitting. Her complexion was like cinnamon, and her hair was light-brown, almost copper colored. She wore a white cotton top and a long Khaki dress with brown sensible shoes on her feet. Her smile was inviting and Dawn could tell that Joe knew her because he returned the same smile to her.

The woman sat a tray on the table and said with an accent, "Okay, Joe. Introduce me to your pretty friend."

"Oh yeah. This is Dawn Williams. She's one of my customers. Dawn, this is my Tia Maria."

Dawn accepted Aunt Maria's hand, smiled, and spoke to her.

"Well, here are your empanadas. I hope you enjoy them," Aunt Maria said in a soft voice.

Dawn remembered that Joe had mentioned them before she shooed him away a few days before.

Joe wasted no time and dug into one. With his left cheek full of the dessert, his aunt said, "It's amazing. He eats like a pig and never gains an ounce."

Then she looked over at Dawn and said, "Please tell me you're not one of those skinny women who can eat like a man and never gain a pound."

"Oh, no ma'am," she replied and then took a small bite of her empanada. "This will go straight to my hips. I'll have to do some Tae-Bo tonight."

Aunt Maria laughed and turned to Joe, who had finished demolishing his pastry.

"Hey, greedy," she said. "You ought to invite your friend to church this Sabbath." She crossed her hands over her heart and said to Dawn, "You know he's going to be ordained as a deacon. We are so proud of him."

Joe wiped his mouth and waved his aunt off.

"I'm sure that Dawn has better things to do on a Saturday than to be in church."

Aunt Maria popped him on his shoulder and said, "What did I tell you about that?"

"Yeah, Deacon. Stop being rude to your auntie," Dawn said with a smile.

"Like I was saying before I was so *rudely* interrupted. Joe will become an ordained deacon this Saturday at House of God, Easley."

"I know that church. It's that big brick one right on Easley Highway," Dawn said.

"That's the one," Aunt Maria responded. "Well, let me get back to the kitchen before your Uncle Herman kills Charlie. It was nice to meet you, Dawn. Hope to see you again."

"Likewise, ma'am."

Dawn smirked as Joe wiped his mouth with a napkin. She fixed her eyes on him, thinking about how handsome he was, and how much better he'd look if he'd retire his grass-cutting attire and put on a nice pair of slacks and shirt. Then she took a sip of water and said, "A deacon? Impressive."

"Yeah, it's a big deal to my family, seeing where I come from."

A quiet moment settled between them and the awkwardness started to shift to Joe's side of the table. Dawn was the first to break the silence. "So, church man, did you ever accept?"

"Accept what?"

"The propositions from the lonely housewives and the freaky daughters."

Joe smiled and looked away. A blush blossomed on his light-brown face. He quickly tried to change the subject.

"Go on and finish your empanada. It's getting cold."

"No, answer me, Joe."

He liked the way his name rolled off of her lips. Her rich southern accent intrigued him. He looked into her eyes, cornered the side of his lip and said, "No mami. I don't get down like that. Too much drama."

Dawn liked the way he called her *mami*.

Another moment passed in which Dawn and Joe smiled at each other but it seemed like hours. Many things ran through her mind. Getting to know him better. Her attraction to him. We're those feelings reciprocated?

But then reality hit as reality has a habit of doing. She wondered how much money Joe made cutting grass. Did he own the landscaping business or was he just someone's lackey? And the more she thought about it, the less she smiled.

Her cell phone buzzed from her purse. She took it out and glanced at the screen and then let out a sigh.

"I guess my sister is done shopping. That's her sending me a text message."

Joe let out a semi-somber, "Oh." And then he stood with her and smoothed out his work pants.

"I guess I'll see you around then," she said.

"Next week like clockwork," he answered.

"Thanks for the empanada. It was delicious."

"Anytime."

"I'd better get going. Don't want my sister to leave me out here."

Joe walked Dawn to the door and opened it for her. His smile was genuine. Dawn's was a little less than that.

Her cell phone buzzed again. She took a look at it. It was from the same person: her mother. She was texting to tell Dawn to call her. It wasn't Brook texting her at all.

She had to lie to Joe and find some reason to leave. Even though he was handsome and definitely hardworking, he probably lived paycheck to paycheck. She hated herself for the way she felt but she honestly didn't want to struggle. Regardless of all of his faults, Cory gave her comfort. She honestly liked being comfortable.

Chapter 23

Brook left the shop early, went home to shower and beautify herself, and then threw on a cream sundress with matching sandals. When she arrived at the Hyatt, Jeff met her in the lobby wearing a white, silk short-sleeve button down shirt, a pair of wrinkle-free slacks creased hard down the middle, and a pair of snake-skin square toe dress shoes.

The two of them decided to catch a matinee and then an early dinner at Vince Perone's. They had been together since four in the afternoon enjoying each other's company. Brook felt like she was in heaven and Jeff was her angelic tour guide.

Brook felt free to laugh and be silly, free to speak her mind, free to feel sexy. Just free. But as the sun retreated and the moon faintly made its presence known, she thought about how the evening would end, how Jeff would react when she told him that she was actually married.

"This is nice and all but wait until you come up to Minnesota. Fifty thousand some-odd lakes, shawty. What do you know about that?"

"I never said that I was coming to Minnesota. You are mighty confident," Brook responded.

"I'm too charming for you to refuse."

"You are full of yourself, Mr. NFL star. But I must let you in on a little secret. You are not as charming as you think you are."

Jeff jokingly lowered his head and said, "I'm not? Gee, thanks for telling me. That's why you're a true friend. Anyone else would have had me thinking I was the joint, but you keep it real with me."

Brook giggled and replied, "You know it."

They had almost reached the top of the hill when Brook lost her footing. She stumbled a little and then caught herself before she fell, cursing her sandals all the way. Jeff rushed to help her up. His hands were strong, yet gentle and a tingle rushed through Brook's skin when he touched her.

"I must be somewhat charming," he said. "You're falling for me already."

When Brook regained her balance, she found herself in Jeff's warm embrace, looking up into his eyes. They were getting close to each other in a way that she did not fully understand. She wanted to feel his lips pressed against hers, to take in his aroma for hours. Her thought at that moment was how she wanted to be intimate with him.

All of a sudden her heels lifted from the back of her sandals. Her hands reached for Jeff's cheeks to bring him closer to her. Before she knew it, she was kissing him. Before she could take it back, he was kissing her.

As the sun set, Brook stepped into a new season of her life. She didn't want it to be ruined by the truth, so as they finally finished their kiss, she decided she wasn't going to say anything about Walter and their situation. She didn't want to spoil a good thing.

"Wow, I wasn't expecting that," Jeff said after he took a deep breath.

"I'm sorry," Brook replied. "I guess I got caught up in the moment."

"Don't be sorry. Honestly, I've wanted to do that since you picked me up earlier. But I didn't think that it would happen."

"Why is that?"

"Because...I'll be honest with you. You are beautiful. And I am intimidated by your beauty."

"So what you're saying is that you're a punk?"

"What?"

Brook playfully taunted him, "You're a scaredy-cat. You're a big ole scaredy-cat."

Brook almost lost her breath when Jeff pulled her to him. He lifted her up and began kissing her passionately. He engulfed her. She warped to another world where nothing else mattered but being with the man she should have been with from the beginning. Jeff was delicious to her. Brook was divine to him. Through heavy breathing and shameless kisses, they told each other how they felt about one another.

He gently lowered her and she rested her head on his chest.

"Wow," she said as he gently turned her around so that her back rested against his frame.

The moon was full and the air was calm and sweet. Tender thoughts flowed through Brook's head as Jeff held her in his arms, thoughts faithfully framed on the many possibilities that were in store for them. Walter was no longer a part of the equation.

"Brook," Jeff finally called after taking a deep breath.

"Yes?" she answered in a sweet tone.

"Who was that man with you in that picture on your desk?"

Time stopped and so did Brook's pulse. She was prepared, for a time, to table the whole Walter issue. But it had reared its ugly head and she had to address it. She didn't want to lie to Jeff; she didn't want to bring clouds of untruth to their young and tender relationship. She had to tell him the truth and bear the consequences of whatever would happen.

She instructed Jeff to take a seat on the park bench that was right behind them. Then she took hold of his hand while she stood. She told him of her and Walter's estranged relationship and the infidelity. She told him the reason why she wasn't completely forthcoming in the beginning. She spoke to him slowly and softly, hoping that he was taking everything in. Then she took a seat beside him and smoothed the sides of her auburn-tinted hair.

181

She cleared her throat and asked, "Well, what do you think?"

Jeff rubbed his hand over his chin, and gave Brook a serious eye.

"I feared that would be your reaction," she sighed.

"No, no. But let me ask you something, and I want you to be totally honest with me."

"Okay."

"I know how you say you feel about him; the two of you haven't gelled in a long time. But do you think there is a chance the two of you will resolve things?"

Brook didn't answer right away. Her first thought was "No" unequivocally, but then she started soul-searching. She still loved Walter, no matter how much she tried to convince herself that she didn't. So to be completely honest she replied, "I don't know."

Jeff slid back and inhaled a deep breath of cool Greenville night air. He rubbed his waves, and looked at Brook. Then he quickly turned away. She softly took his chin into her hand and brought his eyes to hers.

"What does that mean for us?" she asked.

"Don't know."

The next moment was muted until Jeff leaned back on the bench and said, "I saw the picture right when I was leaving. I almost started not to say anything. I hate I did now."

"No, I'm glad that you mentioned it. I don't want secrets between us because I believe we have something here. I feel something when I think about you. Tell me you don't feel the same way."

"I can't tell you that. Wouldn't be the truth."

"So what do we do? I don't want to stop seeing you. I want to be with you."

A small smile was beginning to form on Jeff's face.

"Then we'll have to be careful. Slow things down a taste. You are still married."

"I agree."

"Let's just see what happens. Let's see what blossoms out of a friendship."

They both stood and Brook hugged Jeff, much in the same way she did long ago in her grandmother's living room; only then, all those years ago, she never realized that when she let him go, he was in essence the one that got away. But this time, she was determined. She was not going to let him get away again.

Brook and Jeff's date ended as enchantingly as it began. He opted to see Brook home and then call a cab for the ride back to his hotel. She thought that was very sweet of him. She also thought that it was sweet that he decided not stay for a night-cap. He wanted to take things slow.

Brook glanced at the answering service. She was sure that there would be at least two dozen messages from Walter. But much to her surprise, the only message was from her mother. There was not one message from Walter.

Brook checked the caller ID. She thought that maybe he just didn't leave any message when he called. But his number was not on the caller ID. Brook called Walter's suite. There was no answer. Then she called the front desk, thinking that she did not have the right room number.

The phone rang a few times and then the desk attendant gave a perky, "Hello, Embassy Suites Verdae Boulevard. How may I help you?"

"I need to be connected with one of your guests and I've forgotten his suite number. His name is Walter Riggins."

"Alright, hold one minute, ma'am."

Brook heard the clicking of keyboard accompanied by annoying humming. Finally the attendant responded.

"I'm sorry. Mr. Riggins checked out this afternoon."

Brook fell silent. They weren't supposed to meet until she got off from work, which was usually after six p.m.

"Is there anything else I can help you with, ma'am?"

Finally Brook surrendered a confused, "No thank you. You've been very helpful."

Straightway, Brook dialed Walter's cell phone. She was promptly sent to voice mail. She dialed the condo in Atlanta. The answering service clicked on after one ring.

"I didn't stand *him* up. He stood *me* up," Brook said.

She shook her head. Blew out a gust of disgust. "He stood *me* up. *Me!*"

The phone rang.

"Hello?"

"Hey you." It was Jeff. "Just called to let you know I made it back to the hotel." Brook said nothing. "Hello? You okay?"

"Yes," she said. "Now I am."

She was no longer upset that Walter stood her up. She was actually glad about it.

Chapter 24

Karen was finally going to do it with William. He felt her hand trembling. He heard her heart racing.

"I didn't think that I'd be this nervous," she said, her voice weak in all of the anticipation.

"Don't worry. We're just going to plunge right on in. I promise you this. As time goes by, the nervousness will go away and it will all seem natural to you."

"You think so?"

"I know so," he assured her. "Are you sure that you're ready for this?"

"I'm ready. But I'm so scared."

"Don't worry. I've got you."

That is the one thing that Karen didn't do when she was with William. Worry. He made her feel safe. She could be herself when around him and that was the main reason that she decided to take that big step with him. He made her feel comfortable enough to open up.

"This is it," he said softly, at almost a whisper.

"Go ahead in," she replied.

She opened. He entered.

They moved slowly at first taking their time, progressing carefully. All of a sudden, she stopped.

"What's the matter?" William asked. "You don't want to do this anymore?"

"No," Karen replied softly, a tear forming in her eye. "I just can't believe that I'm finally going to meet my father."

"I told you that the nervousness will go away with time."

William and Karen had become best friends. After extensive treatment with Dr. Arthur Malone, through hard work and tears, Karen was freed from her dependency on the anti-anxiety medications. She learned how to handle her fears and frustrations. William was with her every step of the way.

Yes they had become close but nowhere near where William wanted to be.

"Maybe you should just tell her how you feel," his friend Maxwell said to him once as he washed his Dodge Charger outside of their beach house on the Isle of Palms.

"Aren't you the same person that told me to take it slow? Remember what happened with Tiffany," he said, mocking Maxwell.

"I'm just saying. You two spend a lot of time together. And you seem to be on the same page. You sort of owe it to her to let her know how you feel. Shoot! You owe it to yourself."

William took it all in, imagining how it would turn out if he said something to Karen about his feelings. But in the end, just when he had built up the courage to say something, he froze. He couldn't understand why he did. But he froze up every time.

"Room 212. This is his office," William said to Karen.

They stood in front of the door for what seemed like an eternity. He didn't want to rush her so he waited patiently until she raised her hand, curled up her fist and began to rap on the door lightly. He barely heard the knock and he was standing right next to her.

"You're probably going to have to knock a little harder than that."

So she went to knock again. But just as she did, the door knob jiggled.

The hinges creaked until the massive door was fully open. Finally, a tall, brown skinned, middle-aged man appeared. His hairline, receding. He wore small, black-rimmed glasses that gave him an aura of intelligence. He had broad shoulders and was immaculately dressed in a blue three-piece suit and black wing-tipped shoes.

186

He fixed his eyes on Karen the second the door opened. William looked on as the two of them stared at each other. And then all of a sudden, the man in the three-piece suit broke the silence.

"Oh my goodness," he said, his eyes wide and bright, "Momma!"

Chapter 25

After many years of wondering how it would be, Karen sat at a dining table across from her father, Dr. Dennis Jordan and his wife Teresa. Her good friend William was right by her side. They were all seated together at a table in the Stern Center, a food court located on the campus of College of Charleston.

"You're right, Dennis," Teresa said as she gazed at Karen. "She is the spitting image of your mother."

Dennis smiled at his wife and then looked at Karen, seemingly searching for the right words to say to her. Finally he cleared his throat and said, "I'm sure you must have a lot of questions."

Karen nervously played with her hair and tried with all of her might to control her emotions. But after a few moments, she let the tears flow and with it, the question that she most wanted to know.

"Did you know about me all this time?"

Dennis' eyes began to melt. Teresa began to cry as well.

"Heavens no," he replied. "I didn't know that you were actually born because your mother left The College so abruptly. But I always had this funny feeling, though."

Dennis took a deep breath and gazed into his daughter's eyes, hoping to see some inkling of forgiveness. He felt that he could not simply request it. He would have to beg for it in ways that had not been invented. So he patiently waited on her response.

Karen dried her eyes and asked, "Did you love my mother?"

Dennis looked over at his wife, who quickly nodded to him.

"It's alright, Dennis," she said as she stroked his hand. "Answer her. She needs to know."

"Yes, I loved your mother very much."

Dennis said those words with a lump in his throat and Teresa cringed when she heard them. It still stung her a little.

"Your mother was, in essence, a genius. The things she could do on piano—she was really ahead of her time. Honestly it felt like she was teaching me. The music is what brought us together. Sometimes we'd have jam sessions, me on my alto saxophone and your mother on the baby grand. We'd jam for hours."

Dennis stopped strolling down memory lane long enough to notice that he was smiling and that Teresa's eyes were closed, damp with the tears she held back.

"It was your mother's youth and my ignorance that led to our affair," Dennis said, afterwards biting his bottom lip and taking a quick glance at his wife.

Then he placed his hand on Karen's and said, "I can't just ask you to forgive me. But if you allow me, I want to work for your forgiveness. I want to earn the right to be your father. Would you give me that chance?"

As Dennis and Teresa locked hands with Karen, the only thing that she could offer was a nod of 'yes'. But that was all they needed.

The both of them stood and brought their new daughter into their embrace. Karen began crying loudly, so much so that other patrons were beginning to take notice. She began breathing heavily and fanning herself.

"Are you alright, sweetheart?" Teresa asked her new daughter.

"I'm fine," Karen answered. "I just thought that I would go through life alone. I didn't know that I had any family left."

Teresa gently took her by the hand and said, "Sweetie, you have no idea how much family you have."

Chapter 26

When William pulled into his driveway, he could hear the crisp sounds of ocean waves crashing against the shore. He could also hear laughter coming from around the house, Maxwell and Tamara's playful banter filing out from his first floor patio.

William was happy for Maxwell because he had found his one: the woman he could laugh with and make love to. He wanted to do those things with Karen. He thought she was his one. But the conversation they had earlier that evening proved him wrong.

Several months had passed since Karen had met her father, Dennis, and his wife, Teresa. She met her new siblings, Char and Omar, and the rest of the entire family at a big barbecue that her father threw in her honor.

Char, the eldest, was the musical director at Abundance Holiness Church. She looked like her mother, with her strong, East-African features and smooth, brown skin. Char was a natural leader, very matter-of-fact, very no-nonsense. She inherited her father's love for music, and ungrudgingly passed it on to her children.

Omar, or Big Omar as the family called him, took after his father in looks and his mother in personality. He was the intelligent accountant, with thin-rimmed glasses and a burly frame. His speech was eloquent and his mannerism pleasurable. Karen recalled the first thing that he said to her.

"Thank you so much for being born. I thought that I was going to have to go through life with Char being my only sister."

That statement earned him a punch in the arm by Char.

The entire Jordan family took Karen in. Char and Omar embraced her as their baby sister. Their children, they had seven between them, embraced Karen as their aunt, and of course Dennis and Teresa embraced her as their baby girl.

However, the warmest and sweetest embrace came from the matriarch of the family: a short, sweet soul with sand-colored skin, hazel eyes and reddish brown hair with naturally blonde streaks. She was 'Momma' to Dennis and Teresa. She was 'Nana' to Char, Omar and the great-grandchildren. She was also Nana to Karen.

"Let me look at you," Nana said to Karen when they first met.

She gently caressed her face and then ran her fingers through her hair, which was identical to her own. She kissed her forehead gently and said, "You'll never be alone again."

Indeed, it was a wonderful time for Karen. She spent a lot of time at the family home in Hollywood, South Carolina, twenty minutes outside of Charleston. There were cookouts, church-meetings, and fishing trips. The women would always out-fish the men. She had a family, people that embraced her, loved her, and made her feel special. She was thankful for finding her family. She was also thankful for finding William.

Their friendship had blossomed over time. They were so close that William would often accompany Karen when she visited her family in Hollywood. He had become just as much of a staple with the Jordan family as Karen. And each time they visited Hollywood, the same question would surface.

"Are you sure y'all aren't dating?"

Or

"Do you go with my Aunt Karen, or what?"

Karen's reply was always the same.

191

"We're just friends."

William would just pretend that he didn't hear the questions. But he heard them every time.

It was a cool Sunday afternoon and the Jordan family had taken a trip to Myrtle Beach for fishing and relaxation. As they fished from an old wooden pier at the rim of the Atlantic, Karen's nephew, Little Omar, asked William the usual question. "So you and my Aunt Karen are just friends?"

"Yeah," William replied.

The young boy threw his line out into the ocean and said, "Humph."

"Why do you ask me that?"

Little Omar smirked, shook his head, and said, "Aunt Karen has you in the friend zone." William couldn't believe that he just said that. "I feel bad for you, son," Little Omar added, right before he got a big bite that caused him to yell and scream for help.

Big Omar assisted his son with his reel, which was bending at the tip. Then both of them started walking along the pier, as the large fish was carrying them wherever he wanted to. Karen and Char joined the bunch with excitement in their eyes.

"Get it, Little Omar! Don't let him get away!" Karen shouted as she joined William.

In all the exhilaration, William still focused on Little Omar's comment.

The friend zone.

"What's wrong, buddy?" Karen asked him.

Her question, and the title that she gave him, didn't do much for his mood.

***

"Why are you so quiet?" Karen asked William as he drove a comfortable 65MPH down Highway 17 South.

"You've been acting funny ever since Little Omar caught that tarpon. Are you jealous that even *he* caught something, while you rode the goose-egg?"

Karen laughed and ran her fingers through her fiery reddish-brown locks.

William abruptly pulled into the parking lot of a Hess Station, put the gear in park, and turned off the engine.

"Karen, I need to ask you a question, a question that may change things between us. I don't want to make this awkward, but I have to know and I have to know right now." His words were crisp and clear. When he started his statement, Karen was facing him. But by the time he had finished it, she was facing straight ahead. She breathed rapidly and held on to her seatbelt with both hands. "Karen, where do we stand?"

No response.

She held her position, frozen in a way.

"Karen?"

"I heard you."

"Look, I know I'm about to make a big fool of myself but I have to put it out there. What's the possibility of you and me becoming more than just friends?"

"None," she answered quickly.

William's heart dropped to depths he didn't think reachable. Karen loosened her grip on the seatbelt and turned to face him.

"We're good friends, and I wouldn't want to jeopardize that. I mean, I see you as like, well—a brother."

William digested those words slowly, thinking about them during the entire trip back to Charleston. By the time he returned to Isle of Palms, he felt humiliated and defeated. He had to back away from Karen. He couldn't remain friends with her after their conversation at the Hess Station. No matter what, things would be awkward.

William tossed his keys on the counter and then stepped out onto his balcony. Just as he sat down on one of his long chairs, his cell phone rang. He looked at the caller ID and chuckled. Then he took a deep breath, hit the answer button, and said, "Hello?"

"Hi, William. I know that we're just friends. But I still want to spend time with you. Are you okay with that?"

"I'm cool with that," he replied. "Let's check out a movie tomorrow night."

"I'd really like that. I'll see you then."

And then William hung up the phone, thankful for the opportunity to get some things off of his chest.

Chapter 27

Karen was waiting by the concession bar of the Regal Movie Theater in North Charleston when she saw William walk into the lobby. She waved and called out to him. Then William walked over and gave her a hug like he usually did when he saw her.

"Um..." she said nervously. "...what are you doing here?"

"There you are, William."

Those words came from his ex-girlfriend, Tiffany: the woman he was meeting at the movie theater.

Just then, a large group of young girls rushed out of the bathroom and came running to Karen's side.

"Ms. Cole, did you get us some popcorn?" one of the girls asked as she wrapped herself in Karen's arm.

Still waiting for William's response to her question, she shyly smiled and said, "Well *I'm* here because these little munchkins talked me into taking them to a movie. These are some of the girls that live at the group home where I volunteer."

"Oh! That sounds so nice!" Tiffany said loudly, attempting to get William's attention.

"Where are my manners?" he said, scratching his head. "Karen, this is Tiffany. We used to date each other. Tiffany, this is my good friend Karen."

"Okay. I've heard so much about you," Karen said as she shook Tiffany's hand. Tiffany only replied with a smile.

After the awkward hand shake, Karen fixed her attention on William. Her eyes were locked on his.

"I don't want to keep you from your date," Karen presumed.

"It's nothing like that," William retorted. "We're just two old friends catching up."

Karen's heart raced within her chest. But under no circumstances would she let him know that.

"We're going to check out Gullah," he said. "It's that movie that was filmed in Charleston a few years back."

"Oh, the romance movie?" Karen replied, disliking the fact that he was going to watch a romance movie with another woman. "Well that's a little much for the kiddies."

Then William said, "Well, I guess I'll see you around."

I'll see you around? Karen repeated to herself.

And then William and Tiffany walked off in the opposite direction while Karen stood there in shock.

Chapter 28

"Perk up!" Maxwell demanded of William as they stood next to each other by the grill. "This is a big day for me. You're my best man, so I need you to smile or something."

"Aw, I'll be fine," William replied. "And you know I'm happy for you and Tamara."

Maxwell and Tamara were hosting an engagement barbecue at the condo on Isle of Palms. He proposed to her a few days earlier.

"So tell me about what happened at the movies last night," Maxwell requested.

"There's really nothing to it. I apologized to Tiffany for how we ended things. She apologized for putting that brick through my windshield. We both agreed that we weren't compatible."

"I'm not talking about what happened with Tiffany. I'm talking about what happened with Karen. I would have paid to see the look on your face when you saw her there."

William shook his head and looked off into the horizon.

"I just can't figure her out," he replied. "We spend a lot of time together. We have a lot of fun. I thought that we could take it up a notch. I guess I was wrong."

Then William looked down at the bottle of Corona from which he hadn't drunk one drop.

He said, "I guess I have to move on, huh?"

Maxwell only replied with a shrug.

"But I can't move on, Max. I can't get her out of my head. She's stuck in there."

William put the bottle down on the table. He spoke to a few people as they walked by and nodded his head to the music occasionally.

Then he sighed and said, "I'm sorry, but I'm going to head on out of here before Karen shows up. I really don't want to bump into her."

"Too late for that," Maxwell replied as he looked over William's shoulder. "Here she comes right now."

"Congratulations, Maxwell," Karen said as she walked up.

Then she turned to face William and said, "Hey, you."

"Hey, yourself. You look beautiful as always."

"Oh stop," she said, playfully rubbing William's bare shoulder.

"How was your date last night? I trust you were a perfect gentleman with Tiffany."

William tilted his head to the side and cornered his lip into his cheek.

"I told you; it's nothing like that," he countered.

"Uh huh," Karen said with a grin. "So, Maxwell, where's Tamara?"

"She's over by the volleyball nets down the way," Maxwell said as he pointed down to the beach.

"Oh I see her," Karen replied. "Well, William. I guess I'll see you around."

And then she walked down to where Tamara was playing volleyball with some friends.

"Do you see what I mean, Max?" William asked in desperation. "That girl is driving me nuts!"

Maxwell patted William on the shoulder and said, "Stick around for a while. Things may turn up."

***

Karen joined Tamara by the volleyball nets.

"Hey, girl! I'm glad you could make it," Tamara said.

"Look at you in your two-piece bikini!" Karen replied.

"Yeah, I'm slimming down for the big day."

Karen eased up beside Tamara and whispered, "Look. I really need to talk to you."

"Oh. Okay," Tamara replied, sensing Karen's angst. She signaled to one of her friends to sub for her and suggested that she and Karen take a walk up the beach.

***

"And then he had the nerve to say, 'I'll see you around,'" Karen said as they walked. She was pretty upset. "I'll see you around? Like we're just acquaintances. Like I'm nothing to him."

"What *are* you to him?"

"Duh! I'm his—"

Karen paused.

"You're his what?" Tamara asked as she continued walking. "Go on and say it. You're his woman! But he doesn't know that because you told him you thought of him as a brother. A *brother*? Really? I mean, what do you expect from him? Considering all of the time you guys spend together, you tell him he's like a brother to you. You said yourself that you've kissed him. You're sending him mixed signals."

Tamara didn't even realize that Karen had stopped walking. She was a few feet behind her, crying softly.

"Oh Karen," she said. Then she walked back to Karen and put her arms around her.

"I can't lose him, Tamara."

"Why don't you just tell William how you really feel about him?"

"Because he's going to want to take it where I'm not ready to go, just like every other man I've dated.

"But you've said yourself he is unlike any man you've ever known."

"I know. I know. And truth be told, I have deep feelings for him. He's been there for me in ways that are hard to explain. I don't want to risk losing him."

Tamara wiped the tears from Karen's eyes and said, "You have to tell him how you feel. You have to take that risk, right now!"

***

Karen walked up behind William and placed her hand on his shoulder.

She said, "Can we go up to your place and talk? Please?"

She gave him her hand and led him up to his condo.

He opened the door to let her in and asked, "Can I get you something to drink?"

"No thank you. I'm fine," she replied softly.

"What did you want to talk to me about?"

Karen walked over to the couch and asked William to join her. Then she said, "We had a conversation a few days ago. Do you remember what we talked about?"

"I do."

"Well, since that time, it seems we've drifted apart. I don't like that. I don't want that for us. I really value our friendship."

William stared into Karen's hazel eyes. Then he shook his head and laughed.

"What's so funny?" she asked.

"You are unbelievable. Do you know that?"

"Excuse me?"

"Is that why you wanted to come to my place and talk? To reiterate that you want to be my friend? You could have done that downstairs at Max's."

"I'm not so sure if I like your tone, William."

"You know what? I think that you are lying."

"Lying? Lying about what?"

"You're lying and you're a coward."

"I am not scared of anything. I'm definitely not scared of you!"

"I didn't say that you were scared of me."

"You have some nerve. Do you know that?"

"Karen, why did you want to come up here for real? Huh? Be real with me!"

"You know what? Forget it! This was a bad idea!"

"You're exactly right! This was a bad idea! I think you need to step!"

"Fine!" Karen shouted. And then she got up and started walking away.

"Karen! Wait!"

William jumped to his feet. They had never argued before. And for a moment, neither of them knew quite where to go from there.

William broke the silence by saying, "I'm sorry." He rubbed his hand over his nearly shaven head. His heart could be seen racing through his tank-top. "Look Karen, I'm in love with you..."

"I'm in love with you, too."

"...and I can't go on being just friends. What did you say?" William asked, as his brows rose just slightly.

"I said I'm in love with you, too."

Then she stepped closer to him until her five-foot one inch frame stood right in his six-foot four inch space. She caressed his face lightly with both hands, tip-toed, brought his lips closer to hers and said, "And I definitely do not see you as a brother!"

And then they kissed.

Their kisses were light at first, only their lips touched, afraid of what was next, of what could be. Karen fell limp in his arms as he sat her on the couch, still kissing, still caressing.

Karen's hand traveled across the smoothness of William's chest. Then she raised her leg and positioned it between William's. It had been so long since she had been this close to a man, since she had felt so free, just kissing a man.

As their tongues danced slowly, William's hand found its way inside of Karen's sarong. His hand had a mind of its own, moving from the inside of her knee to the middle of her thigh. Her legs were so warm. Heat increased as William's hand made its trek, from the skin of her thigh to the lace of her bikini, to—

"Whoa, whoa, whoa," Karen said as William lifted himself from her pulsating frame.

They both sat motionless for a moment. Then William straightened his shorts while Karen positioned herself on the edge of the couch. She straightened her hair and let out a gust of air.

"Why? Why? Why?" she asked in a defeated tone. William was reaching out to her to lightly touch her leg when she continued. "Everything was beautiful. I saw you every day. You made me laugh. We shared things, how our days went, what we felt about issues. Now, it's going to be over. I won't hear from you and I won't have you in my life anymore."

"What are you talking about?"

She positioned herself to face him and took his hands in hers. Then she said, "I'm a virgin."

"Okay."

"I've never had sex before in my life."

"I know the meaning of the term, Karen."

"No, listen. I don't want to have sex until I'm married. That has been a problem with every man I have ever dated." William lowered his head and gave out a sigh. "See, I told you. You're going to leave me now. That's why I never pressed the issue that I loved you."

"Look, I don't want to go on being just friends. You want to wait until marriage? That's fine. I just don't want to be your buddy. And I definitely don't want to be your brother. I want to be your man!"

He took her into his arms. They hugged each other. Karen rested her head on William's chest and she listened to his heartbeat, her heartbeat. She wasn't afraid anymore. She wasn't worried about William bailing on her. She realized that he was her soul mate. He wasn't going anywhere.

A little later, William rejoined Maxwell by the grill as Karen went to tell Tamara the good news that they were officially a couple.

"Are things looking up?" Maxwell asked.

"Yes sir, they are," William replied.

"See. I told you so."

Chapter 29

Karen rested the soles of her bare feet on the dash of William's Lexus. The moon roof was open, allowing the cool autumn breeze to caress her tresses. The leaves were starting to turn colors and the weather was starting to cool down in Charleston, giving a great reprieve from the sweltering heat that summer produced. It was officially fall and change was in the air.

"Where us going?" Karen asked as she smiled playfully at William.

He only smiled back in reply.

Some time ago he asked Karen what her answer would be if he proposed.

She didn't hesitate, but boldly answered, "Yes!"

"No hesitation?" William replied. "I like that."

"We'd be good together," Karen added. "I'd make you a good wife."

William had already spoken with Karen's parents, receiving blessings from both her father and adopted mother. He'd already purchased the ring. He was going to wait until the weekend, but he couldn't. The excitement bubbled inside of him.

"We're going to Clear Waters," he said, answering her question about their destination.

Clear Waters was an exclusive eatery located on Shem Creek that served West Indian entrées. William had taken Karen there on their first official date.

"But it's Wednesday night. I thought that place was only open Thursday through Sunday."

William pulled into the small gravel parking lot.

"No. They're open tonight."

He was the perfect gentleman, rushing to open her car door, taking her by the hand as they walked to the restaurant's entrance, opening the large wooden door for her.

Karen and William were met in the foyer of the restaurant by a young West Indian gentleman with dark skin. He was dressed in an all-black tuxedo and shiny square-toe dress shoes.

"Welcome to Clear Waters. Right dis way," he said with a thick patois.

The restaurant, just like the parking lot, was completely empty. Karen began adding everything up in her head and she stalled in her tracks, holding her hands over her mouth when she saw how the restaurant had been decorated.

"Oh my goodness," she said with a gasp.

"Come on," William said as he guided her on. "Let me do this."

Their table was in the center of the dining room under a sparkling white cloth decorated with elaborate designs. The maître d' was going to pull Karen's chair back when William prevented him.

"I've got this, Bruh." he said.

"Handle your biz-ness" the maître d' replied.

"Please have a seat, my lady," William said as he pulled Karen's chair away from the table.

She sat down, still covering her mouth with hands that trembled slightly. He got down on one knee, causing her hands to tremble even more. He pulled a black box from his pocket and held it up to her, looking deeply into her eyes. And then he began his proposal.

"God made you for me. Indeed our relationship is the fulfillment of destiny. I never told you this before, but I dreamt of you before we even met. That was a sign from God that you were the one for me, my angel."

William opened the box displaying the diamond engagement ring.

"Karen Cole. Would you be my wife?"

This was all a formality. For no sooner did William ask the question did Karen release a resounding "Yes!" that filled the room and lit a new fire in William's heart. They embraced and then kissed each other passionately. They no doubt would have gone on and on with their kiss and embrace for hours had they not been interrupted by a loud and large, "Congratulations!"

Karen opened her eyes to see that the room was now filled with family and friends: the Jordan family, the Wards. And of course Maxwell and Tamara were there, telling anyone who would listen that they were responsible for William and Karen getting together.

The evening wore on with much merriment. Karen surveyed the room to see that she was surrounded by family and friends, people who loved and adored her. But her heart was a little heavy because she wished her mother and Ma Geneva were there.

Karen needed some air. She didn't want to cry in front of the gathering for fear that she would give off the wrong impression. She was happy, happier than she had ever been in her entire life. Yet being in the midst of such love and warmth reminded her that she had been disconnected from very special parts of her life: her cousins, the family that she grew up with.

Karen successfully stole away to the patio, an elegant wooden structure that overlooked the marshes. The moon light flickered over the dark waters and the high grass moved with the wind. Karen looked out into the darkness and made every attempt to fight back tears.

"I would have invited them, you know," William said. He had stepped out onto the patio, his voice bringing comfort to Karen. "I actually looked through your contacts on your cell phone. Their numbers weren't there."

Karen sniffled a bit and replied, "I know their numbers by heart."

"Then call them. They're family and I want them to be here for our wedding." Then William placed his hands on Karen's shoulders and said, "Call all of them."

Chapter 30

Heaven.

Cicely lived there as she rested next to Vincent Mann on sweat-dampened Egyptian cotton sheets.

Heady.

She felt that way as Vincent Mann sexed her with animalistic passion.

Harlot.

Cicely's promiscuity and pilfering of seeds that rightly belonged to Vincent Mann's wife earned her that moniker. The theft was no accidental occurrence. She gave Vincent Mann the best of her loving because she wanted to own every ounce of him.

Harlot.

Cicely wore that name. She earned that name.

After collecting himself and gathering his strength, Vincent Mann sat up at the edge of the bed. He glanced back at his harlot, the woman that sexed him crazy. He sighed.

"You're too much, Cicely Shaw. Too much for a man like me."

"You bring it out of me. When I'm with you, I have no inhibitions. It's like I become your personal porn star or something."

Her lover found the strength necessary to pour a glass of wine. He motioned to Cicely to see if she would join him in the nectar of Dionysus. She declined even though it wasn't her desire to do so. She very much wanted to sip a few glasses, let the buzz fill her head and make her more receptive for round three. But instinct had taken over. She had to make wiser decisions.

"He couldn't possibly stay with his wife much longer," Cicely whispered to herself as she closed her eyes. "Especially not now."

Vincent Mann, fighting wobbly legs, returned to the bed puffing on a Cuban cigar. The stench from the cigar tickled and annoyed Cicely's nostrils. She opened her eyes; her instinct kicking in immediately. She faked a cough and placed her hands over her mouth.

"What? The smoke bothering you?" He looked back at her. His tone implied that it shouldn't bother her because it never bothered her before.

She sighed and pulled her locks to the side, tucking her hair behind her ear.

"Well, I was going to wait until dinner at The Zebra tomorrow evening, when the ambience would be perfect for my news. But I'll tell you now." She lifted herself so that she sat right behind her lover, her skin sticking to his. Then she whispered into his ear, "I'm pregnant."

Vincent was frozen. "What?"

Cicely's smile was wide. She knew that the news would stun him, bring him joy like never before, especially since his wife was going through menopause. Cicely was going to give him as many babies as he wanted. She was going to fill their mansion with love and laughter.

"We're having a baby. A baby! Vincent?"

"We can't have a baby," he said bluntly.

His words stopped Cicely's euphoria in its tracks. "What?"

"We cannot have a baby."

He spoke to her calmly, without turning to face her. He took another long pull of his cigar and then littered the dimly lit room with gray plumes of smoke.

"Why not?" she asked softly. When he didn't reply, she sat back, resting on her knees, her palms on her thighs. "We're lovers. I love you. Why can't we have a child? That's what lovers do."

Vincent took a sip of wine and then another long drag of his cigar. He turned to face Cicely, his face enfolded in a thick fog of cigar smoke.

"I'm married," he said. "We cannot start a family until I have properly broken ties with my wife. You know that."

Cicely hung her head and Vincent immediately placed his finger on her chin to bring her eyes back to his.

"Soon I'll get a divorce and we can get married and start our own family. It is essential that we do things properly."

Lifting himself from the bed and gradually finding his balance, he stood in front of Cicely. His eyes seemed to glow with a blood red aura as they peered through the smoke.

He said, "You have to take care of it, okay?" Then he walked to the bathroom and closed the door behind him.

Cicely died inside. She held her stomach and sobbed softly because of the emotionless manner in which Vincent dismissed her pregnancy. She desperately wanted to have a baby girl.

She thought she would make a good mommy. She would do things a lot differently than her mother did. She'd talk with her daughter about boys, giggle with her as her baby girl confessed her gigantic crush on the most popular boy in her class. She would also be there when that popular boy broke her daughter's heart. She would be there, period.

Then Cicely thought about her busy schedule. She was a division leader, managing various projects and multiple budgets. She could not be the type of mother she wanted to be, not until she married Vincent. He was right. She had to take care of it.

Chapter 31

Mrs. Dawn Michelle Mack.

Mr. and Mrs. Cory Levaughn Mack.

Dawn spent hours writing her new name in several variations on the pages of a notebook as she sat at her kitchen table alone. The ink pen trembled in her hand. Uneasiness consumed her. She felt unsure about herself and her position.

Mrs. Mack.

That is how she would be addressed, how she wanted to be addressed by the world. She wanted desperately to be officially recognized as the wife of her long time love, Cory: the father of her child. However, to date, only her daughter shared the last name Mack. That was about to change.

Dawn Williams sat alone at her kitchen table as her mother, who was visiting from Fountain Inn, sat in the family room with her granddaughter. Her twin sister, Brook, was leaving for Minneapolis the next day so Dawn welcomed the company. She spent so much of her days alone.

As she scribbled her new name on loose-leaf paper, she reminisced about the last time Cory had visited her Easley home. She prepared dinner, which they ate together at the dinner table, just as families do. Cory played with his daughter and showered her with gifts. Then later on that evening, after Tarsha was fast asleep, he played with Dawn. She was complete with him and she wanted for nothing.

Nevertheless, he was slow to come through on promises he had made of leaving the game and moving out to Easley permanently. So for now, Dawn had to settle for the small amount of time that she shared with her fiancé. For now, one night a week would have to do.

"What are you writing over there?" Diane asked as she began making her way to the kitchen table. Dawn quickly covered her notebook with her hand as best she could.

"Did Brook make it to Minneapolis yet?" she asked her mother.

That question was enough to freeze a worried mother and make her retreat to her purse to retrieve her cell phone, enough time for Dawn to rip the littered pages from the notebook and toss them into the wastebasket.

"Brook's not leaving until tomorrow morning," Diane called out before returning to her phone call with her other daughter.

"Okay," Dawn replied, even though she already knew that.

She lifted herself from her chair, made her way to the refrigerator and retrieved a bottle of Dasani. Looking out into the backyard as she sipped her ice-cold water, she imagined what things would be like if Cory was her husband. They would make passionate love to each other every evening. Perhaps Dawn would even get pregnant and give him the son he desperately wanted.

But that was just a fantasy. In reality, he spoke of marriage less and less. And it was highly unlikely that she would give him a son. Because lately, Cory would wear a condom each and every time they made love, even if Dawn begged him not to.

"Baby—"

The sound of her mother's voice broke Dawn from her deep reverie. Her mother stood beside the trashcan, clutching the crumpled notebook paper that Dawn had thrown away. Her mother saw what she had been writing.

Measuring what she would say to her youngest child, Diane walked over to where Dawn was standing.

212

She gently placed her hands on Dawn's shoulders and tenderly kissed her on her cheek.

"I've been thinking," Diane said, "you could go back to Fountain Inn and finish school. You could move in with me until you get settled."

"Why would I move in with you? Why would I leave my house?"

"Dawn—baby—this isn't your house."

Dawn took a deep breath to display her frustration and asked, "Why does everyone keep saying that?"

Diane led her daughter to the table and asked her to have a seat. She took her hands in her own and looked deeply into her eyes.

"I just don't want to see you get hurt."

"Momma, I'll be fine."

Diane wiped the tear from Dawn's cheek with her fingers.

"My baby. My youngest. Brook came out so fast. We had to wait a while for you to decide to make your grand entrance."

"Momma, I know this story well."

"Oh yeah? Well here's a story you may not know so well." Diane settled in as she began to impart wisdom. "I was so hurt when your father left us. I felt that I needed to find another man to become the husband and father that your natural father wouldn't be. So you and your sister suffered through a whole mess of men coming and going. And quite honestly, I put you girls in a very compromising position growing up."

"Momma, we've had this discussion already."

"No. Let me finish! You are doing the same thing; searching for stability for your daughter and yourself. But just like me, your first find was a mistake!"

Dawn raised her hand in a halting motion. "Momma, I don't want to hear this right now."

"Dawn Williams, I am not finished! You're out here in the boondocks, all on your own. It's like Cory moved you out here to be his piece on the side."

"Ma, I moved out here, on my own accord, because I didn't want to go to jail for killing Nina."

There was a long bout of silence.

"Baby, you don't mean that."

Dawn lifted herself from the table, her face wrinkled with worry and exhaustion.

"Goodnight, Ma. I'm going to put Tarsha to bed."

No matter where Dawn looked, she saw Cory's face. She couldn't escape him and sometimes she wondered if she really wanted to. Looking into Tarsha's eyes as she played with the bubbles from the bath, she saw Cory Mack. She saw him when she looked at herself in the mirror. He was a part of her. Inescapable.

Dawn lowered Tarsha to her toddler bed and tucked her in. Then she began praying.

"Oh God, I need you. I need you now! Please don't let my daughter suffer because of the mistakes I've made."

She wiped the tears from her eyes, kissed her daughter on the forehead, and whispered softly to her, "Good night, baby."

Then she looked at the diamond ring on her finger and she whispered, "Good night, Cory."

Chapter 32

Dawn was awakened by the sound of rich laughter coming from downstairs. Her vision blurred, slightly blinded by the fresh light that broke through the window casement. She realized she had fallen asleep right next to Tarsha's bed and had slept there the entire night.

There was more laughter and she recognized that her mother was the source; however, she also identified a male voice. She stumbled over to the window, took a look outside, and saw a forest-green Ford F150. It was Monday morning. Her good friend Joe the landscaper had come to mow her lawn.

Dawn quickly made her way to the bathroom and freshened up. Then she raced into her bedroom and put on a navy blue Nike tee-shirt, some dark gray sweats, and a pair of Air Cross Trainers.

When she made her way to the top of the staircase, she was greeted with more laughter from her mom as well as Joe's signature smile. As always, Joe donned his light blue work shirt, navy work-pants and steel toe work boots.

"What's so funny?" Dawn asked.

Her mother turned, still smiling. "You actually asked this man *what* he was."

Dawn reached the bottom of the stairs, looked up at Joe, and smiled.

"Good morning, Mr. Suarez."

"Good morning, Ms. Williams.

Diane stood beside them during the exchange, until she received the eye from Dawn.

"I think I hear Tarsha stirring. Nice to meet you, Joe."

"Nice to meet you too, ma'am."

215

Dawn pulled her hair behind her ear and raised her brow.

"So what can I do for you, Joe?"

"Well, there are a couple things. First, and I am so sorry about this, but I've gotten a little behind in my bank runs. I'm sure that's the problem."

"Problem? What problem?"

"I'm thinking that because I've waited so late, the last check that you wrote bounced. I'm so sorry."

"No problem. I'll write you another and void the old one."

"Great. Great."

Joe smiled. He was extremely fond of Dawn's beauty, the way she smiled at him, the way his name rolled off of her lips.

"Umm. What's the other thing?"

"Oh. Oh yeah. I need to weed-eat the drive way, but your 4-Runner is somewhat parked in the grass."

"Ah, Brook must've put it there before she left. No problem. I'll go grab the keys."

"Alright."

Joe waited for her to return so that she could move her truck. He often wondered why he never saw another car in the driveway, perhaps a car that belonged to her boyfriend, to her man as she called him once. He often wondered if such a man existed. Dawn was indeed a mystery to him. For all he knew she had no job. Yet she owned a home in one of the nicest sub-divisions in Easley and she was one of his most reliable customers when it came to payment.

"Here you go."

That was Dawn. She had returned with her truck keys extended in Joe's direction.

"What do you want me to do with those?" he asked.

"Move the 4-Runner," she answered matter-of-factly.

"I don't get it."

"Oh, I'm sorry. If you need the truck moved, you're going to have to move it."

"What?"

"Brook brought my mother here. My mother doesn't drive. I don't drive. I mean I can't drive."

"You can't drive? You have this nice truck and you can't drive?"

"Blah, blah, blah. I've heard it all before. I know. I never learned to drive. I didn't pick this thing out."

"You've never driven? Ever?"

"Never. The truck is too big. I always wanted to learn to drive in something smaller, you know. Like a little Toyota Corolla or something. I nearly signed up for driving lessons, but even the Corolla was too big for me. I know I suck, right?"

"So you think a Corolla is too big?"

Dawn gave a half smile, put her hands on her hips, and shot Joe a look that said 'Isn't that what I just said?'

He took the keys and moved the 4-Runner while Dawn waited. When he was finished, he hopped out of the truck. Without missing a beat he hustled over to his trailer and cranked up his riding mower. Then he put the mower in reverse and carefully backed it off of the trailer. She looked at him and thought, Is he going to give me back my keys or is he going to just get right to work?

She raised her brow and said, "You are gung-ho about cutting grass, aren't you?"

"I'm not going to cut the grass, mami. You are."

She loved the way he called her *mami*.

"Are you serious?"

"Yes. You said a Corolla was too big. This riding mower is perfect to learn."

"You *are* serious."

"And you have a huge yard. So by the time we're done, you'll be a pro. So come hop on."

Dawn was hesitant. But she had to admit it; her back yard, absent of traffic, free of pedestrians, was the perfect place for her maiden voyage.

"Hop on," Joe said with a smile. "Don't worry. I'll be with you, right behind you."

"Okay. I'll go and let my mother know."

"I HEARD ALL ABOUT IT, BABY! HAVE FUN!" Diane yelled from the front porch.

Dawn shook her head at her mother. And then she mounted the front portion of the mower's seat, with Joe behind her.

"Okay, this is how it works. Left pedal is the brake, right pedal is the gas. You use the steering wheel to direct the mower."

"Joe. I know all of that."

"Well alright then. Let's go."

She looked at him and smiled. Little by little, a fear that had nearly crippled her and resulted in an intense dependence on others started to dissipate. Looking at Joe, she felt a deep appreciation for his excellent suggestion. Then she faced forward and saw the yard before her.

"Just start from the outside, go round and round, and ultimately work your way to the center," he instructed.

"You alright back there?" Dawn asked.

"Oh yeah. I'm chilling."

"Okay. Here we go."

She hit the gas and the mower jerked forward a bit. Joe consoled her, letting her know that she had nothing to worry about. He told her that she was in total control of the machine and that the mower would only go where she commanded it.

Just as he instructed, Dawn accelerated in a straight line, leaving a path of freshly cut grass in her wake. She was a professional within minutes, masterfully cutting straight ahead, skillfully reversing the mower to catch spots that she missed. Finally,

218

after an hour's time, she had finished cutting the entire yard.

"There's just one more thing that you have to do now." Joe pointed to the trailer. "Just take your time and guide this bad boy right on the back of that trailer."

"Are you sure you trust me to do that?"

"Oh I trust you. The question is do you trust yourself?"

Dawn's apprehension did not come from the lack of knowledge of how vehicles worked. And she realized that her fear was never about the size of the vehicle. She just needed to know that she could be in control, that she could guide the machine and not depend on others for help.

"I can do it!" she proclaimed. And with that, she slowly and carefully guided the mower back onto the trailer, into the exact spot it was supposed to be in.

"I did it!" she screamed.

Joe pulled her truck keys from his shirt pocket and said, "Let's see what else you can do. I'm going to take you driving."

"What about your job?"

"I'm my own boss. I can finish my other jobs after we're done. Come on. You have nothing to worry about."

Joe handed her the keys and she began the second leg of her journey.

They started out just driving around the subdivision. Dawn took her time, stopping at all of the stop signs and waiting for three seconds, even though there was no traffic. Then Joe showed her how to back up 100 feet. She mastered that. He showed her how to parallel-park. She mastered that.

"Let's take this up a notch, shall we. Take Harris Ave. to the Parkway."

"O—Okay."

Dawn did as instructed. Shortly afterward, she maneuvered the long winding parkway. She felt so free, so in control.

"Um, we're coming up to the light," she cautioned. "Should I turn around?"

"Nope. Take it on out to Highway 123."

Dawn stopped at the light. "But if I did that, I'd be on the highway."

"Yes. That's why it's called *Highway* 123."

"But I'll be on the road with lots of other cars, with eighteen-wheelers."

"Yeah, I know. Um, the light's green."

Dawn looked at Joe with wonderment. He smiled: no fear in his face. She was strengthened from his confidence. Calmly, she accelerated the 4-Runner, making a left onto Highway 123.

She felt free as a bird. She passed the written test many years ago, so she was well aware of the rules; however, she had never applied them. This application unlocked even more levels of freedom for her.

"Take a right at this light here," Joe instructed.

As Dawn masterfully maneuvered the terrain she marveled at the shear ease of this accomplishment and kicked herself for not going through with it sooner.

"Alright. Take a right into this parking lot."

Dawn pulled into the lot, in such a state of amazement that she really hadn't given much thought about where Joe was guiding her. But then it hit her.

"You can't be serious," she said as she brought the truck to a stop.

"I'm *so* sincere."

Dawn looked straight ahead and saw a brick building with a brown metal top. But what jumped out at her was the sign on the front of the building.

South Carolina Department of Motor Vehicles

"You can do it," Joe proclaimed. "I believe in you."

Dawn spent the next passing moments in self-reflection on how silly and unfounded her fears were.

Her fear had crippled her; however the moments that she spent applying the knowledge that she had acquired empowered her. She finally believed in herself enough to take the ultimate step. She parked the car and smiled at her friend. She was going to go for it. She was no longer afraid.

Chapter 33

The driving test was over and ice cream was the perfect pick-me-up for a disappointing outcome.

"Thanks for treating me to ice cream," Dawn said to Joe as she pouted.

"I figured ice cream would cheer you up."

"This really sucks."

"Don't worry about it. I messed up on my first try, too. I had to live with that for ten years."

"You mean I have to wait ten years to do this again?"

"Yeah. That's if you don't lose it. But look on the bright side: you've got your driver's license now. Who cares what your picture looks like on it?"

"You're right," Dawn said as she smiled and looked at her driver's license. "I'm finally driving!"

She played around with her ice cream, really too excited to eat. Every now and again, when Joe wasn't looking, she'd stare at him in admiration, getting that sweet satisfaction of looking at someone when they are not aware of it. She had moved past his handsomeness to something deeper. Looked into his manhood, the goodness in him, the meekness that he owned and the pureness of his aura.

She took a breath and said, "I wish we had known each other three years ago."

"Oh really?" Joe said, turning to face her.

"Yeah. I mean—by now we could be—who knows."

There was a pause between them. Smiles were exchanged before she nervously looked away.

"Okay, so we have some catching up to do. And I know the perfect way for us to make up for all this lost time," Joe said.

He had Dawn's ear. She turned to him, resting her weight on her right hip.

"Oh yeah? What's that?"

"A little exercise I like to call 'In and Out'."

She rolled her eyes and raised her brow.

"It's not that kind of party, Mr. Suarez."

"No, no, no. 'In and Out'. Tell me who you are. Start with your parents and then end up here, in this truck, at Dairy Queen on Highway 123."

Dawn took a second to measure the idea.

"Wow. That's going to take a while to get out"

"No, no, no. Keep it brief. Just tell me your story, be honest, and don't leave anything out. Then I'll do the same. We work from the inside out. When we're done, we will know each other very well."

"Okay. Here it goes. I was born in 1975 to Richard and Diane Williams. To be honest with you, I really don't remember much about my parents being together other than the fights. And I don't mean verbal arguments. My father was really abusive. I remember walking up the stairs to our apartment once. My mother said to us, 'Remember girls, if your Daddy starts beating on mommy again, call the police.' "

Dawn paused. The memory sent a fresh chill up her spine as she recalled things that, for sanity's sake, her mind had blocked out.

"I have a twin sister. Her name is Brook and she is my best friend. We were close growing up, not so much because we shared a placenta, but for survival's sake. After my parents split up, my mom had a slew of unsavory boyfriends: a couple of guys just lying around the house while my mother worked third shift.

"My fondest childhood memories were of the summers that my sister and I spent in Greenville with our grandmother and our two cousins, Cicely and Karen. Life was serene there, no loud music, no threats. It was just an old lady and her orchids, as she called us.

"I went to school for accounting, but never finished. I met a man at a club and he offered me a job keeping books at his auto dealership. But it turns out, that dealership was just a front. I mean this guy was in the drug game, big time.

"I know that I shouldn't have, but I fell in love with the guy. I may regret a lot in my life but I don't regret the little girl that we produced.

"He proposed but it's like an open-ended plane ticket or something because we still haven't tied the knot. But I'm still with him, even though I know for a fact that he's cheating on me with this chicken-head in Greenville." She paused. Looked at Joe. Then she said, "I met this guy. He's a very handsome dude and you may know him. Well it turns out that this man has a very kind and gentle spirit and this man has taught me that I can believe in myself. He has empowered me. I am sitting in this Toyota 4-Runner with that man right now."

Silence settled between them as Joe digested every word Dawn had spoken.

"Okay. Your turn," she said, perking up.

"Alright. I was born in 1974 to Carmelo and Beatrice Suarez. We lived in a little apartment in the Bronx, right above a bodega.

"My mother and father loved each other very much, but some would say that their bond was strengthened by my maternal grandfather's disapproval of my father. You know, he was one of those old school cats, not progressive at all about black and brown mixing it up. But when I was born, everything changed. My maternal grandfather embraced me and he became more tolerant of my parents' relationship.

"So my mother and father thought of me as a little angel. I mean, for real, they believed that I was anointed by God because I reunited my mother and grandfather and healed this great rift that separated the families. So I was about six months old when moms and pops gave me a second name. Angelito. It means 'Little Angel.'

224

"My whole childhood I was worshipped like a little saint or something. And my peeps were real religious too. I could do no wrong. Man I had them all fooled. When I was thirteen-years-old, I bought a gun and started running with the wrong crowd. We'd stick up dealers and what not. And they'd never see it coming because my crew was so young and slick.

"But we were way too flashy. Way too stupid. We hit the wrong set. It seemed like we had half of New York looking for us with the big guns. We were too stupid to even lay low. Instead, we we're hitting up clubs, flashing stolen jewelry, buying out the bar with hot money."

Joe's deep reverie was proof positive that his account of the story placed him back in that Brooklyn night club.

"The air was thick with ganja smoke. Biggie Smalls bumped hard. Ladies barely dressed. Me and my homeboys were crazy high, tore up from the floor up. Eyes barely opened. They should've been open." Somberness settled on Joe's countenance. "We never saw them coming." Joe gripped Dawn's hand tightly. "It was like an army of them with black masks and semi-automatic weapons. They lit that club up like Christmas; didn't care who they hit. Every single one of my boys died that night. But here I am."

Silence settled. Dawn was amazed at the account because the person Joe described was nothing like the hard-working, Godly man that sat in the passenger seat of her 4-Runner.

"That's why my parents sent me down to South Carolina to live with my Uncle Herman and Aunt Maria. I hated them for it at the time. But if they hadn't done that, I might not be alive today. I gave my life to Christ at the age of sixteen. I started my own business at eighteen. I met a very nice young lady who lives in Easley. You may know her."

"I think I know who you're referring to."

225

"And so, here I am, in this Toyota 4-Runner with one of the most beautiful women I've ever met."

"Aw, that is so sweet," Dawn said as she blushed.

"So that's how it works. We pretty much know each other now."

"And now that you know me, do you think that I'm a gold digger?" she asked.

"What? No! I think you just put your trust in the wrong things. But you are definitely not a gold digger."

Joe repositioned himself so that he fully faced Dawn.

"Do you think badly of me now that you know who I was? I mean, do you think I'm a menace to society?"

"By no means. I think you just needed a hug growing up."

"Aw shucks, a hug."

Dawn feigned pity and said "Come here and let mommy give you a hug."

Joe playfully obliged. But as they reached across the front of the vehicle and felt the warmth of each other's embrace, they realized that something was materializing. Their cheeks touched. Her tresses touched the edge of his lips and he tasted the sweetness and smelled the aroma of flowers.

They embraced for what seemed like hours, holding each other tightly. Sounds stopped and time ceased. A threshold had been crossed, an awkward place that offered no script. The embrace had been building for some time, waiting to be born. Now it was selfish. It innocently delighted itself until sound returned, until time resumed.

Dawn was first to break free. Joe slowly followed suit.

"I'd better be getting back," she said.

"Yeah. You're right."

Not much was spoken on the way back to Dawn's house. However, every now and again, she would glance at Joe. He'd return the glance. She glowed to him and he wondered, given the circumstances, if there was a chance for more.

Dawn pulled into her driveway and put her truck in park, ready to put her cards on the table with no reservations. She had to do it. It ate away at her internally; so much so that she disregarded the risk involved in being completely open.

"There's something I need to tell you," she said.

"Yes?"

"Do you remember that day that I invited you into the house and offered you the apple turnovers?"

"Yeah, I remember that."

"And how I was all nice to you?"

"I remember."

"And you insinuated that I was trying to seduce you?"

"Yeah."

"Well, when I told you that I wasn't trying to seduce you—I lied." Dawn bit her lip and fidgeted with her hair nervously. "I better go," she said, pulling the latch and opening the door. Joe wanted to reach for her. But he didn't have to. Dawn paused and faced Joe, looking deeply into his eyes. "Why did you do all this today, Joe? I mean, no one has ever been that patient with me. You spent your whole work day teaching me how to drive. Why?"

Joe was matter-of-fact with his response.

"I once asked my dad what I should buy a girl to show her that I was really interested in her. He said to me, 'Son, it's not about what you buy for her or how much money you spend on her. If you really want to show her that you care, you give her something rare and precious. You give her your time.' "

Later, both would attest that they weren't quite sure who initiated it; however, it was Dawn who leaned toward Joe, gently placing her lips on his, giving him the softest and sweetest kiss he had ever received.

She slowly pulled back, biting her lip, breathing in the Egyptian Musk that radiated from Joe's skin. Joe sat frozen, eyes closed.

"Thank you, Joe Suarez." Then she got out of the 4-Runner and went into the house.

"Well, well, well," Diane said with a smile. "I want details, young lady." Dawn beamed and showed her license.

"Wow. He's good." Then she went over to the window and peaked outside. "Dawn, what did you do to him? He's still sitting in your truck."

But by then, Dawn had left the room, humming a new tune.

Later that evening, she sat at her kitchen table with a notepad, writing out her future name as girls often do when they are smitten. But this time, she smiled as she scribbled, filling the pages of the notebook with the name—

Mrs. Dawn Michelle Suarez.

Chapter 34

Brook had never been on an airplane before. Perhaps that was the reason for her angst. Try as she might, she couldn't stop her hands from trembling. Butterflies danced in her stomach. Her heart fluttered. Sweat started to form on her brow and Brook was never the type to perspire. Yes. It was flying for the first time in her life that had her on edge and not the fact that she would soon be reuniting with Jeff after having been apart for three months.

It was a fairly large plane. Most of the passengers were flying out on business. Brook surmised this by their dress and by the way some of them were keeping their laptops open, aiming to work until the last possible minute before the plane began to taxi. Others spoke feverishly into their cellular phones, either barking out orders or downloading information. None of them seemed as amazed as Brook that they were all going to leave the Earth's surface shortly. No one seemed to care, that is until the old lady boarded the plane.

The first thing Brook saw on the old lady was the gold tooth that glimmered in the light as she smiled. And the old lady smiled at everyone, waving as if she was fondly acquainted with them.

"Praise the Lord! How are you doing?" she asked each and every person she passed. Most of the travelers ignored her. Some shooed her away as one would a pesky gnat. But she was not fazed. She kept on smiling and nodding her head, bad wig and all.

Brook should not have but she made eye contact. The old lady lit up, her smile expanding, her gold tooth effervescing. She looked at her boarding pass and then looked back up in Brook's direction.

Oh no, Brook thought. Please don't sit by me.

But the aged grinner headed towards her, smiling and greeting and being ignored all the way.

"Please don't sit by me," Brook whispered. "She's going to sit by me and probably talk my ear off the whole way."

"Row 10," the old lady said with way too much joy in her voice for Brook's taste. "Seat B. I'm here baby. I am here! How you, sugar?"

Brook didn't smile and offered no warmth. But her unfriendliness did nothing to steal the elderly grinner's joy.

"Listen. I'm in seat B, the window seat. But I'd much rather sit in the aisle."

"No ma'am I'm fine with the aisle seat."

"I wouldn't hear of it. You just slide right over and enjoy the view all the way there, baby."

"That's quite alright, ma'am."

But then Brook looked up and really focused on the old lady, her gold tooth glistening, and her eyes wide with excitement. She realized that this exchange could very well go on for the entire trip.

"Okay ma'am. I'll take the window seat."

Brook scooted over and the old lady eased herself down into her seat.

They exchanged names. The old lady's name was Ella. Brook marveled at the nonstop grin she possessed. Little by little Ella's smile began to unsettle Brook, adding to her angst all the more.

"Your first flight too, huh?" Ella asked, still smiling, still unsettling.

"Guess you can tell," Brook replied. "I'm nervous as I don't know what."

"I can tell. I can tell. I can hear your heart beating from over here." Then all of a sudden, Ella stopped smiling. The change in her expression startled Brook.

"No, that's not it!" Ella surmised. "Who is he?"

"Who is who?"

"Who's the man that'll be waiting on you in Minneapolis? Because that's why you're nervous."

Brook reared back and widened her eyes.

"Go on, child," Ella said. "You'll feel much better if you tell me about him."

Brook gave a half-smile. At first she was hesitant to speak. But ultimately, she felt more and more comfortable with Ella.

"Well he's a good man," Brook said. "He's helped me through a rough time in my life."

"Um, baby. You have never seen me before and chances are you will never see me again once we get off this plane. Don't be vague. Spill it out. You'll feel better."

Perhaps Brook should have viewed Ella's request as odd. But a certain ease overcame her. She couldn't quite put a finger on it. So she did as requested.

Brook took a deep breath and said, "My husband and I have been separated for almost a year and—"

"He cheated," Ella said, interrupting her.

"Yeah. How'd you know?"

"Go on, baby."

"Well, I really thought my husband Walter and I would be together forever. I said that in my vows. But I caught him red-handed. It hurt so much."

If Brook was really paying attention, she would have noticed how completely disinterested Ella was with the Walter part of the story.

"The separation proceedings didn't go as badly as I thought they would. Walter was more than generous, offering to buy my half of our business."

There was more disinterest from Ella.

"I guess the hurtful thing about it all was that in my heart I thought Walter was the one. When I found out that he was unfaithful, I guess I sort of lost faith in love."

"I see!" Ella blurted out. "This new man, you're not sure if you can trust him."

231

"Jeff?"

"Yes. Tell me about him. Tell me about Jeff."

Ella's smile slowly returned. Brook should have been troubled. But perhaps it was something someone said once. She couldn't quite place why she would even open up to a stranger in this way.

"Jeff is great. But that's just the thing. He's too great. I mean he says all the right things, makes all the right moves."

"Go on," Ella beckoned as she slid closer to Brook.

Brook whispered, "We've sort of been dating for as long as I've been separated. And he has not once made a move on me."

Ella tapped her index finger on her chin.

"Interesting," she said.

Brook continued on to say, "It's almost like he's—

"Perfect?" Ella completed her sentence and a chill shot up Brook's spine. "What's so wrong with that, baby?"

"Nobody's perfect," Brook replied matter-of-factly.

Ella fanned the air in disgust and exclaimed, "I hate when people say that!"

Brook leaned back and carefully measured her. Then she remembered it was Ma Geneva that said the saying, yet she couldn't remember the saying itself.

Ella continued.

"If people couldn't be perfect then why does the Bible say 'Be ye perfect'? You see, people have the wrong idea of perfection. It's not about drawing the perfect straight line or never making mistakes."

What was that saying, Brook thought to herself.

"Tell me more about Jeff," Ella requested.

"He's a good man and I think he was the one that got away. But he's so perfect that I feel like he's too good to be true. I guess I don't want to be hurt again, you know."

Brook laid everything out and it hit her all at once. She remembered the saying. 'Be not forgetful to entertain strangers: for thereby some have entertained angels unawares.' Ma Geneva quoted that scripture all the time. Is that why she felt so comfortable talking with Ella. Was she an angel?

"Snorrr. Snort. Snorrr."

Brook looked over to see Ella with her eyes closed and her mouth wide open. Her angel was sleeping.

"Can I get anything for you ma'am?" the flight attendant asked, catching Brook off guard.

"Nothing for me. But my friend may need a pillow."

Brook spent the rest of the flight thinking deeply about Jeff and how things seemed to just fall right into place for the two of them. Maybe Jeff was perfect.

Finally Brook's bag came around the luggage carousel. She thought about her encounter with Miss Ella, the elderly woman who smiled incessantly. She thought about what she said to her as they parted ways. First she apologized for falling asleep on her, blaming that on a narcoleptic condition she suffered from.

Then she said, "I'm praying for you and your Jeff. I sense a special anointing on your relationship."

As Brook reached for her bag, she heard a deep and rich baritone voice say to her, "Let me get that, Shawty." It was Jeff. He was right on time.

They embraced and gave one another light kisses on the cheek. With bag in left hand and Brook's hand in right, Jeff asked, "Do you have everything you need?"

Brook looked up at him, smiled, and said, "Yes. I do now."

Chapter 35

The sun was setting before Brook and Jeff finally made it to his neighborhood on Lake Minnetonka. Brook was so excited to be in Minneapolis when she touched down that she immediately wanted to sightsee. Jeff was more than happy to play tour guide.

He took Brook to downtown Minneapolis, where he showed her First Avenue and 7th Street, the club that Prince made famous. From there, he took her to the University of Minnesota, where the terrain was draped in maroon and gold and the streets were printed with golden gopher paws. He showed here where the mighty Mississippi river ran free. It was the first time Brook had seen the majestic river. She was somewhat amazed by the sheer force of its flow as she looked toward the south of it, recognizing that this body of water connected the Great Lakes to the Gulf.

They ate dinner at Su Yings, an authentic Chinese eatery which, Jeff attested, served the best sesame chicken in the world. Later they drove out to Bloomington to Mall of America. Jeff convinced Brook to ride the Brain Surge and she screamed for dear life from the first spin until the ride stopped. She screamed, she laughed, and she smiled. Jeff was content to be the one who made Brook's eyes light up.

When the two finally made it to Lake Minnetonka, the sky was dim, but lent enough light for Brook to see the immaculate homes that sat comfortably on the golf course community that surrounded the lake. A family of egrets greeted them as they entered a gated area of the community.

"You're doing pretty nice for yourself, player," Brook said, thoroughly impressed by the surroundings.

"It's pretty nice here. A few of my teammates bought homes out here too. It's nice and chill, you know."

The day had gone perfectly, as most days went when Brook spent them with Jeff. It seemed like the sun always shined, the stars enjoyed the pleasure of cloudless skies and it never rained at all. Brook began to wonder to herself, I think all of the traffic lights have been green for us the entire day.

Just then, the heavens opened and rain began pouring in thick sheets. Brook could barely see the road in front of her. I guess he's not Mr. Perfect after all, she thought. Or was he?

"Here we are," Jeff said and before he made the turn, his drive way was illuminated with blue halogen lights on both sides. It was like a runway, the lights exposing a crystal clear path to his house. Brook marveled at the two-story brick structure that was unlike any home she had ever seen.

The rain poured down even harder. Brook was prepared to make a run for it into the house, but with a push of a button, what appeared to be a large tinted glass window opened up and Jeff guided his Benz right inside. Now Brook was undone. Jeff put the car in park and opened his door.

"I'll get your things," he said with a smile. Brook got out of the car and watched as the solid glass garage door slowly closed. Before, she could hear large claps of thunder. She could hear blankets of rain crashing to the asphalt. But as soon as that glass garage door closed, it was as if the rain continued harshly, but only at a whisper. Brook gazed at Jeff, who in perfect form, made no big deal of it at all.

***

It wasn't long before Jeff had Brook bent over on his kitchen table. She was bent over laughing at the comment he made. The two were about to play spades. And when Brook counted the cards and noticed that the queen of hearts was missing, Jeff said, "The queen of hearts isn't missing." He pointed at her with a serious gaze and said, "There she is. You're the queen of my heart."

They both looked at each other silently at first. Then all at once, Brook broke out into a fit of laughter, kicking and screaming and eventually ending up doubled over on the kitchen table.

"Are you done laughing?" Jeff asked.

"Ha ha! He he!"

"Are you? Are you done?"

Brook continued laughing vehemently.

"I was being sentimental. Or I thought I was, at least."

"Come on now," she said as she caught her breath. "You have to admit that was corny."

Jeff looked away, smiled, and said, "Yeah. Maybe a little—I guess I slipped up on my pimping."

"Yeah, you slipped up."

Brook grinned as she began dealing the cards. Then she said, almost at a whisper, "I was beginning to think you were Mr. Perfect or something."

"What?"

She paused. Looked up at Jeff through her lashes and licked her lips. Rolling her eyes, she attempted to dismiss the statement.

"What were you saying, Brook?"

She placed the deck on the table. She gazed at Jeff, taking measurements of how she should proceed.

"Okay. It's like you're squeaky clean. You always say the right things, give the correct responses."

Brook dropped her gaze and paused.

"Go on," Jeff requested.

She tugged and twirled her pony tail, a sure sign of her nervousness.

"I mean we've been talking for several months now. You haven't put me in a position to have to turn you down."

"Oh. I see where this is going."

"You've been a boy scout, on your best behavior. Even when we kiss, you only go so far. It's not like I haven't wanted it. Because I have."

"No doubt."

"And then there's this long distance thing that we have. I mean—no man is that strong."

"Brook, make it plain."

"You want me to break it down for you?"

"Yes ma'am, I do."

"Alright then. You are a big time NFL star. You have this splendid house. You're up here all on your own. I know you have needs. I know that you wouldn't have a problem getting your needs met by any woman. And with me not here—"

"Come here." Jeff pulled his chair out and patted his lap. "Please?"

She hesitated at first, uncertain about whether or not she wanted to know, yet certain that it was what she needed. She eased her petite frame into Jeff's lap, her soft hips resting safely on his massive quadriceps.

She looked into his eyes and asked, "Jeff is there someone else? Tell me. I can take it. I'm a big girl."

He sighed. Planted a soft and gentle kiss on her forehead and brought her closer to him. He didn't mention the fact that her insecurities stemmed from her past relationship. He didn't say she was wrong to think that of him. He never said that he wasn't like most men. Nor did he tell her that she had nothing to worry about. Instead, he asked Brook a series of questions.

"Do you know when I bought this house?"

She paused for a moment then said, "When you were traded from Atlanta?"

"No. I bought this house a week after you and I visited Reedy River Falls; after our first date. Do you want to know why I bought this house?" She was motionless, quiet, giving him all of her attention. "Back in the day, and I mean way back, like in the days of Mary and Joseph, when a man found a woman that he wanted to wife, he'd first go to the woman's father and ask for her hand in marriage. Then he'd build or buy a home for her. So just like Joseph would have for Mary, I asked your heavenly father for your hand and he said yes. Then I bought this house for you. We're doing this the right way. It's way more than just a physical thing. This is spiritual."

He brought her lips to his and what began as a gentle kiss elevated to a passionate impartation, as tongues touched, danced even. Brook's cell phone rang but neither heard it. The kiss had them. Passion possessed them. It seemed as if the kiss would last forever. But just as she knew he would, Jeff stopped before the heat became unbearable. Their relationship was spiritual, between him, her, and God. No other woman to worry about.

***

Later that evening, Brook rested alone on the king size sleigh bed that would be theirs, a bed that no one had ever slept on. Jeff had divulged so much to her. He bought the house for her. They would be married.

Momentarily, she wondered why Jeff hadn't proposed. But then she realized that he couldn't do that now. She was still married to Walter. In that instant she realized two things: Jeff *was* Mr. Perfect and it was time to formally end things with Walter.

She reached for her cell phone. Simultaneously it rang. It was Dawn on the other end. "Brook. Where are you?" she yelled.

"I'm in Minneapolis, remember? Where are you? What's all that loud music?"

"I'm at a jazz club. On a date."

"Didn't know Cory liked jazz."

"I'm not with Cory. I'm with Joe."

"Joe? The man that cuts your grass?"

"Yep."

"What about Cory?"

"What about him?"

"Ooh!"

"I'm tired of waiting around the house for Cory. He's doing his thing. I'm doing my thing."

"Dawn, you need to be careful."

"Brook, I need this, you know. And Joe is so nice."

"Umm Dawn. Joe's not trimming your special bushes, is he?"

"No!" Dawn answered. "I really like him."

"That license thing was nice," Brook replied.

"You see? I'm really having fun. It's been a while since I had fun."

"You sure he's not trimming your special bushes?"

"No!" Dawn said with a giggle. "It's nothing like that, big sis."

"Well you sound like you're having fun."

"But that's not why I called. Have you talked to Karen? She said she tried to call you."

Brook checked her phone.

"Yeah. I see she called. What's up?"

"Oh nothing much. Just a November wedding."

"Oh okay...What?"

They both screamed in unison.

Dawn caught her breath and said, "She just called me. I'm so excited for her. She wants us to be in the wedding."

"But of course," Brook replied. Then she was silent for a moment.

"Um, Dawn. Do you think she called..."

"Cicely? I don't know. What do you think?"

The answer to that question was no. Cicely definitely would have seen the call because she had been staring at her touch screen the entire evening. She had been waiting at the restaurant for an hour, sitting alone at the bar turning down men who made advances as well as drink offers from the bartender. She alternated between her touch screen and the flickering flames from the candles, waiting on Vincent to call. It seemed as if he kept her waiting a lot lately.

Vincent finally bopped into the restaurant, lighting up the scene with his smile. Cicely's eyes bore holes through the air; her glare was full of hostility. He ignored it. He did a lot of that lately as well.

Vincent greeted the hostess with a little too much friendliness, kissing her on the cheek as he stared at Cicely from across the room. Though he was an hour late, he still took his sweet time making it to the bar where she sat. She rolled her eyes but Vincent was immune to that.

"You're late!" Cicely's words were cold and laced with attitude. It didn't matter to Vincent one way or the other at that point.

"No. You were early," he replied with a smile and without missing a beat, he ordered himself a gin and tonic. "Yeah and let me get a Cosmo for the lady."

"No thank you," she interjected. "Another orange juice will be fine."

Vincent gave a strange look. Cicely quickly countered with a smile.

"I'm really looking forward to Cozumel," she said speaking of the quarterly company retreat. Vincent coughed loudly and then immediately downed his drink. "I bought this hot little number that shows off all of my curves. I can't wait until you see it."

Vincent glared at Cicely through the bottom of his glass.

"I've been meaning to talk to you about that," he said. "The Saint Francis account in Charleston needs some real attention. I'm thinking a face to face meeting with my star salesperson."

"Yeah. But what does that have to do with Cozumel?"

"The CIO is extremely busy. I scheduled a meeting with him, but he could only meet the week we're in Mexico. So I need you. That's a $2 million account and to be honest, we need to close it."

Cicely's look was a mixture of pouting and frustration.

"But Vincent, we have spent zero time together in the last few weeks. I was looking forward to Cozumel. I mean, I know that..."

"You know that my family life is keeping me busy. My oldest boy is a shoo-in for Florida next year. My youngest is not far behind him."

"And then there's Heather," Cicely said, rolling her eyes as that name rolled off of her tongue.

Vincent pressed forward. "Yes, Heather. My wife. You keep forgetting that I am still married."

Frustration began to settle into his countenance. "Look Cicely, here's the bottom line. We need this account. You're my best closer. The only time the CIO can meet with us is during the week of the Cozumel retreat. If you close this account, you *will* be rewarded."

Cicely sat motionless, her arms folded. Vincent finished his drink and motioned for the bartender. Sliding the bartender a crisp fifty dollar bill he said, "I've have to get going. Kelly has all of your travel arrangements squared away."

"I thought we were having dinner tonight. I thought we were spending the evening together."

"Cicely, I need you sharp for Charleston. We need that account." He stood to his feet and continued. "Take a few days to prepare and then go make us that $2 million."

He landed a cold kiss on her cheek. Then he turned to walk away with no 'I love you' at all. That hurt Cicely deeply. But just as she was about to release her tears, Vincent stopped and returned to her. She smiled, expecting a salutation of warmth from the man she adored. But instead of telling Cicely that he loved her, he said, "Did you take care of that thing we talked about?"

He spoke of the abortion.

All expression left Cicely's face.

"Yes. I took care of it."

"Good," he replied. And then he was off.

Cicely was exploding inside, unable to contain herself. She ran from the bar to the ladies room, collapsing in an empty stall, weighed down by her burdens. She was there, where Mr. Inman warned her never to return, in bondage, a slave to a man.

Nausea overwhelmed her. Her muscles tightened and her jaws tingled. And then suddenly, and violently, Cicely heaved chunks of her lunch into the commode. Water splashed into her face as she gripped the porcelain. Her stomach hurt from the intensity of her retching. And she rested on the floor of that bathroom stall, feeling dead inside.

Chapter 36

"Walter, we're separated. There's no reconciling what we had. I want to move forward with the divorce."

Brook had been rehearsing the words she would eventually say to Walter ever since she ended the call with Dawn. The evening she had shared with Jeff, the words he spoke to her, supported what she had been feeling for some time. She was ready to move on.

Brook was finally satisfied with the words that she had chosen. Her aim was to be straight and to the point. She wouldn't mention Jeff at all. Not mentioning Jeff would avoid any emotional uprising from Walter and lend to a smooth exit out of their mistake of a marriage. After all, Walter probably wanted to move on just as badly as Brook. He could then legally be with his mistress, the stunningly beautiful model that Brook saw in the photos.

It was about ten in the evening. Brook decided to make the phone call outside. The fresh air would calm her. She also wanted to avoid the chance of Jeff overhearing the conversation.

A set of glass doors led from what was to be Brook and Jeff's master suite to a balcony that overlooked the lake. She draped her housecoat over her shoulders, grabbed her cell phone, and stepped out to the balcony. The view was incredible. She could see the moon's reflection on the dark waters of the lake. The stars were like millions of candles that ornamented the surface of the water. The scenery took her breath away. Brook could only smile as she dialed Walter's number. Soon she would share this view with Jeff; the view and so much more.

"Um, hello?"

The phone barely rang once before Brook heard Walter's raspy voice.

"Walter? This is Brook."

There was silence on the other end. That was good for Brook. It meant that he was trying to hush his mistress; he had definitely moved on.

"Am I interrupting something?" Brook asked. There was still silence. "Walter, it's okay if you're with her. I'm cool with that."

"I'm not with her—I mean—well I'm alone now."

Not good. Brook needed a clean get away. The mistress was essential to that plan.

"What? Did she leave you?"

Silence owned the next few moments until Walter replied, "Yeah."

Darn it! Brook thought to herself. The conversation was not going as planned. Nevertheless, she pressed forward.

"Walter, I actually need to discuss something with you."

He sniffled. "Yeah?"

"I would like to proceed with the divorce."

"No."

"Excuse me?"

"No divorce."

Agitated, Brook began to light into Walter.

"No? You broke your vows. You made a fool of me. And you have the nerve to say no?"

"Brook," Walter said with exasperation. "We need to talk, face to face, as soon as possible."

Chapter 37

For Dawn, that evening was the eve of sweet ecstasy. Dancing slowly on the parquet floor at Club Trio. The music of Juan Pablo Torres oozing from overhead speakers. Her body, warmed by strong arms. She was high on a drug called Joe. Eased by a euphoria that was so foreign to her. They danced and she thought about their moment. Their bodies melting into a mixture. That touch that sent chills up her spine. For the first time in a long time she wasn't lonely. And she did not want to be alone.

She said, "Spend the night with me."

Joe looked down into Dawn's big brown eyes, mystified by her beauty. And thirty minutes later, though he knew he shouldn't have, that regret would undoubtedly join him for breakfast, he found himself following Dawn into her bedroom. He found himself lying with her. Boundaries were crossed. As they rested together, bare fleshed on disheveled sheets, Joe looked deeply into his lover's eyes and said, "I love you."

To which she replied, "And I love you."

And as the music ceased and flickering flames melted candle wax to wick, Joe and Dawn curled up next to each other and lent themselves to a deep sleep.

***

"Dawn."

It was the gentle whisper of her name that roused her. Without doubt it was Joe, waking his lover, wanting more of her. However, she opened her eyes and saw that Joe was still asleep, still snoring.

"DAWN!"

245

That was a scream. And it definitely didn't come from Joe.

It was Cory, the father of Dawn's baby.

He hovered over them, his eyes red with anger, his teeth clinched, his nine-millimeter pistol pointed directly at Joe's head. Dawn jumped up.

"Cory, please don't!"

BANG!

Joe's blood was everywhere, on the sheets, splattered across Dawn's face. She couldn't scream. Cory pointed the gun at her head and Dawn closed her eyes tightly. She braced herself for the impact and then the phone rang.

She opened her eyes. The room was dark, cold, and quiet. And they were all alone. Joe being shot was all a dream.

He didn't even budge when his cell phone rang again. He continued snoring even louder.

"Joe, your cell phone. Joe!"

Finally, he rustled from his slumber. Still bare, he reached down to the floor to pick up his cellular. Grogginess consumed him.

"Um—hello?"

"Jose! Jose, where are you?"

The frantic voice on the other side of the receiver was Aunt Maria. Joe could barely make out what she was saying because of her panic. He looked at the clock and saw that it was a little past three in the morning. Phone calls at that time of morning are rarely good.

"Jose! Joe, I've been trying to reach you! I called your house three times, no answer. Where are you?"

"I'm at...um..."

"Joe. It's your cousin!"

Aunt Maria continued in Spanish, her panic not allowing the proper words to come fast enough in English. She spoke of her son, Charlie.

246

"Joe, he's been shot! He's in bad shape. He may not make it. You have to come now!"

***

It wasn't long before Joe and Dawn made it to the emergency room at Greenville Memorial Hospital, where they met Joe's family, all with somber looks on their faces. Aunt Maria trembled, her eyes bloodshot red from crying.

"He's gone, Joe! Oh my God. He's gone!"

He took her hand and brought her into an embrace. He began sobbing fitfully, still in shock from the news. He needed to see him, even if for one last time. So Joe walked into the room where Charlie's remains lay. It was dim and quiet, the respirators and regulators long turned off. Charlie's head was bandaged. Dark brown liquid lined the surface of white bandages. Joe touched the side of his face. Strangely, it was still warm to the touch.

Joe thought about what Aunt Maria had told him when he asked her what had happened. Charlie was spending the night with one of their clients, a wealthy woman whose husband was usually away on business; however, the husband was not away the previous night. Charlie never saw him come into the bedroom, never saw the .38 caliber pistol, never heard the shot.

***

It was ten o'clock by the time Joe and Dawn returned to her home in Easley. Joe was quiet the entire trip. Dawn didn't know quite what to say so she shared in his stillness. He pulled into the driveway but he didn't shut off his engine, neither did he put the truck in park. He only stared straight ahead at the immensely beautiful home that stood before him.

"Joe—are you coming in?"

He continued staring at the house, the house where he had just spent the night, a house that wasn't his.

"Joe?"

"What is this, Dawn? What are we doing here?"

"What do you mean?"

"What am I to you?"

"You know what you are to me. You're my lover."

That answer made Joe gulp and hang his head. He looked at the house and then back at Dawn.

"Whose house is that?"

She rolled her eyes and sighed. "It's my house. Why are you asking me that?"

"And what is it that you do for a living again?"

Dawn paused, measuring her response. "I was with the father of my baby. He purchased this house for us. We aren't together anymore."

"Are you sure about that?"

"Yes I'm sure."

"Dawn, keep it real with me. What man buys a home for someone that they're not with, and continues to pay all of the bills, even the lawn care bill?"

"Joe. Where is all of this coming from?"

"My cousin got his brains blown out last night because he was sleeping in another man's house, because he was in another man's bed, with another man's wife. Charlie never saw it coming. Boom! He's not here anymore. How long is it going to be before that happens to me?"

"That's not going to happen because that house is mine. And I'm not leaving my house for Brook, my mother *or* you!"

For the next few moments, only the hum of the truck's engine could be heard.

"Dawn, I think we need to cool it."

"What?"

"Get out of the truck."

"No, Joe. I want you to come in the house with me. You don't need to be alone right now."

"Dawn, please just go."

She folded her arms and sat stiffly in her seat.

"I'm not going anywhere."

"GET OUT!"

Shock hit her initially. Anger quickly followed as she gathered her things in haste and got out of the truck. The passenger door of Joe's F-150 wasn't even closed before he backed out of the driveway. Dawn threw her hands up and stomped into her house, angrier than she had been in a long time.

***

Dawn walked through the rooms of the spacious four bedroom house that Cory had bought for her. She walked through the living room, through the family room, through the kitchen. She walked up stairs, traveling in and out of every bedroom, through the bonus room. She needed to process the events of the previous evening. She asked herself why everyone was so eager for her to give up everything she worked so hard for. The house was hers. The car was hers. She had earned them.

Her deep reverie was interrupted by the sound of the doorbell.

"Joe," she said. It had to be Joe. He had come back so they could work things out.

Dawn raced down the steps. She was so ready to jump into Joe's arms. To kiss him, comfort him in his time of need. She didn't bother checking herself out in the mirror. She didn't concern herself with fronting, with hiding her smile to protect her feelings. Clothed in humility and vulnerability, she opened her front door.

"Nina?"

Nina stood in the doorway. Nina was the other woman in Cory's life.

"Hello, Dawn. Well, are you going to invite me in or what?"

Dawn's heart raced within her. However, she mustered all of the strength she could and calmly allowed Nina to enter her home.

Nina's feet hit the hardwood floors hard, her stiletto heels clicking with each step. She looked around the house from the foyer, her eyebrows raised, her mouth curled downward.

"I'm impressed. You've done a nice job decorating the place."

"Thank you," Dawn replied with sarcasm. She was shocked that Nina took great liberty to roam the floors of her home.

"Um, Dawn. Is there someplace we can sit and talk?"

"I guess. Right this way."

Dawn led Nina into the family room and asked her to have a seat on the couch. Surrealism painted the entire scene. Dawn was in the same space with Nina, her archenemy. Nina sitting beside her like nothing had ever transpired between them.

"Dawn, I'm going to get right to the point. I'm sure you've heard by now that our family has grown, is growing, with the birth of my son, Cory's *first born son.*"

Dawn could feel her blood pressure rising as Nina continued.

"And because our family is growing, we've decided that we need a bigger home. I told Cory, and I think this is a wonderful idea, that instead of going out and buying a house, we could just move into the house we already own. This house."

"Excuse me?"

"Now Dawn, I know that you have a little temper problem. But let's be grown-ups about this. It's no secret that Cory has several women. We are not the only ones. But I have always been, and will always be his number one."

250

"Uh, Nina. I think you better leave now, before someone gets hurt."

"Dawn, call him. Call Cory right now and see if this isn't what he wants. You can use my phone."

Dawn rolled her eyes and pulled herself from the couch. She really wanted to do battle, but instead she chose the high road. She went into the kitchen, picked up the cordless phone, and dialed Cory's number.

"Cory?"

"Yeah. What up?"

"Why is this tramp in my house?"

"Dawn, what are you talking about?"

"Nina. She is here talking about moving in here."

"What? Put her on the phone."

With class, Dawn carried the cordless phone to Nina, who greeted her with a smirk.

"Hello?" Nina said as she put the receiver to her mouth.

Cory lit in to her. Dawn could hear the cursing, the yelling, the B-word. Cory spared nothing. Dawn was pleased. He was putting Nina in her place.

"Now put Dawn back on the phone!"

Nina gave the phone back to her.

"Here you go."

Dawn was happy that Cory cursed that tramp out; however, she was puzzled because that tramp was still smiling.

Cory said, "Look Dawn. You weren't supposed to find out like that. But listen, man, we need the extra room. And since I'm not in the game anymore, money isn't as fast. We need the space. Now I can put you and Tarsha in an apartment for now."

Dawn hung up the phone.

Nina said, "We need to do this as soon as possible. I know there are a few openings in the projects so you need to jump on that."

She would have said more. But before she knew it, Dawn smashed the cordless phone against the side of her head. Nina dropped to the floor and the phone broke into several pieces. Dawn had no idea that she had that in her, no idea that she had hit Nina hard enough to knock her out.

"Ma'am you have the right to remain silent."

Dawn never saw the cops who stood in the doorway. Never realized that Nina had the Sheriff's office accompany her to the house. But there she was, being escorted by Sheriff's deputies down the driveway in handcuffs, being led to a squad car and away from her house.

Chapter 38

The scene was Gladys Knight & Ron Winans' Chicken and Waffles. Brook caught the first flight out of Minneapolis/St. Paul to see her estranged husband, Walter.

"I'm glad that you came to see me so fast, Brook. I really appreciate you coming."

Brook was not in the mood for small talk.

"Here we are, Walter. Face to face. I want a divorce."

"Um...can we take this slow? You owe me that."

"Owe you? You cheated on me!"

"Why did you have me pick you up from the airport?" Walter asked. "The drive from Greenville to Atlanta is only two hours long. But you weren't coming from Greenville were you?"

"No I was *not* coming from Greenville. I flew in from Minneapolis."

"Who were you with?"

"I was with Jeff."

"Your boyfriend Jeff?"

"Yes my boyfriend Jeff!"

"Funny. Last I checked you were still married to me."

"I cannot believe you."

Brook grabbed her bag and would have rushed out of the restaurant, but Walter's grasp prevented her.

"Brook! I need you!"

She stood frozen. A small scene was starting to form with patrons at neighboring tables watching closely. A greeter made his way to their table.

"Is everything okay, ma'am?"

Brook looked down into Walter's eyes and saw something in them that she had never seen before. Desperation.

"Y-y-yes. Everything is fine."

Brook took her seat. She noticed that Walter was shaking.

"Walter."

His shaking increased. Brook could see that he was coming undone.

"Walter. Talk to me. What's wrong?"

"I'm sorry, Brook. I'm so sorry."

"What's wrong, Walter?"

"I can't grant you a divorce."

"Why can't we get a divorce, Walter?"

The silence was deafening. As patrons enjoyed crispy fried chicken, macaroni-n-cheese, and succulent waffles, Brook sat across from her estranged husband, waiting for his response.

Chapter 39

Kelly Reagan was a five-foot seven inch beauty of mulatto origin. Brown freckles were lightly sprayed across the bridge of her nose. Her hair was red; however, she had started highlighting with blonde streaks a few months before she accepted a position as Administrative Assistant to Vincent Mann at Mann Information Systems.

Cicely enjoyed chatting with Kelly. She enjoyed her spirit. Indeed she often reminded her of Karen.

Karen.

Cicely thought a lot about her lately.

"You seem like something's troubling you, Ms. Shaw," Kelly said as Cicely stopped by her office.

"Just bummed out, you know. While everyone else is in Cozumel, I'll be in Charleston. Not too happy about that."

"Yeah. I feel real bad about giving you this, then."

Kelly passed the travel arrangements to Cicely.

"I know you have to go down there and handle business," Kelly said. "But I really wish that you could come to Mexico. We could kick it down there, you know. Have a girlfriend's excursion."

"Kelly. You are so sweet. You really remind me of..."

"Of who?"

Cicely paused for a moment; however, for her it seemed like an eternity. She thought about the last encounter she had with Karen, the male stripper and the phallic display. She thought about the beat down at Ma Geneva's house. She wasn't proud of any of it and it was weighing heavier and heavier on her with each passing day.

"Who do I remind you of, Ms. Shaw?"

"Someone I knew long ago."

"Like I said, I hate you can't make the trip to Mexico. So I threw in a few upgrades for the Charleston trip: first class seats all the way, presidential suite at the Charleston Inn, and a fully stocked mini-bar in your suite."

"Well, I don't know about the mini-bar, but for everything else, thanks so much."

Kelly smiled and continued.

"I know how Mr. Mann is cracking down on the extra stuff, but what he doesn't know won't hurt him."

"I know, right?"

Cicely's eyes watered slightly. She had been so emotional lately.

"Kelly, you are so sweet. I...I really appreciate it."

"We ladies have to stick together, you know."

"You're right. You are so right."

Cicely grabbed her briefcase and started toward the elevator.

"Well I better get going, Kelly. I have a plane to catch."

"Okay. See you in a week."

Cicely already had her bags packed. Her plan was to drive to the airport directly from the Mann building. But then her Blackberry buzzed.

"Hi. May I speak with Cicely Shaw, please?"

"I'm Cicely Shaw."

"Hi Ms. Shaw. My name is Winton Crosby and I'm the CIO here at Saint Francis."

"Oh hello, Mr. Crosby. I should be in Charleston later on tonight. I'll be staying at the Charleston Inn and I'll have a car bring me to the hospital in the morning."

"Yes Ms. Shaw. That's why I was calling you. I know this is short notice, but there's been a family emergency and I am actually leaving town tonight as well. I simply cannot meet with you tomorrow. As a matter of fact, I'll probably be gone until next week."

"O-Oh. I'm sorry to hear that."

256

"Look, we're going with Mann Information Systems. I mean, you have the contract. I'm sure we can iron out any of the points that Vincent wanted to deal with when I get back. I'm really sorry Ms. Shaw. But this really couldn't have been avoided."

"Okay, Mr. Crosby. I'll see you week after next."

"Great. I'll have my assistant schedule everything with you later. Have a good evening."

And then Crosby was gone. Cicely was excited. She could go to Cozumel after all. She could be with Vincent Mann.

She began going through her contacts to find Vincent Mann's name so that she could call him. She couldn't wait to tell him the good news; they had the $2 million contract. But more importantly, that she would be able to spend time with him in Mexico. Then Cicely had a better idea. She would trade in her upgrades for a flight to Cozumel. She would give Vincent the surprise of his life.

Chapter 40

20 McGee Street, Greenville, South Carolina. Greenvillians know that address well. Visitors can't help but see the large white building as they enter town from the south on Interstate 385. It is the County Detention Center or the McGee Street Inn, a place Dawn never thought she would visit. But there she was, in the intake area, making her first phone call. And even though it was Dawn that was in jail, her mother was the one who was hysterical. Dawn was surprisingly cool about the situation.

"Dawn Williams! I told you about your temper. 'Cool it, Dawn.' Didn't I say that to you?"

"Momma, they record these phone calls, you know."

"Well how much is your bail?"

"$100,000."

"Oh my goodness."

"But I only have to post $10,000."

"Oh my goodness."

"Momma, don't worry about it. I'm going to call Cory. I'll be out in a couple of hours."

"Cory? Are you in denial?"

"Not right now, Ma. How's Tarsha? Does she know where I am?"

"She's fine and no she doesn't."

"Good. Let's keep it that way."

"Dawn. I could ask Sue to lend me the money for your bail."

"Momma, Cory is going to bail me out."

"Dawn...baby..."

"I have to go, Ma."

Dawn disconnected the call. She didn't have much time and she needed to connect with Cory. Surely he would send his lawyer down with the bail.

She dialed Cory's cell. She waited, and waited, and waited. And then the call was disconnected.

"Ma'am, your time is up."

That statement came with coldness from a female guard.

"Just one more call. There had to be some technical difficulty. The call was never connected."

As Dawn made her reply, she redialed Cory's cell phone. She waited, and waited, and waited. And again, the call was disconnected. Dawn gently placed the phone back on the wall jack. She was confused.

"I'm trying to call my child's father so he can arrange bail, but the call won't go through. I tried twice."

"Ma'am, times up." Without any emotion, the guard took Dawn by the arm and guided her back to her cell.

The walk back to the holding cell was a long one. They passed the cell that held a woman that was accused of killing her three children with a hatchet. She passed by a cell that held a tall, muscular female with tattoos from head to toe. Dawn wondered if she was really a woman. Finally they reached Dawn's cell. It was the size of her linen closet. The guard opened the huge door.

"Step inside ma'am." With wintriness, the guard guided Dawn into the cell. And through emotionless eyes, she looked at Dawn and said, "There were no technical difficulties with the phone. You know that right?"

And then the door slammed shut in front of Dawn's face. The guard was right. Cory chose not to accept the collect call. Twice.

***

Three days had passed and Dawn was still sitting in her tiny jail cell. There was no word from Cory and more importantly no bail. Dawn broke down because the truth finally hit her in the face. And this was the truth: from day one, Dawn had been the mistress while Nina was the wife. It was a bitter pill for her to swallow, but swallow it she did. And instead of being sad about Cory or the house in Easley, Dawn was unhappy because she had lost Joe.

Three days had passed since the beginning of her incarceration, her incubation. Indeed concrete walls became her cocoon. And three days after she entered her cocoon, she heard the large latch on the massive metal door swing back. It was the emotionless guard.

"Dawn Williams, you made bail."

Dawn never really considered who posted her bail. Her mother, against her wishes, must have borrowed the money from Aunt Sue. She knew it wasn't Cory. It definitely wasn't Cory. When she made it to the front gate she was extremely surprised to see who had picked her up.

"Karen?"

"Hi, cousin."

Karen was a sight for sore eyes.

Long after hugs were exchanged, after tears fell mutually, the two cousins found themselves on Interstate 385 on their way to Fountain Inn. They used the drive time to catch up. Karen informed Dawn that she had come to the upstate to visit her cousins and aunt when she found out about her arrest.

"Karen, I really appreciate you bailing me out. My mother doesn't have the money and I didn't want her to borrow it from Aunt Sue." Karen didn't respond in any way. "Don't worry. I'm going to pay you back. Ouch!"

Dawn rubbed her chest as if she were suffering from heartburn.

"So have you talked to Brook?" Karen asked, quickly changing the subject.

"Nope. Not yet. Not quite ready for the lecture. Besides, Brook's in Minnesota visiting her boyfriend,

Jeff. I don't want to disturb her with my drama. Ouch! What's going on with my chest?"

"Are you alright?"

"Yeah, I guess it's just heartburn from that horrible jail house food."

"It's a trip that Brook ended up with old school Jeff Blitzer," Karen said.

"I know. All I think about is how we played spades in Ma Geneva's living room. Who knew?"

"Fate if I ever seen it."

"Yep."

The next few minutes were held by silence.

Fate.

Dawn began thinking about how she had acted so foolishly. She wished that she could have replayed the events three days prior. Perhaps she would not be in so much trouble. Maybe she would still have Joe.

"Karen, I've really screwed things up. I've been blind for so long. I lost my freedom. I lost Joe."

"I don't know, Dawn. Joe seemed to be a pretty understanding guy...you know...from how you describe him."

"He's a wonderful man. I was too blind to see it, holding on to a life built on falsehood. I was a fool."

"Don't be so hard on yourself. Everybody makes mistakes."

"Yeah everybody but you."

"Ha! That's a good one."

"Now, I'm not hating or anything like that. But you have done it the right way. No drama. And saving yourself for marriage, do you know how much drama you avoided by doing that?"

Then Dawn cut a sly look in Karen's direction.

"Yeah you're Miss Perfect. But I know one thing."

"First of all, I'm not perfect," Karen said as she snapped her fingers. "Second of all, what do you know?"

"I know why you're getting married in a month. Because you can't hold out any longer."

Karen laughed. "True. True. Sometimes I want to jump William's bones. I cannot wait to get me some!"

"Ooh. There *is* a freak in there."

"You know it!"

Dawn was teary-eyed with laughter. She wiped the tears from her eyes and said, "This is good, Karen. I missed this. You, me, Brook...Cicely."

Karen's smile disappeared.

Dawn read Karen's expression perfectly and shot her a look of shyness and guilt.

"Um Karen, did you by chance tell Cicely that you're getting married?"

"I haven't spoken to Cicely since Brook's bachelorette party."

Dawn looked away and allowed silence to settle for a moment, but only for a moment. Remorse rose within her. She said, "Karen, I'm sorry. But I told Cicely about your wedding the same night you told me."

More silence.

Karen shifted in her seat. Memories began to overtake her. Hurt resurfaced. Finally she said, "She probably wouldn't come anyway."

Seeing that the mood was somber, Dawn decided not to press the issue.

It wasn't long before Karen pulled into Helmsley Parkway, a Fountain Inn subdivision scattered with three bedroom ranch style homes, most over 30 years old.

She pulled into a badly cracked concrete driveway and into a modest carport where only an old dryer sat next to weather-worn cardboard boxes.

"I never thought I'd be back here," Dawn sighed, speaking of her mother's home.

"I have a confession to make."

Karen spoke those words as if something were eating her up inside.

"What's up?"

"I didn't put up the $10,000 for your bail."

"You didn't? Well who did? It *was* Aunt Sue, wasn't it?"

"No."

"Brook?"

"Not Brook either."

Dawn looked confused because she just knew that it was not Cory that put up the bail. "Who was it then?"

Karen replied, "Joe bailed you out."

Dawn felt that sharp sting in her chest again.

***

Nearly 150 miles away, in a plush condominium not far from downtown Atlanta, Dawn's twin sister Brook held her chest as well. It stung as if her heart was breaking.

Brook slowly made her way back up the steps as she headed for the master bedroom, a space that held so many memories for her, mostly memories of the love she made with Walter.

Walter was sleeping soundly, lying bare chested on top of extremely disheveled sheets. Brook was wearing one of his old tee shirts and nothing more. She sighed. It was time to handle her business.

She dialed Jeff's Blackberry. She was sure that he wouldn't answer since he would be on the practice field. As she waited for his prerecorded message to end, she cleared her throat and searched her heart for the right words to say.

"Jeff. I'm in Atlanta—I'm sorry that I had to rush off like that but—I don't know quite how to say this, so I'll just come right out with it. I can't see you anymore. I'm with Walter now. He's my husband and we're going to try to work things out between us. Please don't try to contact me in any way."

And then Brook ended the call, sat down on the bed, and had herself a good, long cry.

Chapter 41

"SURPRISE!" Cicely yelled at the top of her lungs as she entered Vincent's suite in Cozumel. She smelled sweet incense burning. Candles decorated the room. He must have known she was going to be able to make the trip after all.

She heard movement in the bathroom, water splashing.

"I'm coming, baby!" she yelled.

And then she began undressing herself on her way to where surely Vincent waited for her. However, it wasn't Vincent in the tub.

It was Kelly Reagan.

She was in the tub, covered in bubbles, staring right back at Cicely in disbelief.

Both gasped and simultaneously asked, "Where's Vincent?"

And then Cicely put two and two together. Her eyes reddened. Her blood boiled. She glared into Kelly's eyes, that sand colored complexion, that red hair with the blonde streaks.

She screamed, "How dare you, Karen!"

"Who's Karen?" Kelly replied in shock.

Cicely balled up her fists and began stomping towards the bathtub.

"I'm going to finish this once and for all," she snarled through clinched teeth.

Kelly cowered back as far as she could as Cicely tried to pull her out of the tub. Cicely's intent was to grab Kelly by her hair and fling her around the room until she snapped her neck. But just when Cicely got a good grip, Vincent rushed into the bathroom and grabbed her by her arm. His grip clamped tighter and tighter with each second, so much so that Cicely yelped as she buckled helplessly to the floor.

Veins bulged in the middle of Vincent's forehead.

"Kelly," he said calmly, "get out of the tub, go into the bedroom, and close the door behind you."

She hesitated and then replied, "But I'm naked."

"Now!" Vincent screamed at the top of his lungs. Kelly jumped out of the bathtub and raced into the bedroom, her backside jiggling as she ran.

As soon as the door slammed Vincent flung Cicely to the floor. She quickly regrouped and jumped to her feet. She had never backed down from a fight and she was certain that she was not going to start now.

"Don't put your hands on me like that again!" she roared. "Are you crazy?"

Cicely showed much fire. Vincent wasn't fazed in the least.

"Why are you here?" he yelled. "Why are you not in CHARLESTON?"

"BECAUSE CHARLESTON POSTPONED!" Cicely fired back, her fists balled tightly for battle. "Forget all that. Why are you cheating on me?"

"Cheating on you?" Vincent threw up his hands. "You know what? From this day forward, the physical portion of our relationship is over. It will be strictly business between us from here on out."

"What? Are you breaking up with me?"

"Keep your job. You can stay in the company house if you like. But we are done."

Cicely's disposition switched from anger to desperation in a split second.

"We can't be over, Vincent! We..."

Kelly Reagan tried to make out the rest of their conversation; however, their uproar eased to a whisper. She put her ear to the door, hoping to hear something, if anything. But they had gone so quiet. Kelly wondered if they were making love. But then...

BANG!

It sounded as if someone's head were slammed against the door. And indeed that's exactly what had

266

happened. Kelly backed away from the door, holding her ear to ease the stinging that resulted from the loud sound that she heard.

On the other side of the door Vincent had become somewhat of a monster. He wrapped his hands tightly around Cicely's neck as he continuously banged her head against the door.

"Please, Vincent," she pleaded.

But he wouldn't ease up. He choked her violently, causing her to scratch at the floor underneath her. She gasped, feigned a scream.

"Please, Vincent. Please don't kill me!"

Vincent released his grip, gathered her up, opened the bathroom door and threw her down on the floor so that she landed right at Kelly's feet.

"You're on your own! You hear me! You're fired. And I want you out of my house or else! Get out of here NOW!"

Vincent screamed at Cicely so harshly that spit flew from his mouth. And even though Cicely was furious that he choked her and repeatedly rammed her head into the door, she was too afraid of him to retaliate. For the first time in her life, she was frozen by fear and shame. So she hung her head in defeat as she lay on the floor at Kelly's feet.

Then Cicely looked up and eyed her nemesis. Shame turned to anger, fear to contempt. She glared at her mortal enemy, with her signature reddish brown hair and despicable blonde streaks. Revenge consumed her as she thought to herself, if I can't be happy, neither will she.

Chapter 42

Dawn felt weird waking up in the 10 by 10 bedroom in which she grew up. She spent the entire evening curled up next to her daughter in the same twin bed she'd had for as long as she could remember. By some standards, she had taken a great loss: losing her home, her truck, having to move back in with her mother. But to Dawn she saw the experience as a sort of liberation.

Even though she appreciated her situation and felt like she had lost nothing and gained everything, she still had an eerie feeling that something was horribly wrong. She was supremely somber and could not understand why at the time. However, she decided to shelve those feelings. She would have to get over it.

The smell of turkey bacon, grits, and scrambled eggs hovered above the cool air back to the bedroom. The scent of freshly brewed coffee presented itself as well. Dawn knew it was her mother's way of inviting her into the kitchen for a much needed and long overdue conversation.

"Good morning, Ma," she said as she walked into the kitchen.

"Good morning, baby."

Her mother had just finished putting breakfast on the table. She hummed some spiritual tune that Dawn had heard before, but for the life of her couldn't place the name. Dawn kissed her forehead and joined her at the table.

"How long have you been up?" Dawn asked.

"Since four-thirty in the morning."

"Oh my goodness."

"It's been two years since I retired from the plant. But I can't seem to shake the getting up early thing. I guess it's just programmed into my brain."

Dawn nodded and took a sip of her orange juice.

Diane hummed her tune a bit more and then asked, "So, how are you feeling?"

"Well, this may seem crazy, but jail may have been the best thing for me. It was a wakeup call. Not sure the blinders would've come off without it."

"Yeah, I can see that."

"I know my legal issues are far from over, but I think that I have been liberated. But to really answer your question about how I feel, I have to say that I feel lousy inside, depressed I guess. I don't really know how to explain it."

"Well, that should pass."

Diane sipped her coffee, peering over the rim of the cup at her youngest daughter. And then she asked, "Have you talked to Brook?"

Dawn took a deep breath.

"No ma'am. I'm really not ready for the 'I told you so' speech."

"Well I'm just going to tell you right now that Brook knows about you being arrested."

Dawn rolled her eyes. "Let me guess. You told her."

"Watch your eyes. And yes I did."

"What'd she say?"

"Nothing much. She sounded upset though."

"Oh boy!"

Silence settled momentarily. Then Dawn looked at her mom and asked, "Joe?"

"Yes, Joe. He came here as soon as he found out. He asked how much your bail was, stepped out for a while, and came back with a cashier's check. Karen was here by then. He told her not to mention him. I knew she would, though."

Then Diane crossed her legs and said, "Forget about all that. What are your plans now?"

Dawn didn't miss a beat with her answer.

"I'm going to go back to school, get a job doing accounting somewhere, save some cash for a car and

269

an apartment. You know, stand on my own two feet for once."

"Sounds like a plan."

Just then, they heard the front door knob turning back and forth. They both looked at each other.

"Are you expecting someone, Ma?"

"No."

They both jumped up and ran to the front door. Just when Dawn made it to the door, her fist balled up tightly for warfare, the door flung open. It was Brook.

Dawn held her heart and smiled.

"Oh Brook, you scared me. What are you doing here? I thought you were in Minneapolis."

But Brook just stood in the doorway, staring intensely at her. Dawn knew what this was about. The older sister had no doubt come home to give the younger a stern talking to. So Dawn waited for the inevitable. And she waited. And she waited. But Brook said nothing at all for what seemed like ages.

"Brook, are you okay?"

No answer. A trembling lip was Brook's only reply. Dawn moved closer and fortuitously so, because Brook collapsed into her arms as their mother looked on. Brook cried vehemently, sobbing so ferociously that her body jerked violently in Dawn's arms.

"What's the matter?"

But Brook couldn't answer. Dawn began crying herself. Their mother stood frozen with her hands over her mouth.

"Shhh. Shhh. Talk to me, sis."

And suddenly, Brook managed to form a coherent sentence.

"Walter's dead. He died last night...and I might...I...might..."

Dawn consoled her twin. Then Diane joined them on the floor and they all cried together.

***

It took a while for Brook to calm down enough to discuss at length the situation. But when she had calmed down, she joined her mother and sister at the kitchen table, all holding tissues, each wiping tears from their eyes. Brook explained it all to them.

"I took Walter to lunch so we could discuss moving forward with the divorce. That's when he lowered the boom. He told me that he had AIDS and that he didn't have long to live. Of course I didn't believe him. He looked fine to me.

"So he said that he was going to prove it. He took me to the house and showed me all the meds he was taking, the medical declaration. I was floored. I had no idea that he'd been sick. Then he started coughing real bad, I mean like he was going to cough up his lung or something. Well he might as well have done that. Because before I knew it, Walter was vomiting all over the place, all over himself and me.

"Then he said that he needed to rest. I snapped out of my shock long enough to get those nasty clothes off of us and I helped Walter into bed. But I flew from Minneapolis with no luggage. I had nothing to change into. So I put on one of Walter's old tee-shirts while the clothes were in the washer. When I got back upstairs, Walter was fast asleep. And he never woke up from that sleep."

Silence settled while Dawn and their mother digested the information. And then Dawn asked, "What about Jeff?"

"I broke up with him. There's no way we can be together now."

"But there's no guarantee that you have it. You should get tested so you'll know for sure."

"I DON'T WANNA KNOW!"

Brook screamed those words and startled Dawn and Diane.

271

"I let Jeff go. I'll be alone for the rest of my life—I don't want to know. Promise me you won't tell anyone about this."

They nodded and then Brook said, "I'm going to go to the back and lie down."

And then the house was quiet, too quiet for Dawn. She needed to get away for a while and blow off some steam. She needed to vent her frustrations. So she grabbed Brook's car keys and hit the door. There was unfinished business in Easley, business that she needed to handle once and for all.

***

It didn't take Dawn long to reach Easley at all. When she reached the house, she pulled into the driveway, shut off the engine, and took the keys out of the ignition. It wasn't her house but she didn't care. Things needed to be said that wouldn't wait another day.

She stepped out of the car and started walking toward the house. Butterflies did somersaults in the pit of her stomach. Her heart fluttered with anxiety because she had no idea how things were going to turn out.

And then came the moment of truth. Joe emerged from the backyard holding a weed eater. He had just finished edging the Emerson Family's yard and was heading for the riding mower.

They both stood in the driveway staring at each other for a while. Silent. Measuring the next moment. Joe removed his sunglasses, his light brown eyes dancing. He was the first to speak.

"How did you know where I'd be?"

"I didn't," Dawn replied. "I figured I'd ride around Easley until I found your truck."

A few seconds of silence followed, during which Dawn nervously looked around and fidgeted with her hands.

Then she mustered up enough courage to ask, "Why did you bail me out of jail?"

Joe sucked his teeth and replied, "You already know the answer to that question."

There was more silence.

"Well I'm going to pay you back, every single cent."

Joe didn't respond.

Dawn's nervousness waned little by little; yet she still struggled for the correct words to say. Joe decided to let her off the hook.

"Come here," he said and she followed him to the riding mower. "Hop on," he requested. Dawn acquiesced, sitting on the seat right in front of Joe, her hips nestled into the hollow of his thighs, such that he had to wrap his arms around her to reach the steering wheel. Joe started the mower and they were off, cutting a fresh path into the thick green grass ahead of them.

"This is a new mower," Dawn observed.

"Yeah. Top of the line. The Bentley of riding mowers."

"It's real quiet."

"Yeah. That's why I like it so much."

The more they rode, the more comfortable Dawn became. She felt good. She needed to talk to someone and Joe, as always, proved himself to be a good listener.

"There's trouble with the family, my sister mainly," Dawn confided.

"Oh yeah?"

"Yeah. Brook's husband died."

"Sorry to hear that."

"They weren't together. But there's extenuating circumstances. I can't get into it too much."

"No doubt. We'll just have to stay prayerful about the situation. It'll all work out."

"I hope so." The scent of cut grass was intoxicating. So effervescent. Behind them lay assaulted green blades who welcomed the mowing, needed it maybe. So they freshened the air to show their appreciation. "How are you and your family..." Dawn asked, "...losing Charlie and all?"

"Taking it one day at a time, you know. My Tia Maria is holding up as best she can. She asked about you, actually."

"Really?"

"Yeah. She decided that she needs to slow down a bit. She's looking for someone to do her books."

"Well, shoot, that's right up my alley."

"Cool. I'll let her know."

Dawn enjoyed their discourse, even the spaces inhabited by silence. She took a deep breath and said, "You know I'm going to pay you back, right?"

Joe didn't respond and Dawn accepted the fact that he just wasn't going to respond to that statement.

Then she rested the back of her head against his collar and asked, "It's not over between us, is it Joe?"

He curled the right side of his mouth into a smile, kissed Dawn's hair, and replied, "Mami, it will never be over between us."

Dawn smiled. She loved it when he called her *mami*.

Chapter 43

Immediately after a long and tedious day at the Department of Social Services, Karen would give William a call at the lab, if even just to alert him that she was off from work. That's just something she did and had done for quite some time. That particular cool autumn evening would be no different, not in respect to the day's end salutation. But other aspects of the evening would stray the loving couple far from their norm.

William answered on the first ring.

"Hey, honey," Karen said.

"What's going on, babe?" he replied.

Other pleasantries were exchanged, such as a brief synopsis of each other's day, how he would not be working late after all, how they had one more week before they exchanged vows before God and family. Somewhere in the conversation, William mentioned that he was checking into the Embassy Suites when he got off from work.

"Why is that?" Karen asked.

"Your memory is horrible. Remember, I closed on the condo sale this morning."

He continued, saying that his things were all moved into the new house that they were buying in Mount Pleasant.

Karen asked, "Why don't you just stay at the house?"

"Because I want us to move in at the same time after the honeymoon."

Karen's next suggestion triggered a chain of events that would change her life forever.

"Well, why don't you just stay at my apartment until the wedding?"

"Come again?"

"Embassy Suites for a week? That's a lot of money. Come and stay with me. You can sleep in the guest room."

William thought about it for a while and then he said, "Nah, I don't think that would be such a good idea."

"What, you don't trust yourself?"

"No, I don't trust you. I've seen how you've been looking at me lately."

Karen had to laugh.

"Oh you've noticed?" She growled like a lioness stalking her prey. "Come on William. I promise I won't bite you...too hard."

"See there?"

"No seriously. We've come this far. We'll be fine if you stay at my place. I promise."

After giving the idea some thought, William replied, "Alright then. I'll see you in a few."

"Great," Karen said, totally unaware of what lay ahead.

***

The hour that followed was uneventful. Karen called William to see if he was cool with spaghetti with meat sauce and salad. Of course he was. He informed her that he was on his way and she replied that she couldn't wait to see him. She looked forward to seeing him. She always did.

Karen was shocked to hear her doorbell ring just five minutes after she last spoke to William on the phone.

That was fast, she thought. Then she wondered why he didn't just let himself in, considering he had a key. Nevertheless, she approached her front door, smiling from ear to ear.

"Hi honey!" she exclaimed with eyes closed and arms open wide.

"Cousin!"

Karen opened her eyes to see Cicely standing in her doorway with her arms opened wide. The next thing Karen knew, she was being embraced by the woman who hated her guts.

***

William smelled the savory scent of spaghetti before he even opened the front door.

"Mm mmm!" he said to himself. Opening the door, he was met by Karen. "Baby, you've got it smelling good in here. And I am hungry, too."

He spoke those words, quickly kissed Karen, and rushed past her toward the kitchen.

"Um, William..." Karen called softy. She was trying to catch him before he stepped in, but his hunger rushed him past her. He didn't even see Cicely sitting in the living room.

"Hello," Cicely said as she rose from her seat.

William stopped short. He smiled and then looked at Karen.

"Um...this is my cousin, Cicely. Cicely, this is my fiancé, Dr. William Ward."

William offered his hand and smiled.

"Oh, okay. Nice to finally meet you. I've heard so much about you."

"I'm sure you have," Cicely replied.

"So, I see that Karen told you about our wedding." Cicely gave a sly glance to Karen, but it was so quick that neither she nor William saw it. "I'm so glad you could make it," William went on to say, "but, um, you're a whole week early."

Cicely placed her hand in William's and responded, "Well I'm here on business. So I decided to kill two birds with one stone."

Cicely gave Karen another sly glare. Karen caught that one.

When William's hand touched Cicely's, it tingled. He still smiled; however, his brow rose as if he was puzzled.

He tilted his head, carefully inspected her, and then he asked, "Have we met somewhere before?"

"No, I don't think so." Cicely playfully batted her eyes and patted her breast with her free hand. "But don't sweat it. I get that all the time."

"No. I've seen you before somewhere," he said, still shaking her hand, still gazing at her in wonderment.

"Ooookaaay," Karen interrupted as William snapped out of his reverie, released Cicely's hand, and nervously smiled.

Karen picked up Cicely's coach bag and handed it to her.

"Like Cicely said, she's here on business. So I'm sure she has to get going to check into her hotel."

"Where are you staying?" William asked as Karen's eyes grew wide in disbelief.

"At the Charleston Inn, near the Medical University."

Karen broke in. "Yeah. Her meeting is early in the morning. So she should be leaving."

"The Charleston Inn?" William interrupted. "That's a nice place and all. But you could stay here with me and Karen."

If it were possible, Karen's eyes would have popped from their sockets as she looked shockingly at William.

Cicely smiled and said, "That would be great. That is, if it's cool with Karen."

Karen raised her brow, smiled desperately, and asked William, "Can I see you in the bedroom, please?"

"Sure. We'll be right back, Cicely."

As soon as they were in Karen's bedroom and the door was closed, she said, "William, have you lost your mind?"

"Huh?"

"*Huh?*" Karen mocked. "She—Is—Not—Staying—Here!"

"Karen," William said with disappointment.

She shushed him with her hand and said, "I haven't spoken to this chick in ages. The last time I saw her she waved a male-stripper's stank privates in my face. And all of a sudden, she shows up at my doorstep?"

"You haven't spoken to her? I thought you said that you called her and invited her to the wedding."

"I lied, alright. The point is, she is NOT staying in my house and that's that!"

William shook his head. "Karen, I'm disappointed in you. I thought you were past all that."

"William, you just don't understand. No one has ever hated you like that."

He gave it a few ticks, measuring his next words carefully. "Hear me out on this," he said, "Cicely spending time here would allow you to really get over the past as well as add to your spiritual, mental, and physical growth as an individual. There are many plausible benefits to you doing as much as you possibly can to form a cohesive bond with the person who has served as an antagonist to you for much of your life."

Karen stared at him for a few seconds, wondering what planet he was on.

"William, honey, please chill with the psycho-analytical babble for one second, if you can..."

"Babble?"

"...Cicely cannot stay here!"

Karen turned away and plopped on her bed. William joined her side and kissed her forehead.

"Do this for me, babe. Let Cicely stay for dinner. We'll talk; figure out where her head is. And if you still don't want her to stay after that, so be it."

After taking a few seconds to think about it, Karen reluctantly agreed, and wanted to go on record as doing so.

Dinner went forward without much incident. The three mostly spoke about the state of the economy. They conversed about the state of music, the lack of musicianship and cleverness in writing. Uneventful indeed was dinner conversation.

The evening wore on and Cicely yawned and said, "Well, the hour is growing late. I need to get some rest for my meeting."

"You can sleep in the guestroom." Karen said that with a smile, or as much of one as she could muster.

William smiled and said, "And I'll sleep on the couch."

"Cool. I'll go get my things," Cicely said. And then she was off.

When Cicely returned with her suitcase, Karen showed her to the guestroom. Then she went to the linen closet to retrieve a pillow, some sheets, and a blanket for William. On her way to the living room, she saw that William was in the kitchen washing the dishes.

"Don't worry about those," Karen said. "I'll get them in the morning."

William winked at her and said, "You see? Everything went well. I told you so."

Karen returned the wink, gave him a soft kiss on the lips and said, "Goodnight, William."

With that, William made his sleeping space on the couch. He made himself as comfortable as he possibly could. And then he closed his eyes and drifted off to sleep.

***

"William."

The whisper of his name aroused him from sleep. He opened his eyes and saw nothing but chocolate legs in front him, the scent of Chanel radiating from them. Cicely was standing right in front of him, wearing a silk nightgown that barely covered half her thighs.

"William, I need you," she whispered.

Groggily, he lifted himself and cleared his throat.

"Um—Cicely. What time is it?"

"It's about three in the morning. I can't sleep. I looked for the milk in the fridge and couldn't find it. You think you could help me find it?"

"Um, sure. Give me a sec."

"I'll be waiting in the kitchen," Cicely whispered. And then she sauntered off, switching way too hard.

William got his bearings and slowly followed her into the kitchen. He opened the fridge and took a look inside.

"Karen usually keeps the milk on the top shelf in the front. But you're right. It's not here. Oh wait a minute—here it is."

William found a half gallon of milk shoved in the back of the bottom shelf of the fridge.

Cicely smiled and said, "Excellent. Do you like chocolate?"

"Pardon me?"

"Chocolate syrup. Does Karen have any?"

"I think she does," William replied going back into the fridge and retrieving the container. "Oh I see how you like it," he said. "Chocolate milk, warm?"

"Yes. That's how I like it," Cicely responded with a sneaky grin.

"Well that's my specialty. Do you want me to hook you up?" he asked naively.

"Yes. Please. Hook me up," Cicely replied.

William gathered all of the necessary items: two porcelain coffee cups, silver spoons, the milk, chocolate syrup, and marshmallows, of course. He began whipping up his specialty and then he took a quick look at Cicely, who ironically, was staring intensely at him. He looked away and returned to his work.

"So Cicely, you say you went to Furman?"

"Yeah. Beautiful campus. Have you ever been there?"

"Actually no. I don't recall ever being in that area. And that's what's so puzzling. I could swear that we've met before. I never forget a face. You don't recall ever seeing me somewhere?"

Cicely crossed her legs, displaying the fullness and thickness of her thighs. Then she replied, "No, sweetie. I would definitely remember meeting you."

William handed Cicely the cocoa and said, "Careful. It's—"

"Hot? I know. But don't worry. I can take the heat." She licked her lips. "Please. Sit with me, William."

He took a seat and then took a sip from his cup. Cicely, whose legs were still crossed and exposed, looked longingly at him. She dipped her forefinger into the hot chocolate. And then she sucked the froth from her finger nice and slow.

"So, William. What have you heard about me?"

He raised his brow. "What do you mean?"

"Earlier you said that Karen had told you a lot about me. The things that she told you, were they good things, or were they bad things?"

"Just things. Why do you ask?"

"Come on now. I'm sure that she's had a lot to say about me. And I know that it hasn't all been good."

William smiled and took another sip from his cup.

"Just things," he replied.

"The truth of the matter is I have been a bad girl, a very bad girl. And it's no secret that Karen and I aren't close at all. But now, I'm at a point in my life where I would like to move beyond all of that."

"I think that deep down inside, Karen wants the same thing."

Cicely raised her brows and nodded.

"So how'd you hook up with Karen, anyway?"

"Long story short, it was fate. I dreamt of her before I had even met her. Sounds strange, huh?"

"I've heard stranger."

"Honestly, Karen is an amazing woman. She's the tender earth in which I plan to plant my seeds."

"Woo!" Cicely said. "It's getting hot in here!"

William laughed and replied, "But seriously. I'm a lucky man to have Karen in my life."

Cicely eased her hand on top of his and whispered, "No. Karen's the lucky one."

He looked down at his hand, held in the softness and warmth of Cicely's palm.

"I better put these things away," William said nervously.

He retreated to the fridge to return the milk and chocolate syrup.

"I want to be the lucky one," Cicely said after she eased up behind him.

William spun around to see her standing right in front of him, cleavage exposed, lips pouting.

"Excuse me?"

"Come on, William. There's some electricity between us and you know it!"

"I don't know what you're talking about."

She moved in closer, pressing her body against his.

"Cicely, you need to back away from me."

"Please, baby. There's chemistry between us. Let's just do it here, right now. Karen doesn't have to know."

And then Cicely took William's face, bringing his lips to hers.

"Oh no!" he exclaimed. "I know where I've seen you before."

"WHAT IS GOING ON IN HERE?" Karen screamed. She walked into the kitchen to find Cicely, half-naked, pressing her body against William.

Cicely looked away, sheepishly. William remained frozen in reverie. Karen threw her hands up and retreated into her bedroom. Hurriedly, she threw on a pair of sweat-pants and athletic trainers. Then Cicely rushed into Karen's bedroom, holding her chest as she ran.

"Oh my goodness, Karen. I'm sorry. But listen. All we did is kiss, I promise. Nothing more."

Karen waved her away and ran out of her apartment into the night. The next thing she knew, she was racing down Interstate 26, traveling at nearly 100 miles per hour.

Her phone rang. It was William.

"Karen. Where are you going?"

"Did you kiss Cicely?"

"Yes. But—"

Click!

Karen disconnected the call.

She raced down the highway; out of Summerville, through North Charleston, through the Neck Area. Before she knew it, Karen had run out of highway and was hitting the curve that led to the Crosstown way too fast. She heard tires screeching. The car was out of control, spinning round and round.

She screamed at the top of her lungs, only able to see flashes of white light. She knew that she would surely be hit by oncoming traffic or that she would run off the road and hit a building. So she braced herself for the inevitable. But then, all of a sudden, the car stopped spinning and Karen found herself sitting in the driver's seat, her car sitting neatly against the curb, undamaged.

She gasped for air. Her heart raced within her chest and she began wheezing, became dizzy. This would be the panic attack of all panic attacks. She fumbled through her purse, looking for that amber bottle. It had been so long since she had taken her medication and she wasn't even sure that she would find it. But she had to try. She felt like she would die if she didn't take it.

Only after all of the contents of Karen's purse were strewn on the seat and on the floor, did she find the amber bottle. She quickly popped the top and poured a couple of pills into her palm. She didn't remember the last time she had taken her meds. She had been delivered from them. So somewhere in the madness of her badly littered car, somewhere in the darkness of early morning, she pondered to herself, "If I have been delivered, then why I am about to take these pills again?"

She threw the pills on the floor board. Her breathing returned to normal. Her heart no longer pounded. Her bearings were restored. And then she shouted, "I was at *MY* house! Why did I run from *MY* house?"

She would run no more.

She called William. He picked up on half a ring.

"Karen. Thank God. I've been worried about you. We need to talk."

"Where are you?"

"I'm at the Embassy Suites in North Charleston."

"Meet me in the parking lot in FIVE minutes!"

Click!

Karen again disconnected the call.

***

Karen whipped into the Embassy Suites parking lot. William was waiting for her, standing right beside his car. She got out of the car and stomped over towards him, simultaneously taking the engagement ring off of her finger. Then she threw it into his face and screamed, "IT'S OVER!"

"Wait, Karen. Let me explain."

He tried to grab her arm, but she was too quick in snatching away from him. In fact, by the time he made

285

it to the front of her Honda Accord, she was in the driver's seat, behind the steering wheel, with fury in her eyes.

William threw his hands in front of him in a motion to get Karen not to leave.

"Move!" she screamed

"No. Let me explain!"

"I'm going to hit you if you don't move!"

"Then, you're going to have to hit me." William folded his arms in defiance.

Karen sucked her teeth, rolled her eyes, and jammed the car into drive. She hit the gas and William raised his hands again.

"KAREN, NO!"

She had only moved the car an inch before she slammed on the brakes. She screamed and then she put the car back into park.

With his hands still extended forward, he beckoned, "Just give me two minutes. That's all I ask."

Karen gripped the steering wheel, her attitude mingled with hatred and annoyance.

"Two minutes," she replied. And then she unlocked the door.

William eased down into the passenger seat, closed the door carefully, and took a deep breath.

"The clock is ticking!" Karen commanded.

"Okay. Okay. Listen. It all makes sense now, my dreaming of you, though I had never met you."

"TICK! TOCK! TICK! TOCK!"

"Karen, please hear me out!"

She rolled her eyes; however, she motioned for him to continue just the same. William gulped because he didn't think she would believe what he was about to say. Nevertheless, he proceeded.

"Karen, I don't know how to say this, I don't even know if you'll accept this as truth, but...I've been to Greenville before."

Karen gave him a blank stare.

286

"You don't get it," William said. "It was so long ago and the visit was so brief that it totally slipped my mind. But I've *actually* been to Greenville."

"William, get out of the car."

"Wait! When we met, you told me that you were raised in Greenville, South Carolina. When you asked me if I had ever been there before, I told you no. But that's not true. I've been there, and just didn't remember it.

"My family was there. We visited some old college friends of my mom and dad: the Halls. We were only there for a day—yeah, I remember it now. The Halls had a son, Clarence. Clarence took me and my brothers to this basketball court to shoot hoops. Four girls showed up, to watch us play, I guess.

"I started talking to one of the girls, you know, just being a boy. I asked her if she'd ever tongue kissed before. This girl was bold, bolder than any girl I had ever seen in my life. I was so scared. I had never ever kissed before and she told me that she had. I couldn't look like a punk in front of my older brothers. So I took that girl up under the bleachers and I kissed her. That girl was Cicely, your cousin."

William was right. It all began to make sense to Karen. She had never told him about that incident because quite frankly, she didn't remember it herself until then. And then she let go and hugged her man tightly, as if she were hugging him for the first time.

"So, you didn't kiss Cicely tonight?" she asked, a tear beginning to form in her eye.

"No. I would never do that to you."

They held each other for a while, enjoying each other's warmth, realizing that it all could have been over. William took a deep breath, released a sigh of relief and then placed the engagement ring back on Karen's finger.

"You're not getting rid of me that easily," he said.

Karen smiled and pulled her hair behind her ear. Then she punched William in the shoulder, not hard, just enough to get his attention.

"I told you that letting Cicely stay at my place was a bad idea."

"I know. I know. And you know what? I'm starting to think that she planned all of this on purpose."

Karen looked at William like he was crazy.

"Duh!" she said. "You know William, for an intelligent man, you sure are slow."

"Ouch!"

"But seriously though. You just learned a valuable lesson."

"What's that?"

"Listen to your wife."

William smiled and planted a kiss on Karen's lips.

"I think I *am* going to stay at the Embassy Suites this week after all," he said.

"I think that's a good idea," Karen replied.

And then she was headed back to Summerville. She had some house cleaning to do.

Chapter 44

Karen returned to her apartment to find Cicely lounging on her couch, wearing a pair of tattered blue jeans, a wife beater tee, and a pair of Air Force Ones. Her feet propped up. She was reading a magazine like nothing had ever happened. When Karen entered the apartment, Cicely only looked up enough to roll her eyes.

"I want you out of my house."

Karen was supremely calm when she spoke those words, words that were not acknowledged at all by Cicely. So Karen walked over to her, gently tapped her on the shoulder, and again politely asked her to leave. But Cicely slapped Karen's hand extremely hard and sneered, "Get your hands off me!"

Karen jumped back and this caused Cicely to leap to her feet.

"Yeah, come with it!" Cicely shouted. "I'll beat you down in your own living room!"

Karen retreated to the front door, her steps quick and purposeful. She thought about the beat down in Ma Geneva's living room. The pain she felt then as Cicely pounced on her. It was as fresh in her memory as yesterday. So yes, she retreated to the front door.

But perhaps *retreat* is not the proper word to use for Karen's movement. Indeed she appeared to be running from Cicely. But in actuality, she was rushing to lock the front door. She locked the knob, the deadbolt, and then the chain latch. She wanted to make sure that Cicely couldn't escape.

Karen had finally snapped.

There was no warning scream, no dancing around, and no squaring off. In fact, Karen ran and leaped over the couch, airborne, a ballistic missile, catching Cicely off guard. She came down hard, jarring Cicely's jaw with her forearm. Cicely was stunned, buckling to the floor, breaking the coffee table in two as she collapsed onto it.

Karen mounted her chest, pinning her arms down with her knees. She began beating Cicely in the face, her fists instantly breaking skin. Cicely wiggled one arm free and dug her claws into the back of Karen's thigh, squeezing for dear life. Karen yelped in pain and rolled off from Cicely, holding the back of her leg.

Cicely jumped to her feet, regrouping, regaining her composure. She could taste blood in her mouth. Her face was on fire. But now she had Karen where she wanted her. She balled up her fist and swung at Karen with an uppercut designed to drive Karen's nose bone into her brain. But Karen quickly moved out of the way and in the same step, struck Cicely's ankles with a leg whip that sent her reeling back into a glass picture cabinet. Glass shattered everywhere. Cicely grunted in agony, dizzied, her neck badly scratched by shards. Dazed, yet determined, she squirmed past Karen and made fast for the front door. But of course it was locked from top to bottom. She had nowhere to run. And she never saw the ceramic lamp coming. Karen hit Cicely on the side of her head with the antique lamp, causing it to shatter into what seemed like a million pieces against the wall and on the parquet flooring.

Cicely was done. Her body went limp and she slid down the door to the floor. That's when Karen commenced to stomping her. First she lowered her trainers with authority to the back of Cicely's head. But when Cicely covered her head with her arms, Karen began kicking her in the abdomen. Karen's foot met Cicely's gut with thunderous thuds that caused her to cough fitfully. Cicely quickly shielded her stomach. But the kicks kept coming, each kick driving her further against the front door. Sheer instinct caused Cicely to cover up and shield her abdomen from further damage. When she realized that there was no more mercy within Karen, she cried out to her pitifully.

"Karen, please don't kick me anymore."

Karen kept on kicking.

"Karen, stop kicking me," Cicely sobbed pitifully. "KAREN! PLEASE!"

Karen stopped kicking. She brooded over Cicely, face flush, hair disheveled. She spat on Cicely's face and then stomped away into the guest bedroom. Cicely eased from the floor and began fumbling for the locks. Finally, she managed to open the door and hobble into the breezeway. She felt a harsh wind flash past her which was created by the suitcase that Karen threw out of the house, barely missing her head. Karen's front door slammed behind Cicely and startled her as she limped onto the sidewalk. Mired by extreme pain, she labored to her Land Cruiser, managing to heave her bag into the backseat. She was defeated, deflated. With no fight left inside of her, she retreated down the street and out of Karen's apartment complex.

Before long, Cicely was headed west on Interstate 26. The sun eased slowly over the horizon, little by little, shedding light on the day; however, she felt like nothing could brighten her spirits. She needed to talk to someone.

She dialed her father's phone.

"Hello. You've reached the voicemail of Doctor..."

Cicely hung up. Her father's phone was going to voicemail a lot lately. She dialed her mother, Susan. She always answered, but unfortunately the conversation was always the same.

"Hello, Cicely. What can I do for you?"

"Hi, mother. How—how've you been?"

"I *have* been well. You remember that I hate contractions."

"Mother, I need a place to stay for a while. I lost my job."

Susan sucked her teeth. "It figures," she said. "I told you, Cicely. Go to medical school. People will always need physicians. It is a recession proof profession. That is your problem. You never listen to me."

Cicely quietly took it all in like she always did.

"You can stay at the house on Lake Lanier for now. But you have to address your vocational situation."

"Um, Momma. I was sort of hoping that I could stay with you in Atlanta."

"That is not a good idea. I am at the hospital all of the time and when I return home, I like things just so."

Silence settled. Cicely wanted to cry, but she knew she would get the chiding of her life if she showed any weakness in her mother's presence.

Then Susan continued. "Cicely, you know there is money in your account, right? It is always there. You know that, right?"

Susan spoke about the $10,000 a month that was transferred into her checking account each month: $5,000 from her father and $5,000 from her mother. Cicely usually passed most of that money off to her financial advisor to manage her portfolio.

"Alright, Cicely. I have to go."

"Okay," Cicely whispered, trying to fight back tears. "Momma, I love you."

But Cicely's mother was long gone.

Cicely was rushed with a range of emotions: fear and depression, pain and pessimism, longing and loneliness. She drove slowly down the highway in a brand new Toyota Land Cruiser. She had $10,000 in the bank. She had a net worth of over $2 million. She was headed to a four bedroom mini-mansion nestled on the bank of a beautiful lake. Yet Cicely felt she had nothing to smile about and she had nowhere to go.

Chapter 45

A stormy evening morphed into a beautiful Saturday morning. Dew lightly kissed the lawn at Nana Jordan's Hollywood, South Carolina home. Swallows and owls sung harmoniously in the weeping willows that protected the back yard. The crickets joined them, adding percussion as it were. Theirs was a love song. Love was in the air.

Karen sat in front of the vanity of Nana's bedroom, which on that day, Karen's wedding day, served as a dressing room for the bride. The warmth and love of the women in her life surrounded her. Brook smiled and laughed at jovial conversation as Dawn looked on. Nana stared longingly at her beautiful granddaughter through the mirror, happy that she lived to see this day. Karen's older sister, Char, worked tirelessly with the flower girls.

Char's cell phone rang and she instructed the little ladies to go downstairs and sit still somewhere. Then she sighed in disgust and answered her phone. It was her nephew, Little Omar.

"Hello. Where are you? I called you an hour ago?— Well come up here now. I want to make sure you have that part down pat—Not me, I'm perfect. I'm concerned about you. Get up here now!—Boy, the bad luck thing doesn't apply to you, only the groom. Get up here, now!"

Then she threw her phone on the bed and said, "Geez. When they're babies they're all nice and sweet but when they grow up—"

Little Omar knocked on the door seconds later.

"Get in here, boy!" she yelled.

He entered the room and said, "Hello everyone."

Then he walked over to Karen and said, "Wow, Aunt Kay. You look beautiful. Uncle Will is definitely out of the friend zone now."

That produced laughter by all; however, Char pressed forward.

"Alright, alright, boy. Let's see if you've practiced!"

"Yes ma'am," he replied.

And then they stood side by side, and without humming the key, or counting down, they went right into the bridge of *Share My World* by Debarge.

Brook and Dawn were shocked, mouths ajar. Amazed at the sheer power of their voices and the perfect blend of their harmony. They were awestruck with the way their voices filled the room and touched their hearts; however, Char and Little Omar blew it off like it was nothing. Karen just smiled. By then she was used to it.

"Alright, Little Omar. Meet me downstairs at my car in five. I've got some things I need for you to bring into the house," Char said.

"Yes ma'am," he replied. And then he was off.

"It won't be long now, Sis," Char said. "You're going to blow William away in more ways than one."

"Get your fresh tail out of here and bring the candles and stuff in!" Nana said to Char with a smile. Then she eased beside Karen, still awed by her beauty.

And then, as if it happened magically, Nana seemed to be the only one in the room with Karen. Her words were soft and loving.

"Karen, I thank God that I lived to see this day. I always knew you were out there, when your father didn't have a clue that you even existed. I thank God for bringing you home to us, home to me."

Then time and space resumed as Karen's stepmother, Teresa came into the room holding an old picture frame.

"Oh, she *is* adorable," Teresa said.

And then she presented the picture to Karen as Nana, Brook, and Dawn, looked on.

"You see, Momma?" Teresa said. "I can't tell you two apart."

She showed them all the picture of Karen's grandmother, standing in her wedding dress many years ago.

"Oh I remember that day," Nana said. "I was so nervous that my hands shook. But when I took your grandfather's hand, my nervousness vanished. I grew strong in his strength."

"Oh Momma," Teresa sighed with a smile.

And then she gave Nana a serious look and told her that the caterer had knocked over some things in the kitchen. Nana frowned and said, "I'm about to go upside somebody's head. Fetch me my hitting skillet!"

And then mother and daughter exited the room.

"You were right," Brook said. "She does remind you of Ma Geneva."

"Old-school Ma Geneva," Dawn responded reminiscently.

"I wish she could've been here," Brook replied.

"She is here, in our hearts," Karen smiled and said. Everyone had to agree.

Then Karen let out a shout of victory.

"Woo! I'm getting married. And I'm finally going to have sex! And have babies and raise a family—"

Dawn jumped up and down with glee, joining Karen in her jubilation; Brook, however, did not. Somberness overcame her. She decided that she needed to retreat before she broke down into tears.

"Your hair's done, Karen. You do look beautiful...I have to get some air."

And then Brook quickly walked out of the room.

"Is something wrong with Brook?" Karen asked.

Dawn only replied with a shrug of her shoulders and a raise of her brow.

Brook stepped swiftly to the backyard. She didn't want anyone to see her crying. A pond was nearby, neatly nestled in the midst of great oaks and willows. She rested there, fanning herself in an attempt to keep at bay the rush of emotions she felt. She used her hands to push down some imaginary imps that wanted nothing more than to hear her scream in despair.

Finally, she was calm, looking into the crystal waters, feeling that because of Walter's insensitivity and selfishness, she would never know the joy of motherhood. Worse still, she may not have long to live.

"Oh God," she cried. "I really need to hear from you."

"Brook."

She whipped around.

It was Jeff.

"Jeff! What are you doing here?"

"A voicemail, Brook? Really?"

"Well did you listen to the voicemail? I told you that I was with Walter. But more importantly, I told you not to contact me. *This*—is contact."

"I heard the message you left. But there's one thing you never said. You never said that you loved Walter."

Brook backed away, but Jeff only followed.

She pleaded with him. "Just go back to Minneapolis, Jeff. Okay."

"No. Tell me you're still in love with Walter. Heck! Tell me you love him period. And I promise, though it would be hard for me, I will leave you alone."

Brook said nothing. She stood frozen, her arms folded, her eyes fixed on Jeff's.

"See. You can't do it," he said. "You can't say you love him because you don't love him. You're in love with me."

"Jeff, please. What are you trying to do, huh?"

"I'm trying to love you, woman! I'm fighting for you."

"Fighting for me?" Brook asked past the sobs.

"Yes! Fighting! Because that's what lovers do. They fight for each other."

Then Brook stepped into Jeff's space, her face in his face, and she asked, "Oh you want to fight?"

"Brook," Jeff said as he lowered his tone and backed away. But Brook stayed right on him.

"Who do you want to fight, huh? Do you want to fight Walter?"

Jeff stood his ground, yet looked off into the sky.

Brook grabbed the lapel of his sport jacket tightly and screamed, "WELL YOU CAN'T FIGHT WALTER CAUSE WALTER IS DEAD! AIDS related complications! He may have given it to me!"

Brook released her grip, lowered her head into the palm of her hands and cried softly.

"Just go, Jeff. You want a wife. You want children. I can't give you either—because I may be sick."

Brook just knew that he would run away from her after hearing that news. She just knew that he'd be gone when she opened her eyes.

But she was wrong.

Jeff was still there. He lifted her head and brought her lips to his. He kissed her softly, tasting her lips, breathing in her air. Slowly, he released her, looked deep into her eyes and said, "You're fine."

"How do you know that, Jeff? How can you be so sure about that?"

"Because God cannot lie."

Jeff brought her into an embrace and said, "Brook just—let's just love each other, and let God take care of the rest."

"Okay," Brook agreed. "Okay."

With that said, Jeff and Brook walked back to the house, hand in hand.

***

297

"Wow, Karen. This time tomorrow, you'll be Mrs. William Ward."

That was Dawn. She beamed, yet played with her fingernails nervously.

"I know right," Karen replied. "Karen Ward. I love the sound of that."

A nervous hush settled between them until Dawn spoke up.

"Karen, I'm probably the last person who should be preaching to you about this, seeing as I'm a jailbird and all. But, that thing with Cicely…" Karen sighed and closed her eyes. "Don't get me wrong, cuz. Considering what she did, I would've probably beat her down too. But don't hate her. Nothing good comes from hatred. Believe me, I know. The only person you end up hurting is yourself." Dawn allowed Karen time to digest those words and then she said, "I'm going to go and check on Brook. I'll be right back."

Dawn left the room and as soon as the door closed, Karen hung her head. She had mixed emotions about the incident, sentiments she had to admit she couldn't process at the time. So she shelved those thoughts and decided to enjoy the day instead. Her day.

She heard the door open and close.

"That was quick," she said, supposing that Dawn had returned. However, Karen looked up into the mirror and saw Cicely, standing with her back against the door.

Karen looked around the vanity for something sharp. She spied a pair of scissors and gripped them tightly.

"What are you doing here?" she asked.

"There are some things I need to say to you," Cicely replied.

"Cicely, if I were you, I would choose the next words you say to me very carefully."

Cicely saw Karen's hand clutching the scissors. She grew sheepish, looking from left to right, not able to look Karen directly in the eye through the mirror.

"Karen—um—you look fabulous."

"WHY YOU LITTLE!"

Karen jammed the scissors deep into the wood surface on the vanity and jumped from her seat. She totally forgot that she was wearing a wedding dress as she lunged toward Cicely, ready to do her harm.

Cicely cowered back into the door, turning to the side, folding her arms tightly.

"KAREN, I'M SORRY! I'm sorry for all the mean words I said and for all of the hateful things I did. I'M SORRY! I'm so, so, sorry."

Karen surveyed Cicely from top to bottom. She noticed how she was standing with her arms folded tightly over her stomach.

"My goodness, Cicely," Karen said. "You're pregnant!"

Cicely's eyes grew wide.

"How—how did you know that?"

Karen covered her mouth with her hands.

"You're pregnant, aren't you?"

"Yes. About ten weeks."

"Cicely, please come sit down."

Karen went to Cicely and guided her to the bed. She placed her hands on Cicely's stomach. And then she remembered that just a week ago, she was kicking Cicely violently in her abdomen. She gasped.

"Oh no! I kicked you in the..." She pointed to her stomach, "...the baby...I..."

"I'm fine, Karen. And the babies are fine."

"Babies?"

"Yes. Twins."

Karen hugged Cicely and kissed her forehead.

"I'm so glad you're okay. I don't think I could live with myself if it were otherwise."

"No. No. No. Everything's fine," Cicely said as she began to cry. "But I am *so* scared. The father wants nothing to do with me, or the babies. I can't tell my mother. I just feel so alone."

"Well that's where you're wrong. You are not alone. I'm here for you."

Karen held Cicely in her arms, rocking her back and forth, comforting her.

"Karen. I need to tell you why I was so mean to you all of those years."

"Hush, now. That doesn't matter anymore."

But Cicely needed to clear the air.

"I owe you that," she said. "I owe myself."

So Karen sat back and gave Cicely her full attention.

Cicely sniffled and said, "I remember Aunt Adele's funeral, your mother's funeral. I remember seeing you grieve. You didn't even want to see her body. You looked like you were afraid, desperate, and unsure of your future. You were standing by your mother's casket. And the only thing I could think about was how lucky you were."

Karen furrowed her brow and asked, "What are you talking about?"

"Karen, you had it all, everything I wanted, everything I needed."

"But Cicely, you're the one that had it all growing up: money, the finest clothes, a big house. While I was poor, living from house to house. I lost my mother!"

"No you didn't. That's just not true."

Cicely looked at Karen with bloodshot eyes and she confessed, "My mother doesn't love me. She has NEVER loved me. In fact, growing up, the only time I felt the warmth of a mother's love was during the summer. But you had that love all year long."

It all began to make sense to Karen. Cicely took a deep breath. And finally she said, "I love my mother; believe me, I do. But I have to be honest with you.

That day, at Aunt Adele's funeral, I wished that it was my mother in that casket instead of yours."

Karen's heart dropped as she processed everything that she heard. Cicely's words were harsh but genuine and Karen couldn't judge her for them.

"You think I'm a monster, don't you?" Cicely inquired as Karen held her in her arms.

"No, I don't think that at all. I really understand."

"So, are we still cousins?"

"No," Karen said. "We are sisters."

Karen's father, Dennis, tapped the door and peaked inside.

"Everything okay?" he asked.

Karen looked at Cicely and then at her father and replied, "Yes sir. Everything is as it should be."

"It's time, baby-girl," he said.

Cicely gathered herself and stood to her feet. Afterwards, she helped Karen to her feet.

"Go get him, girl," she said as Karen beamed.

Karen took her father's hand and said, "I'm ready. Take me to my man."

***

Suffice it to say that the wedding ceremony was beautiful. It was everything that Karen and William thought it would be. The songs were performed wonderfully and the scriptures read powerfully. Even if someone in the wedding party made a mistake, it was chalked up to good humor, which added to the jubilation of the service.

Memorable were the moments designed to honor those loved ones who had gone on. Nana, escorted by Little Omar, carried with her a framed portrait of Ma Geneva. That brought tears to Karen, Brook, Dawn and Cicely.

Then there was the rose for Adele, Karen's mother. Karen placed it in the space where she would have sat were she there. And then Karen gave an identical rose to Teresa. She cried because she wasn't expecting that.

But perhaps the most memorable moment was the song that Karen sang to William. No one in her family, not Cicely, Brook, or Dawn, had ever heard Karen sing. No one even knew that she could. But on that day, Karen sang Bishop T. D. Jakes' *You Are My Ministry*, hitting high notes with perfect pitch and belting out runs that ran chills up William's spine.

That was the first time that Karen had sung in front of people. If someone were to ask Karen why, she would probably tell them that she never had a reason to sing. But on that day, that special day, Karen sang from her heart, like never before. On that day, she had every reason to sing.

Epilogue

And they all stood together, side by side: Karen, Cicely, Dawn, Brook, and of course Brook's fiancé Jeff. They stood patiently in an examination room, waiting for Dr. Abbott to return.

They were sure of many things. They were certain that Dawn would only have to serve 100 hours of community service for her assault on Nina and that she and Joe would get married later that summer. They were certain that Karen and Cicely were fully reconciled and that Karen would be called 'Aunt Karen' by Cicely's twin boys. But there was one thing that they were unsure about: the results that Dr. Abbott would soon share with them when she returned. Had Brook contracted that deadly disease?

But perhaps to say that they were unsure would be inaccurate. They believed in God. They believed Isaiah 53:5. They stood on Mark 16:18. They held firm to Psalm 91 in its entirety. So when Dr. Abbott entered the examination room carrying that manila folder, they grasped hold to each other's hand, and patiently waited for the results.

An Ode for Brook
A Sister Gone Too Soon

A Poem Written and Recited by Dawn Suarez at the Home Going Service for her Sister Brook

My dearest Brook, beloved twin
Her sun has set, for me, too soon
And now I'm hurt. I'm missing her
I remember well the fear we felt when we found out the inevitable.
But it was her incredible courage that calmed us, consoled us, gave us comfort.
And she held on, fighting as long as she could, 'til strength failed her, 'til Heaven found her. And she lay down to rest a while. I'll learn to accept that fact, somehow.
But I am being selfish for saying she was gone too soon. For indeed, she lived a full and fruitful life. She walked this earth for eighty years, more years than God promised. She mothered seven wonderful children: four boys and three girls, who grew up in a home filled with love, in the fear and admonition of the Almighty. At one time, my sister feared she'd never have children, yet she was called granny by her great-grand-children. And she was wife to an incredible man who loved her unconditionally. She'll join him now in the sweetness of sleep.
My dearest twin, Brook Amelia Blitzer. I selfishly say that she was gone too soon because I've never lived without her, never had to walk without her. But I remember what she said to us as we stood side by side, hand in hand in a doctor's office long ago.

"No matter where you rest, no matter where you roam. Take solace in this knowledge. You will never walk alone."

304

Acknowledgements

First giving honor to God. I thank Him for the Windows that He opened and the Blessing that He poured out. To my beautiful wife, Felicia. You are my orchid and I love you. To my children, I love you. You make me smile. To my parents, thank you for loving me. I praise God for the both of you. To my pastor and first lady (who are also my in-laws), thank you for making me one of your own.

To the family that shapes me, to the friends that embrace me and to the colleagues that challenge me to be the best I can be, thank you, thank you, thank you!